Praise for Libby Fischer Hellmann

Havana Lost

"A many-layered adventure...smart writing, done in accomplished style by an author who never talks down to her readers."
—*Mystery Scene Magazine*

"A riveting historical thriller... This multigenerational page-turner is packed with intrigue and shocking plot twists."
—*Booklist*

"A sprawling tale... the story of the Cuban revolution, as well as the Cuban military efforts in Angola, is fascinating..."
—*Publishers Weekly*

"Hellmann's writing has matured considerably since her early novels. Her plotting has become more solid and assured, her characters more realistic, her settings wonderfully described. This is a fine, extremely well told novel."
—*Deadly Pleasures*

A Bitter Veil

"The Iranian revolution provides the backdrop for this meticulously researched, fast-paced stand-alone ...A significant departure from the author's Chicago-based Ellie Foreman and Georgia Davis mystery series, this political thriller will please established fans and newcomers alike."
—*Publishers Weekly*

"Hellmann crafts a tragically beautiful story... both subtle and vibrant... never sacrificing the quality of her storytelling. Instead, the message drives the psychological and emotional conflict painting a bleak and heart wrenching tale that will stick with the reader long after they finish the book."
—*Crimespree Magazine*

"Readers will be drawn in through the well-researched inside look at Iran in the late 1970s and gain perspective on what the people in that time and place endured. *A Bitter Veil* is so thought-provoking that it especially would be a great title for book clubs to discuss."
—*Book Reporter*

"*A Bitter Veil*... is a social statement about what can happen when religious fundamentalism trumps human rights, but that's hardly a drawback in this suspenseful, well-researched book. It might even serve as a warning."
—*Mystery Scene Magazine*

Set the Night on Fire

"A top-rate standalone thriller that taps into the antiwar protests of the 1960s and 70s...A jazzy fusion of past and present, Hellman's insightful, politically charged whodunit explores a fascinating period in American history."
—*Publishers Weekly*

"Superior standalone novel...Hellmann creates a fully-realized world...complete with everyday details, passions and enthusiasms on how they yearned for connection, debated about ideology and came to belief in taking risks to stand up for what they believed."
—*Chicago Tribune*

"Haunting...Rarely have history, mystery, and political philosophy blended so beautifully...could easily end up on the required

reading list in college-level American History classes."
—*Mystery Scene Magazine*

Easy Innocence

"Hellmann brings to life the reality of bullying among teenage girls with enough twists and turns to keep you reading. Highly recommended."
—*Library Journal, Starred Review*

"Just what's needed in a mystery... Depth of characterization sets this new entry by Hellmann apart from a crowded field."
—*Kirkus Reviews*

"There's a new no-nonsense female private detective in town: Georgia Davis, a former cop who is tough and smart enough to give even the legendary V.I. Warshawski a run for her money."
—*Chicago Tribune*

Also by Libby Fischer Hellmann

Havana Lost
A Bitter Veil
Set the Night on Fire

◆

THE GEORGIA DAVIS SERIES

ToxiCity
Doubleback
Easy Innocence

◆

THE ELLIE FOREMAN SERIES

A Shot to Die For
An Image of Death
A Picture of Guilt
An Eye for Murder

◆

Nice Girl Does Noir (short stories)

◆

Chicago Blues (editor)

Nobody's Child

NOBODY'S CHILD

Libby Fischer Hellmann

The Red Herrings Press

Chicago

Copyright © 2014 Libby Fischer Hellmann
All rights reserved.

Cover design by Miguel Ortuno

Interior design by Sue Trowbridge

Names: Hellmann, Libby Fischer
Title: Nobody's child / Libby Fischer Hellmann
Description: Chicago, IL; The Red Herrings Press, 2014
Identifiers: LCCN 2019408554 I ISBN 9781938733468 (Pbk.) I 9781938733475 (Ebook)
Subjects: Human trafficking — Fiction. | Chicago (Ill.) — Fiction. | Murder — Fiction. | Human trafficking. Illinois — Chicago. | Mystery—Private Investigator
Classification: LCC PS 3608 E46 E17 2008 DDC 813/.6
LC Record available at https://lccn.loc.gov/2019408554

For Jan Gordon

who has my everlasting admiration and respect

I have nobody to talk to, to confide in and share my problems with. I have nobody to cheer me up when I'm down, nobody to love or love me back. I have nobody. I am alone.
Unknown

Chapter 1

T hey swarmed into the store like a plague of locusts. The rows of pants, jeans, and shirts were stacked in neat piles ready to tempt shoppers. The floors were swept, the windows sparkled, and punk music flowed out of the loudspeakers. Reggie Field, the store owner, didn't much like punk. He preferred Dylan, the Byrds, even Motown, but oldies wouldn't work for his customers.

He sipped the last of his latte, mentally congratulating himself for finally being in the right place at the right time. A serial entrepreneur, he'd failed more than not, but last fall he'd opened a designer discount store in Evanston, a suburb just north of Chicago. Evanston was a mecca for college kids, not only from Northwestern and the teachers college whose name he never remembered, but Loyola students and high school wannabes too. The store took off, and fourteen months later, he turned a profit. He'd been thinking about opening another store.

He was contemplating whether to flirt with his new salesgirl—it was only her third day, but she was cute, curvy, and blond—when the doors flew open and a horde of young males streamed in. There had to be more than twenty, all converging on the store. Reggie froze as they surged past him without a glance and slithered down the aisles. They planted themselves beside the counters, the wall units, even the display mannequins. Where had they come from? How had they managed to appear en masse, like they'd crashed a boring party and were taking over?

Wearing oversized jackets, backpacks, baggy pants, and gym shoes, these kids weren't the preppy college kids who usually shopped here. A few had earbuds that trailed white cords and were bobbing their heads. Others grinned and laughed and shouted over the store's speakers. The pungent smell of weed drifted over. All within a minute.

The new girl tried to ask one or two if they needed help, but they pushed past her, knocking her off balance. Reggie set his latte down next to the register.

"Hey. Watch it!"

But no one answered, and he soon saw why. The kids were too busy raking through piles of clothes and holding them up. It was when they started stuffing them into their backpacks and bags that Reggie ducked behind the cash register, pulled out his cell, and called 911.

"Designer Discount Den. I'm getting ripped off. Right now. About twenty. Maybe more. Get here right away!"

Still behind the counter, he pushed a button and a loud alarm sounded. Any normal person would have been startled by ear-splitting blasts that sounded like the end of the world. Not these punks. They kept grabbing clothes and stuffing them into jackets and backpacks, all the while laughing and high-fiving each other, clearly enjoying the bedlam they'd created. That's what it was, Reggie realized. Sheer bedlam. Everything he'd worked for was turning to shit.

His pulse pounding, his blood pressure sky-high, Reggie tried to think. The best thing would be to get the hell out of the store. Lock the doors with them inside. They'd be trapped. He'd heard of another guy who did exactly that, but the assholes managed to sneak out the back, smashing windows as they ran. And what about his girl? He craned his neck, trying to spot her. He finally saw her, pinned against the wall by two punks. What were they doing? He couldn't tell, but her eyes met his. She looked terrified. Fury knifed through him. He couldn't abandon her—Maya, that was her name—to these barbarians. With a boldness he hardly recognized in himself, he tore himself from behind the counter and shouldered his way through the mob.

"Hey! Get away from her. Right now. Leave her the fuck alone!"

Two guys spun around, releasing their hold on the girl. As she sprinted toward the front door, one of the punks grabbed him from behind, while the other hit him across the jaw. A third belted him with an uppercut to his chin. The last thing Reggie heard as he slumped to the floor was Maya's scream.

Chapter 2

Georgia Davis got the call two days later. She'd heard about the incident—the video was all over YouTube, and the media was full of it. How the flash mob ripped off five grand in inventory, how the owner ended up in the ER with stitches, how the punks scattered so fast the police had no suspects and were begging the public for leads. Even so, she was surprised when Reggie Field's wife phoned.

"I just can't believe it," Shelly Field said a few seconds into the call. "Thirty years in retail and we've never seen anything like this. And the first week of January. Happy Fucking New Year."

"Is your husband home from the hospital?"

"Oh yes. You know how they are. If you're conscious and breathing, they kick you out. You could die on the way home, but they don't care. Reggie's still recovering, of course, and we've had to keep the store closed. I don't know how we're going to make up the losses. It's just—just unlike anything we've ever dealt with." The woman sighed theatrically.

Georgia listened with more than a trace of skepticism. The woman's whines and complaints presumed an innocence about the ways of the world Georgia didn't buy. Thirty years in retail would have taught anyone with half a brain about shoplifting, price gouging, and under-the-table deals. But she didn't have to fall in love with her clients; she just had to tolerate them long enough to make their problem go away. She was a private investigator, not a therapist. Then again, being flash robbed was not your everyday event. She should probably fake a little sympathy.

"You have insurance, don't you?"

The woman went on. "Yes, but they say they're not going to investigate any more than the police already have. And, of course, the police have no idea who it was or how to catch them. Can you believe it? Going on the Internet and TV with our security tape? Do they think these thugs are just gonna give themselves up? Next thing you know they'll offer 'em a reality show."

Georgia stifled a giggle and covered it with a cough. The woman, intentionally or not, had a sense of humor. "Mrs. Field, I'm not sure I can do anything the police haven't already done."

"Call me Shelly, honey. And lemme tell you, they're not doing anything. Look, I realize nobody got killed, and Reggie wasn't seriously hurt, and the insurance—God forbid the rate hike that's coming—will cover most of it. But you know? I gotta believe those punks knew that. And the cops—well, they won't admit it—but this is on their back burner."

The woman was right. Before she became a PI, Georgia had been a police officer for ten years, and despite the fact that she ultimately resigned, put-downs about cops still made her defensive. "It's not that, Shelly; it's just that they have to prioritize. This economy has hit cops hard too. They've got a—a boatload of homicides, arsons, sexual assaults, and fewer resources to handle them. They have to choose." She almost smiled. She wished she'd recorded what she just said so she could send it to Dan O'Malley, her former boss, now the chief of police in Northview. He wouldn't believe it.

"Yeah, yeah. A victimless crime. That's what they keep saying," Mrs. Field said. "But it wasn't."

"I agree. Especially with your husband getting hurt. If violence is involved, no matter—"

"It's not just that, sweetheart." The woman cut her off.

"There's a part of this that hasn't come out. That's why we called you."

"What do you mean 'hasn't come out'?"

"Reggie'll tell you." Shelly hesitated, then issued a sigh. "You gotta remember this was our livelihood. Our entire life. Now Reggie's practically ready to cash it in. Ya can't blame him, you know? We're not getting any younger. But I just hate the thought of going on social security."

"How did you get to me?" Georgia asked.

"One of our neighbors recommended you."

"Who?"

"Um, she—they don't wanna say. But you got a good rep. They say you know what you're doing."

"Where do you live?"

"Glencoe."

Georgia wondered who the neighbor was. She didn't know many people in Glencoe. Only one family, in fact. She tapped her fingers on her desk. It was the second week of January, typically a slow period until the post-Christmas cheer dried up and people went back to their greedy, thieving ways. She had time. And she could always use the money.

"Tell you what," she said. "I'll look into it for a couple of days. If I can't see a way forward, I'll let you know. I don't want to take your money for nothing."

"Well, that's fair. I see why they like you."

It's why I'm barely eking out a living, Georgia thought. Aloud, she said, "How about I swing by later today?"

Chapter 3

There was no "other side of the tracks" in Glencoe, an affluent suburb on Chicago's North Shore. At the southern edge of the village, though, not far from Green Bay and Washington, a small black community had taken root in the 1880s. It was largely dispersed now, but at one time it was the only African American neighborhood between Evanston and Lake Forest. Reggie and Shelly Field lived in a small older brick house near the old St. Paul AME Church, and as she pulled up Georgia wondered if the place had once belonged to a black family.

It was a crisp, sunny day, the roads were wet with melting snow, and the ground smelled earthy. Chicago was in the midst of a January thaw. As she climbed out of her Toyota, Georgia caught her reflection in the car window. She'd bundled up before she left home, but now she loosened her muffler and flicked her long blond hair over it. The shades she wore masked brown eyes, but they made her nose seem sharper and more prominent. Not much she could do about that. The weather was so mild she unzipped her parka, displaying her fisherman's sweater and jeans.

She mounted three concrete steps to a tiny porch surrounded by an iron banister. The screen door had one of those initials in the center, in this case, a cursive *F*. She pressed a buzzer to the right of the latch.

The woman who opened the door was not what Georgia expected. She'd anticipated an elderly woman with no shape and flyaway gray hair. To her surprise, Shelly Field was thin, with black hair and red lipstick. She wore a stylish warm-up suit and had that taut, stretched skin that comes from a facelift or two. Is that where the profits from the store went?

"Shelly?" Georgia said. "I'm Georgia Davis."

Shelly appraised her, frowning slightly. Georgia wondered if she'd expected something different too. Then she opened the door wider. "Come in. Reggie's anxious to meet you."

Shelly's tone, clipped and businesslike, was so different from her phone personality that Georgia was taken aback. No whining, no sour grapes. Did she hide that side of her from her husband? The woman led her into a small living room with overstuffed furniture, white wall-to-wall carpeting, and ornate gilded picture frames. The sharp odor of ammonia drifted over the room, announcing the presence of a cat, which, on cue, jumped down from a chair, blinked, then without a sound swished its tail and skulked out of the room.

Reggie Field lay on a brocade sofa, clutching an iPad. A pair of crutches leaned against the wall behind him. He was a big guy, bald except for few strands of comb-over gray. His hair was longer on the sides and back and had the consistency of steel wool. His nose was tiny and turned up like a pug's. A gauze bandage with adhesive tape covered one cheek, and Georgia saw a nasty abrasion on his chin.

"Thanks for coming," he said, not bothering to paste on a smile.

Shelly sat in the chair the cat had vacated and motioned Georgia into its mate on the other side of the coffee table.

"How are you feeling, Mr. Field?" Georgia asked.

"I'll live. And call me Reggie. Everyone does."

She nodded. "As I told Shelly, there may not be much I can do that the police and your insurance company haven't already done."

His eyebrows arched. "Oh yes, there is. I can vouch for it."

Georgia inclined her head.

He set his iPad down and with a huge effort sat up. His weight settled in his gut, making him look like an overripe pear.

"I'm gonna save you a lot of time." His expression tightened, and he poked a finger at Georgia. "I fired my assistant manager last week. Name of Chase Bartell. He's behind the whole thing, but I can't prove it."

Georgia straightened. "Tell me."

"He was dealing drugs right out of the front of the store. Cocaine, reefer, pills. Caught him red-handed."

Georgia hadn't heard anyone use the word "reefer" in years.

"I got him on the security tape. Fired his ass right away. After the flash rob, I turned everything over to the cops. Told them exactly what happened and who was behind it."

"Then what happened?"

"Bubkes. Nothing. Absolutely nothing. Except that the tape showed up on YouTube."

Georgia frowned.

"Bartell's a snot-nosed rich kid from Northfield. I was doing his parents a favor. They begged me. Said he needed something to keep him out of trouble. So, I think, okay, I'm a nice guy. I'll give the kid a chance. I shudda known. He was doing something, all right." Reggie's face darkened. "The cops wanted to file charges, but the parents hired a fine and fancy lawyer who makes a big deal that the tape isn't clear enough and doesn't really show a drug transaction. And that there's no way in hell anyone could connect his client to the flash mob."

"But you say otherwise?"

"Damn right I do." He shook his head angrily. "I gave their kid a chance. And this is how they repay me?"

Georgia kept her mouth shut. She had worked with video specialists in the past and knew all sorts of magic could enhance images that *would* stand up in court. The fact that the cops or the State's Attorney hadn't gone that route suggested that the Bartells—or their lawyer—had clout or great connections or both.

"Then, well, bottom line, the cops decide not to pursue charges after all, and the kid gets off. Not even a fucking slap on the wrist."

"But you think he was out for revenge and set up the hit on the store."

"I know he was," Reggie said. "The kid was pissed. He threatened me when I fired him."

"Did the police check his cell phone? His Facebook friends? All that?"

"Said they did. Said he's clean. But I'm telling you he ain't. I know the little bastard did it. That's why I called you."

Chapter 4

That night Georgia pored over the surveillance tapes of the flash rob on her computer. Reggie was telling the truth. The digital files on YouTube consisted of a series of staccato images, all wide shots of the store from various overhead angles. She could clearly see the kids stuffing clothes into their pants pockets, backpacks, and jackets, but she couldn't see their faces. Even so, Georgia felt a chill. The marriage of technology and bad intentions had created an entirely new kind of crime: impulsive, passionless, and organized by smartphones on the spur of the moment. It was a powerful warning of what could happen to a society where envy, a sense of entitlement, and electronic toys converged.

She clicked on the file that was supposed to show the drug deal going down. A tall, lanky white boy was at the register, while another kid, presumably Chase Bartell, stood behind the counter. Something changed hands, but whether it was a packet of drugs, money, or just a credit card wasn't clear. Georgia was surprised the cops hadn't pursued it. If she were still on the force, she would have. She went back to the YouTube tape. All the police needed to do was connect one face or phone number to the flash rob. Just one. Had they started to make an effort but then dropped it? If so, the Bartells' or their attorney's clout was serious.

She drummed her fingers on her desk, making sure she tapped each finger the same number of times. Had to make them all come out even. She'd requested Chase Bartell's cell phone records from a contact who did that kind of thing under the radar. While she waited she clicked onto Facebook. Chase Bartell's profile was typical of high school students: grandiose pronouncements, lots of cursing, and a pseudo-cynical philosophy. Nothing hidden or private. Georgia studied his friends list. She found two boys, one African American and one Hispanic, who lived on the South Side. Looking them up, she compared their photos to the surveillance tape. There wasn't a lot of definition, but she thought the Hispanic boy might have been on the tape.

She wrote down his name and his Facebook moniker so she could cross-reference him later. People should only know how easy it was to be a PI these days. She'd worked hard for her license, but so much information was online now, just waiting to be viewed, collated, and analyzed, that almost anyone could set up as an investigator. And teenagers were so oblivious to anything other than themselves, they never imagined their information could be used in a way they hadn't intended.

She got up and stretched. She could take a break. Go down to Mickey's for a drink. If she did, though, she wouldn't make it home until late. And she'd drink way too much. She glanced around her living room. Her décor was bare-bones neutral; she had never been into possessions. With a beige sofa, brown chairs, coffee table, and small area rug, it was obvious that only one person lived here. She wondered if that would ever change. On this chilly January night, for example, she would have loved— She forced herself to stop. It was what it was.

The cheerful chime of her email told her the cell phone records had arrived. She went back to her computer. The kid's cell was registered to Stephen and Marlene Bartell. They had a family plan, and her contact had obligingly provided all four cell numbers. Four phones for three people—what was that about? She checked them all. One had a lot of calls to the 312 area code.

Downtown Chicago. The two others were mostly calls to 847. The North Shore. One phone hadn't been used at all. She'd have to trace them all. It would be tiresome. Then again, that's why she was a PI.

Two hours later, she was satisfied the cells were clean. No suspicious or disposable numbers. And the cops had the same records. That was probably why they'd passed. This case was going to take more than a superficial effort. In fact, since she'd begun, all she'd done was duplicate their work. Facebook and other social media were the first places cops checked when there were crimes by juveniles. The only thing she had going for her was that the cops hadn't cracked the case either.

Chapter 5

Saturday morning Georgia drove to the affluent part of Northfield where Chase Bartell lived. The January thaw was a distant memory; it had snowed three inches last night. The roads were clear and the air carried the brittle chill of winter. Georgia layered up, energized at the prospect of a little old-fashioned surveillance. She fished out her tiny video camera and slipped it in her pocket with her iPhone.

She pulled up to a huge white brick colonial off Happ Road with a three- car garage, an enormous entrance door, and a fenced-in backyard that held a tennis court. She frowned. Why would a kid who lived here, where the sense of entitlement was so broad and deep you could swim laps in it, work at a cheap clothing store in Evanston? His hourly wage wouldn't pay for a tank of gas. Maybe Reggie Field was right and the kid's parents *were* trying to instill some kind of work ethic in him. If so, she should cut them some slack. It had been a good idea. The problem was that they'd succeeded too well. The kid had marshaled his organizational skills and talent to destroy his boss's business.

She ran the Toyota's heat intermittently, prepared to stake out the house all day. An hour later, though, around ten, the kid came out. He slid into a red four-by-four, keyed the engine, and took off. Georgia tailed him at a discreet distance as he turned onto Happ Road, then twisted and threaded his way southeast.

The kid stopped in front of a redbrick ranch home in Wilmette and honked. Georgia parked a hundred yards away. While not as upscale as Northfield, Wilmette was itself a well-heeled North Shore village. What was Chase doing there? Making a delivery? A buy? She pulled out her camera and started recording. Moments later the front door opened, and a fresh-faced brunette bounded out and climbed into the SUV.

The kid turned the car around and headed back down the street. As he passed Georgia, she slumped and averted her face. Once they were gone, she started following again, glad they were teenagers who'd never check for a tail.

They soon arrived in Evanston. Like the suburbs they'd just come from, the affluent part of Evanston was north, the seedier section south. Chase flew through the Northwestern campus down to Main Street. He made two more turns and ended up at a small apartment building with iron bars on the windows. He honked again. Georgia, fifty yards away, picked up her camera and started shooting. An African American kid in extra-large sweats but no coat emerged, hands in pockets. He looked in both directions, then made his way to Chase's car and leaned against the driver's side. The window lowered.

A conversation between Chase and him ensued. No. It was an argument. Twice the black kid poked his index finger at the kid's chest, after which Chase flipped up his hands as if to say, "What do you want me to do?" The black kid motioned Chase out of his car. Nothing happened, and Georgia suspected the girl was telling Chase not to get out. But when the kid gestured again, Chase reluctantly climbed out. Something was happening. A moment later, Chase spun around and beckoned the girl. She got out of the SUV and trotted over. Then she dug out her cell, handed it to Chase, and watched as he made a call.

Georgia got it on tape.

Chapter 6

⚬⚬⚬

I t didn't take long to track the girl's cell. The owner of the Wilmette home was Carol Chernikoff. Georgia emailed her phone contact asking for the woman's records. Her contact wasn't pleased and complained that she was using up her favors; he wasn't a goddammed 411. He had to be careful too. Georgia told him she'd pay extra. An hour later she had the records for two cells: one for Carol Chernikoff, and one for Carol and Emily Chernikoff. Mother and daughter.

The mother's cell showed mostly calls to the 847 area code, the North Shore. Emily's records, on the other hand, displayed a slew of calls to area codes 312 and 773, both in Chicago. Her calls spanned a three-week period, then abruptly stopped. Georgia checked the last day calls were made on her cell. Her pulse sped up. Ten calls. The morning of the robbery.

When Georgia tried the numbers, most of them came back as "unregistered," which meant they were prepaid disposables or burners. Adrenaline pumped through her. She was close. All she needed was one number that wasn't a burner. That belonged to a living, breathing person. A person who just might have gotten a call telling him to show up at Designer Discount Den just after the store opened.

She was carefully examining the cell records when her land

line phone rang. Startled, she leaned over and picked it up. Name withheld. No caller ID. She considered not answering it. It could be the killer who did the drive-by closing in on her. Or not.

"Hello?"

There was no response. In the background she could hear two voices. Indistinct. Sounded like a male, one female.

"Hello? Is anyone there?" It was probably someone butt-dialing her. But that would mean she was on someone's contact list, and she couldn't imagine whose. She didn't have many friends. Except Sam.

"Hey!" she yelled into the phone. "Sam! Is that you?"

A female voice in the background spiked. "No! I won't!"

Georgia heard anger, but underneath the anger was fear. "Sam... are you there?"

A male voice cut off the female. Equally angry. Like he was issuing an order.

The female replied. Petulant, and still scared, but Georgia couldn't make out the words. Seconds later, she was cut off by a sudden crack. Or slap. Or shot. The line went dead.

Georgia stared at her cell, wondering what the hell had just happened. She let out a nervous breath and punched in Sam's number. After three rings, Sam's voice mail kicked in. Georgia left a message. "Call me. Something weird just happened, and I want to make sure you're okay."

She hung up. Who besides Sam had her number on speed dial? Maybe Ellie Foreman. She usually checked in once a month. Pete, her former neighbor who had gone back to his wife but still kept in touch. And her clients. Should she call them to make sure? No, that was overkill. She should just forget the call.

She went back to the cell records. Twenty minutes later she had it. One of the 312 numbers "Emily" called on the morning of the robbery was a landline registered to Tabitha Jefferson in Englewood on the South Side. When she cross-checked the woman's street address on a public White Pages database, the Englewood address listed three other occupants, including someone named Willard, whose age was listed between fifteen and twenty.

All the cops had to do now was establish the daisy chain between "Emily's" calls to Tabitha Jefferson and other calls made by either "Emily" or "Ms. Jefferson." Georgia knew they'd find some. She picked up her phone to call the Fields.

Chapter 7

Savannah—A Year Earlier

The car smelled like stale weed and something sweet that could have been either doughnuts or cookies. Vanna climbed in the front; Dex was behind the wheel. He gave her a toothy smile, which was unusual. Dex was a neo-Goth; he never smiled. His hair was long and stringy, he wore black clothes and even blacker eye shadow, and he claimed to know Dylan Klebold's little brother. Klebold was one of the jerks who shot up Columbine years earlier, then killed himself. Vanna wasn't sure Klebold even had a brother, but it didn't matter. Goths were uncool.

Vanna ignored his smile and looked around. It was dark outside, but a lamppost threw a shadowy light across the car. Still, she couldn't see much. "So where's the shit? I gotta be home by ten."

Dex's grin widened, showing off uneven teeth. He liked to make her wait, even grovel. She felt her eyes narrow. This was the worst part—making nice to guys to get what she wanted. But if she wanted to get high, and she most definitely did, she had to put up with it. Compared to some, Dex wasn't so bad. Not like Jason, the creep she'd been scoring from a few months ago. He demanded a BJ even before he'd talk business. Smelly too.

Vanna ran a hand down her long blond hair. Thick, straight, with just the hint of a curl at the ends, it was a rich shade of honey, but in the right light, it sparkled with lemony highlights. She didn't have to do anything to it—it just *was*. Her mother told her it was genes, that she'd had hair like that too, although to look at her now—at least when Vanna could bear to—you wouldn't think so. Her mother's hair was thin, disheveled, and flyaway. Just like the rest of her. It hadn't always been that way. When her father was still alive, they'd been a real family. Storybook land, home-cooked meals, happy endings. Vanna shook it off. She couldn't think about the past.

She turned toward Dex. "You got something to drink?"

"Maybe." He reached over to the backseat, felt around, and pulled out a bottle. The sweet smell intensified. Sloe gin. He passed it to her, and she took a swig. Tasted like Hawaiian Punch. The hazy memory of a kid's birthday party washed over her. Paper hats, pink party favors, birthday cake, and red punch, so perversely sweet it made her lips pucker. She held out the bottle. "You want?"

He shook his head. She took another swig and stowed the bottle on the floor. You had to be careful with Sloe gin. The first time she drank it, she'd guzzled half a bottle and puked her guts out.

"So what else ya got, Dex?" She was hoping for some meth. The high would help compensate for fucking him or whatever he wanted as payment.

He dug into a pocket and brought out a tiny, grimy crumple of cellophane. Either meth or blow. She stared at it eagerly, already imagining its bitter taste in the back of her throat. She wanted to grab it, do the lines, feel the rush. But she had to wait. Had to be patient.

She tried to be cool, even blasé, but Dex picked up her vibe. He held the package at eye level just out of reach. "Interested in some nose candy, little girl?"

Her insides grew warm and sticky with anticipation. She swallowed her pride. "You gonna share?"

He dangled the package back and forth like it was on a chain and smirked. "What's it worth to you, Vanna?"

If she'd had a weapon, she just might have shot him. Or stabbed him, then run away with the dope. But her only weapon was her body, and it took every ounce of self-control to use it to her benefit. "Tell you what, baby," she purred. "You give me a hit and see what happens."

His eyes gleamed even in the dim light. They'd parked at the back of a secluded parking lot in Littleton, Colorado, near the North Woods restaurant, although technically the area was called South Woods. Vanna didn't give a shit what they called it or what direction it went; truth was Littleton had nothing to recommend it. Probably why they called it "Little." The Denver suburb was just another faceless town her mother had dragged her to. Vanna had no illusions it would be the last. Since her father died, her mother flitted moth-like from town to town, trying to outrun her grief. Houston, Albuquerque, Tucson, now Denver. Always circling the sunbelt, looking for a better life, a better deal, then packing up when everything turned to shit and starting over somewhere else.

Dex took his time opening the package. "It's crystal," he said reverently.

Vanna's heart beat faster, and she ran her tongue over her lips. She couldn't help it. Another minute. That's all it would be.

"You got a blade and mirror?" Dex asked.

"A straw, too." She dug into her purse and produced the required tools. He laid the mirror on the dash, tapped out some crystals. She snapped on the dome light. The stuff looked a little dirty to her, not the white she associated with a better grade.

"What the fuck?" Dex growled. "Turn it off."

"Sorry. Just had to check." She turned it off.

Using the razor blade, he chopped the crystals into powder.

She wanted to tell him to hurry. Instead she said, "What's it cut with?"

He shrugged. "How the fuck do I know?" He pushed the stuff

across the mirror, making four fat lines, then reached for the straw. She didn't mind snorting the stuff, although smoking was a better high. But there wasn't enough time. She waited as he snorted a line. Then another. He squeezed his eyes shut. An ecstatic smile came over him, and he spread his arms.

Vanna took the straw and inhaled the other two lines. The rush started from a place deep inside, waves of bliss pulsing from her nose to her gut, her ribs, the backs of her knees, her toes. The rush pushed her higher, lifting her up, and she started to float above the car. Within seconds she was flying across a blue sky, cushioned by cottony white clouds. She could do anything. She couldn't fall. No pain. No darkness. She was looking down on all the sad children of the world. And all the ones she'd babysat. She wanted to scoop them up, cradle them, bury her nose in the folds of their sweet skin. Tickle their cheeks until they giggled. Tell them it would be okay. She would protect them.

Then she glanced over at Dex. His eyes were open now; he was watching her, breathing hard. He grabbed her hand, moved it over his crotch, and pressed down. His dick was rock hard. An itch tickled her groin. With his shiny eyes, slender build, and big cock, he wasn't so bad. She leaned back against the seat and let the itch climb up through her torso, her breasts, her throat. A motor revved through her body, vibrating, honing the itch. She was a racehorse pawing the ground, anxious to break out of the gate.

She reached over and fumbled with his zipper. When she'd freed his cock from his jeans, it sprang up, an eager soldier reporting for duty. She took it in her mouth. He groaned. She loved this moment, because she knew it was her doing. She sucked him until he started to tremble. He reached down, grasped the sides of her head between his hands, and lifted her off. She knew what he wanted. She lay back across the front seat, spread her legs, and hiked up her skirt. She never wore underwear; it took too long to get it off.

As he entered her, she sighed with pleasure. Everything was fine now. Just fine.

Chapter 8

When Georgia picked up the tail three blocks from her apartment two days later, an uneasy feeling shot through her. How long had he been following her? How had she missed him? She hadn't been paying attention; that's how. Totally unacceptable. Her powers of observation were supposed to be incontestable. First-rate. She tried to rationalize: people didn't follow her—it was usually the other way around; she had been preoccupied; she wasn't on the clock.

No. No excuses. She was no better than the teenagers she'd tailed the other day. More important, excuses wouldn't solve the problem. She forced herself to focus on the now. Do the reconnaissance. Take appropriate action. Passing a bookstore, she stole a glance in the window. A man was about a hundred yards behind her. Burly. Caucasian. Brown jacket, jeans, work boots, wool hat. Shoulders hunched against the cold. Hands slouched in pockets. She couldn't see his face, but he didn't seem to be anything special. Just an average guy. An amateur, too, to be so obvious. Was he connected to the flash rob?

Frigid air stung her face, but she picked up her pace. Chicagoland was in the grip of a bitter cold—the kind of cold that made people grateful for any bit of warmth, even the exhaust from a bus. She was bundled up herself, a bulky, nondescript fig-

ure heading south on Sherman Avenue. It would be hard to recognize anyone. So where did he pick her up? Had he been staking
out her apartment?

She slowed, reviewing basic countersurveillance techniques.
She could climb on a bus, take it down to Howard, then switch to
the El or a cab. Or she could double back to Benson Avenue, cut
through the parking lot, and circle around the bank. She'd likely
lose him either way, but both options would mean staying outside.
The sky was that miserable dirty gray that blankets Chicago from
November until March, and the numbing cold sapped her resolve.
Losing him wouldn't tell her why he'd been tailing her in the first
place.

She stopped outside a coffee shop on the corner of Sherman
and Davis, hoping he'd follow her in. It was a fifty-fifty shot. As
she pushed through the door, a coffee-scented gust of warmth
wafted over her. She went to the front window and waited.

He didn't appear. Georgia frowned. Was he not sure he had
the right target? Had someone ordered him not to approach but
simply report in? Or was he a pervert waiting for the right moment
to pounce? She waited another few seconds, then turned around
and unzipped her jacket. Whoever he was, whatever he wanted,
he could damn well freeze his ass off. She wouldn't.

She headed over to the counter. There were only a couple of
other people in the shop besides Paul Crosby, who was working
the afternoon shift. Tall, slim, with brown hair, Paul had a sweet
face marred by an ugly mole on his left cheek. She worried about
that mole and kept nagging him to get it looked at, but Paul was
cavalier, claiming it was the mark of God. What sort of mark, he
couldn't explain. He moonlighted as a drummer for a blues band,
and she'd spent plenty of nights at Hanson's listening to him jam.
He'd even come on to her once or twice, but they were listless,
halfhearted passes.

Now he was wiping down the espresso machine. She cleared
her throat. He looked up and brightened. "Hey. What's happening, peaches?"

"My bones are cold." No sense telling him about the tail. They'd both know soon enough.

"I got just the thing." Paul began playing with the levers of a giant metallic coffee machine with lots of tubes, valves, and handles. Steam hissed, curled into the air, and dissipated. Black liquid dropped into a cup. He pulled another lever. Something sputtered, and white foam covered the black. He slapped a top on the cup and handed it to Georgia. She took a sip.

"Thanks. This hits the spot." She went back to the window. She couldn't see the guy.

"They're saying more snow tonight," said one of the people in the shop, an elderly man with snowy white hair and beard.

"Feels that way," Paul replied and started on one of his rants about the Chicago winter and how it wasn't for wimps. Georgia barely listened—it was the sort of mindless chatter that passed for genuine communication today. Instead she mentally reviewed her cases. The flash rob case was over. She was still investigating a domestic and a workers' comp claim, in which the plaintiff alleged he'd thrown his back out while working in a Lincolnwood factory, except he'd worked there only a week before he was fired for selling crack in the parking lot.

Still, unless her client was holding out on her, it wasn't a heater. Or dangerous enough to warrant a tail. Neither was the domestic. She doctored her coffee with sweetener, shook off her coat, and sat at a small round table. Someone had left a newspaper, and she idly thumbed through it. The paper, shrunken and plastered with photos and color graphics, wasn't good for much more than lining a birdcage.

Not that she was a big reader. She'd never been a good student; she discovered in high school she was dyslexic. Overcoming it would require a lot of behavioral changes, they said. Georgia decided she didn't have the time or the inclination, so she accepted the stigma that came with the label. She had a disability. She was slow. A retard. It hadn't really mattered. There were plenty of high school boys eager for her expertise in other things.

The door to the coffee shop opened. Georgia went on alert, but it was just a man and a woman, shivering and complaining about the cold. They ordered lattes, sat, and launched into an intense discussion about monetizing websites.

"You should come out to Bill's tonight," Paul called out over their chatter and the hum of the espresso machine. "I'm playing with Louie."

She folded the newspaper and looked out the front window. No one. Had the tail given up?

"Maybe."

"It might be one of our last gigs there. I don't think the place is gonna make it."

"Sorry to hear that." She gazed out the window.

Paul caught it. "Something going on?"

She shook her head. But his question spurred her to action. She zipped up her jacket and put on her gloves. She didn't like loose ends. Time to confront the tail, if he was still there. Find out what he wanted. She took her coffee to the counter and set it down. "I'll be back in a minute. Save it for me."

Paul's eyebrows rose.

"Don't worry." She flashed him a smile.

She hunched her shoulders and went outside. The sky had darkened, and a few errant snowflakes sifted down. She glanced in both directions. She easily spotted the guy, leaning against the wall of a building on the same side of the street as the coffee shop. His gaze was on the coffee shop door; he wasn't even trying to be inconspicuous. Irritation flashed through her. She pulled her jacket close, intending to approach him and demand he tell her why he was following her. But as she turned toward him, a black SUV turned the corner and headed down Sherman.

Suddenly a burst of lightning-fast images exploded. The SUV headed toward the man who'd been tailing her. As it came abreast, it slowed. The man who'd been tailing her froze. A look of horror tore across his face. The passenger window rolled down. Georgia knew what was going to happen.

"Drop!" she yelled. "Get down and roll!"

The man didn't move. He was still staring at the SUV, his features a frozen grimace of fear. Georgia waved her hands and tried to simulate a crouching-down motion. But he couldn't see her. The barrel of a rifle emerged from the passenger window of the SUV. She couldn't make out the model, but when her tail saw it, his mouth dropped open, and he reeled back.

Not fast enough.

A series of loud cracks split the air. The man who'd been tailing her folded up like an accordion. The SUV driver gunned his engine, fishtailed, then shot down Sherman Avenue.

Chapter 9

"**S**o you have no idea who he was or why he was tailing you." The detective's voice was heavy with scorn.

"That's right." Georgia made an effort to keep her voice neutral. An hour had passed, and she was back in the coffee shop. Sherman Avenue was now a crime scene, crawling with uniforms, techs, reconstruction experts, and a photographer. The experts were trying to analyze skid marks, the speed of the SUV, and the bullets' trajectory. The techs were sifting and bagging. The photographer was shooting. The uniforms weren't even trying to look busy.

Detective Raoul Gutierrez, in jeans, heavy sweater, and peacoat, looked to be about her age, early thirties. He had dark hair, a trimmed goatee, and an edgy hostility. Was it because he was Hispanic? Frustrated he hadn't risen far enough, fast enough? She could relate; she'd struggled when she was the token female on the force.

She picked up her coffee, trying to calm her nerves, but realized her hand was still shaking. "Like I said before, I never saw the guy."

The detective caught it. "Is that a fact. Then how do you know he was tailing you?"

She leveled a look at him, all the while thinking she had to pull it together. She was a PI, for Christ's sake. And a cop before that. It might have taken her a while to pick him up, but she *had*. She might have been freaked-out by the drive-by, but she'd seen worse. "I know when I'm being followed."

Gutierrez fingered his goatee like he was vain about it. She took another sip of now cold coffee. She grimaced.

Paul held up his hand. "I'll make you another."

"Thanks."

As Paul brought her a new drink, one of the techs strode inside and hustled over to Gutierrez. The detective stood, gave Georgia his back, and conferred with the guy. The tech flipped up his hands and went outside. Gutierrez turned around.

"There's no ID on the vic."

She shrugged. She'd expected that.

"You sure you have no idea who he was?" He sat again, arms folded.

Gutierrez must be one of those cops who bullied others before they could bully him. She appraised his build. Slender but wiry. Ropy neck muscles. Probably a martial arts expert.

"Nope," she said almost cheerfully, then immediately regretted it. No reason to stoop to his level.

"What about the SUV? You get the plate?"

"Sorry." She hoped it sounded sincere.

"I thought you used to be a cop." His glare was a mix of irritation and triumph, as if he'd scored a three-pointer.

"The SUV took off too fast. But"—she paused and took a sip of her drink—"I did get a partial."

The detective's eyebrows arched. "That so? You planning to share?"

"It started with six-three-three."

"Illinois plates?"

Georgia nodded.

Gutierrez wrote it down.

"You see anyone inside the SUV?"

"Two people. Driver. Passenger."

"Descriptions?"

She shook her head. "They wore ski masks."

Gutierrez took out a ChapStick, removed the top, and rolled it over his lips, carefully avoiding his goatee. He stuffed it back in his pocket. "You're not giving me much."

"Look, Detective. I want to know who the hell was tailing me as much as you. I was the target, remember?" She folded her arms. "After all, if A killed B, and B was following me, A might come after me."

He looked her over with an expression that said he didn't really give a shit. Was he playing bad cop? Trying a sexist ploy? Whatever his motive, she'd had enough. She zipped up her jacket, finished her drink, and hoisted her bag on her shoulder. She was just standing when his cell rang. He fished it out of a pocket and took the call.

"Gutierrez..." He got up again and stepped away from Georgia. She tried to eavesdrop, but he was out of earshot. She looked over at Paul, who rolled his eyes. She glanced through the window. The media vans had arrived. She'd have to be careful. Gutierrez started back in her direction.

"I'll do that. Thanks." He snapped the phone shut and held it up. "You have a friend."

Georgia's eyebrows went up.

"O'Malley. Deputy superintendent up north. Says you're okay."

She didn't mind Gutierrez checking her out; any good cop would. Dan O'Malley had been her peer, then her boss, when she was a cop. They still talked, usually when he was trying to persuade her to come back on the force. She'd been suspended over an administrative matter a few years earlier, set up shop as a PI, then resigned. She didn't *want* to go back. She liked being her own boss. Still, it was reassuring to know someone had her back. She just wished O'Malley had been more vocal when the suspension went down.

"Good." She stood and tossed her cup in the trash. "Anything else? I need to get going."

"Listen, I—well—if you don't mind, let's go over it again." Gutierrez's tone was less hostile now, almost civil. He sat and motioned to the empty chair. Georgia sat. He summarized what she'd already told him: a stranger was tailing her. Could have picked her up outside her apartment. He followed her here but didn't approach. She went into the coffee shop, then came out fifteen minutes later to confront him. He got shot in a drive-by. That was it.

"You got any enemies you know of? Cases you're working on that are hot?"

She thought about Reggie Field and the flash rob at his store. Sure, property had been stolen and tempers had frayed. But tailing her and killing someone who didn't appear to have anything to do with the robbery? It made no sense. Still, she told him about the case.

Gutierrez scribbled on a notepad. She could tell he didn't think it was a strong lead either. She told him about her other cases too.

"So you think the offenders who gunned down the tail will be coming after you?" He asked.

"No clue. But the way I figure it, the tail either wanted to give me information or wanted information from me. The *offenders*"—she almost smiled—"didn't want one of those things to happen. If they're coming after me, I guess I'll know soon enough."

Gutierrez was silent for a minute. "You mind if we call your clients?"

Georgia hesitated. "Yes, I do. My cases are confidential. But I'll canvass them myself and let you know if I find anything."

Gutierrez didn't look happy, but he must have realized there wasn't much to be gained by pushing—more than he had.

"One thing," she said. "The media. Can you keep them off my back? I don't want to end up on the six o'clock news. Have them stake out my place. It's bad for business."

He appeared to be mulling it over. Then he gave her a brief nod. "We'll keep it quiet. But that doesn't mean *they* will." He handed her his card. "Keep me informed. I want to nail these guys."

She nodded back. "Me too."

He almost smiled. Gutierrez might be an asshole, but he was a good cop.

Chapter 10

For dinner Georgia made a grilled cheese sandwich, added chips and dill pickles, and ate in her kitchen. The room wasn't big, but she'd been able to squeeze in a tiny table under a large double-hung window. During the day she liked to watch the sun glitter through the trees, fingers of light and shadow making abstract designs on the walls. Of course, in winter, the sun was gone by four thirty, and despite a cheery day once in a while, this winter had been especially gloomy. After a week of overcast, the media had proclaimed Chicago more depressing than Portland.

She finished the sandwich, took a Snapple into the living room, and went online, hoping to identify, or at least narrow down, who owned the SUV. But first she had to figure out what model it was. She searched SUVs, clicked on the images, and studied the photos. She ruled out a Mercedes—its headlights were too elliptical. It wasn't a Hyundai, Audi, or Ford, either. Toyota and Nissan were close, although she might be sending herself down a blind alley if it turned out to be a Chevy or Honda. Still, she had to start somewhere. She printed out pictures of three or four models and pinned them up on the corkboard behind her desk.

She didn't have an in at the Illinois DMV, but she had the next best thing: a set of databases so reliable they were used by police departments all over the country. Her favorite was FindersKeepers, which allowed her to slice and dice information in any number of ways. She logged on to the website, agreed to a onetime charge of fifteen bucks, and clicked on "Find vehicle."

When prompted for the type of car, she entered "Nissan," "Black" for color, and for model, "SUV." For the year of the car, she selected "All years." She was asked what states she wanted to search. "Illinois." There were several options when it came to license plates: "All," "Starts with," "Ends with," "None." She chose "Starts with" and entered "633." She clicked on "Find."

Three seconds later, she was looking at a list of twenty-three black Nissan SUVs that had Illinois plates beginning with 633. Each listing included the VIN number, the full license plate, the date the auto was registered, make, model, and year, and best of all, the owners and their addresses. She was printing out the list when she heard a car outside gun its motor. She went into her kitchen and gazed out the window. The car immediately took off down the street and out of sight. She could only catch a glimpse of the vehicle, but it was dark and boxy and looked like a van—maybe an SUV.

She shivered and studied the row house across the street. A single mother with young children lived there, and their lawn, in good weather, was kiddie heaven, strewn with toys, bikes, and wagons. Now, though, the lawn was desolate and empty, and the blanket of snow covering it was rutted with scraggly grass. Was the driver of the car visiting her neighbor?

The snow cover threw off a muted blue glow that turned the dark into a faux twilight, but the eerie illumination was oddly comforting, allowing just enough light to keep predators from lurking unseen. Georgia took a good look up and down the street. No more strange cars, no media, no people. That was good. Still, she pulled down the blinds and double locked her door.

She went to her closet and checked her guns. She still had her 9 mm Sig Sauer, but she'd recently bought a Glock 26, a "baby

Glock." The size of a snub-nose, it could be concealed in her pocket or bag. She loved how it felt; its recoil was almost as gentle as the Sig's. Like the Sig it was a 9 mm and could take ten plus one in the chamber. She took it into her bedroom and slipped it in the drawer of her nightstand.

She undressed, got into bed, and tried to distract herself with a graphic novel. She'd been reading them more often: with her dyslexia, they went down easily, and she loved the illustrations. Within a few minutes, though, she put it down. She knew what she wanted; it wasn't a character drawn on a piece of paper. But instead of a warm body curled up beside her, calming and comforting, she had a pulp novel and a loaded gun.

Chapter 11

Armed with a strong cup of coffee the next morning, Georgia went back online to cross-reference SUV owners on FindersKeepers. Some were registered to Chicagoans, but others lived in St. Charles, Peoria, and Carbondale. A smattering of foreign names appeared on the list, mostly Hispanic, but one looked Russian or Eastern European.

Two of the SUV owners had DUIs. Two others had court case numbers, one in Cook County, one in Sangamon. She planned to check them out, although just because someone had a DUI, or even a criminal conviction, that didn't mean they'd killed someone. Then she reconsidered. The police were undoubtedly doing the same thing as she, and they had access to better data. She should spend her time looking into something they wouldn't.

She pulled up her own case files. Maybe she'd been too cavalier with Gutierrez yesterday. It was possible that someone involved in one of her cases had been following her. The domestic, the case of the wife who ran away, could be promising. The man tailing Georgia might have been a relative of the runaway wife or husband, and if *he* was involved with sleazy characters, he might have been targeted by the men in the SUV. In the workers' comp case, the guy who'd been fired *was* clearly involved in illegal activities. What if he was seeking revenge for being fingered? Or what if he stiffed his dealer?

She spent most of the day interviewing her clients, prodding them to suggest people who might have been tailing her for some reason. She asked if anyone they knew drove an SUV. She came away with a long list of people to check out, but most seemed dubious, even wacky. For example, a legitimate customer at Designer Discount Den was upset by the invasion of her privacy because of the YouTube video, although how anyone could connect *her* to the flash rob was unclear. And someone had filed a workplace sexual harassment charge years ago against the pharmaceutical executive.

Still, you never knew.

By the time she finished, it was after four. She drove to her gym, a small converted warehouse with foggy, sweat-soaked windows, a boxing ring, and surprisingly good exercise equipment. She did some cardio, worked out with weights, then did two rounds in the ring. Her spotter, who was also the boxing coach, was a knotted, gray-haired man who looked like Burgess Meredith's father. He kept telling her she should shadow box in front of a mirror. Concentrate on her footwork and punches. Step, slide, jab. Step, slide, punch. "And don't forget to dip when you slide, and bob and weave when you're still. And—oh—remember to stay relaxed at all times," he added cheerfully.

She decided he was the perfect coach; she was ready to slug him by the time they were done.

Chapter 12

Mickey's, an old-style bar and grill in Evanston, was owned by Owen Dougherty, who bought it from Mickey so long ago that no one remembered who Mickey was. Which wasn't a bad thing for the customers who'd been flocking to it for years. In the years Georgia had been hanging out, though, little had changed, which wasn't good for future business. Evanston had been inundated by high-end establishments, and two new hipster places had opened on the same block.

But Mickey's sported the same scarred bar, scuffed booths, and even the same waitress, a single mother of three who was studying for her CPA at Kellogg. Owen wore the same apron and draped the same bar towel over his shoulder, except when he took off for Arizona during the winter and left his son-in-law in charge. Georgia wondered if Owen's snowbird status was an omen.

She walked in, trailing a gust of cold air, which was snuffed out by a delicious warmth scented with grease. Samantha Mosele sat in a booth, sipping a glass of wine. Sam was a brunette with precise features and dark, merry eyes. She'd recently cut her hair, and her short curly bob gave her an elfin quality. She and Georgia had met years ago when they were both taking courses at Oakton. They'd remained friends, unusual for Georgia, who was a loner by nature.

She slid into the booth. "You get my message?"

Sam frowned. "What message?"

Sam wasn't the most dependable person in the world. Georgia told her about the phone call two days earlier.

Sam shook her head. "Wasn't me. I've—um—been busy."

"I thought I heard a man and a woman. Arguing."

"Well, I've been with a man. But I definitely wasn't arguing."

Georgia drummed her fingers. If it wasn't Sam's cell, butt-dial or not, whose had it been?

"Hey, I'm hungry," Sam said.

"Thirsty, too, I see."

"I'm celebrating." Sam tipped her glass toward Georgia. "New client."

"Website?"

Sam nodded. A graphics designer, Sam was coming into her own, developing and maintaining websites. "An appliance company. They're moving their commerce online. And here's the best part. Lots of updates and revisions, all the time." She waved toward the waitress, who was bussing plates at the next booth. "Another round for me and my friend."

Gemma came over. "Howdy, stranger," she said to Georgia. "Where you been?"

"Being a couch potato. You?"

"Just started my last semester. With any luck, I'll have my CPA by fall."

And you won't be working at Mickey's, Georgia thought. Another omen. Aloud she said, "I'll have a Diet Coke with lemon."

Gemma floated back to the bar and returned with their drinks. After setting them down, she motioned to the menus. "You need some time?"

Georgia shook her head.

"The usual?"

Georgia smiled. She loved that someone knew what she wanted without her having to ask.

Gemma turned to Sam. "And you?"

"Double it."

Gemma disappeared into the kitchen.

"So what's new?" Sam asked.

"Strange doings." Georgia explained about the tail who was gunned down.

Sam looked shocked. "What are you doing about it?"

Georgia told her she'd cross-checked the plate online, followed up with interviews, and was about to do more data mining. "But since it was a homicide, the cops are doing the heavy lifting."

"Aren't you worried? I mean, someone follows you and then gets shot. And you get a strange phone call. That's a little too close for comfort, right?"

"Maybe. Maybe not."

"You need to be careful."

"Let's drop it, okay? I just want a nice burger."

Sam shrugged and started in on her second glass of wine. "Have you ever calculated how much time you spend at the computer every day?"

"Way too much." Georgia said. "But that's what PIs do these days. Checking sources, databases—"

"Excuse me." A male voice cut her off. "My friend and I would like to buy you a round. Would that be okay?"

Georgia looked up. She'd noticed the two guys at the bar when she came in. About her age, they had the Chicago winter look: jeans, boots, heavy sweaters, down vests. One had dark hair, and dark eyes with just enough lines at the corners to suggest a life well lived. The other was blond, with a scruffy growth of something that wasn't quite a beard. He also had a nice butt, which Sam was happily eyeing. Georgia and Sam exchanged brief looks; then Georgia turned to the one with dark hair, the one who'd spoken.

"It's not necessary. I just drink Diet Coke with lemon."

Sam pursed her lips at Georgia, then looked at the guy with an eager smile. "But I drink Chardonnay..."

Dark Eyes grinned and went back to the bar. As he did,

Gemma brought their food: burgers, very rare. Georgia tore into hers and shoveled fries into her mouth. Meanwhile, Nice Butt slid into the booth next to Sam. "I'm Noel."

Dark Eyes returned with a Chardonnay for Sam and a Diet Coke for Georgia and sat next to Georgia. "I know it wasn't necessary, and my name is Jay."

Sam introduced herself, and then, after a pause, so did Georgia. Sam took a sip of her drink. "Thanks." She smiled at Jay, clearly enjoying the attention. "So," she said, "if we can only know one thing about you two, what should it be?"

"How about that I think you have the most beautiful eyes I've ever seen?" Noel said.

Sam made the sound of a raspberry. "You're gonna need to do better than that." She turned to Jay. "What about you?"

He paused. Then, "I raise chickens in my backyard. And I give my neighbors the eggs."

Georgia, pleasantly surprised, turned toward him. "How'd you get into that?"

He answered by talking about sustainability and reducing his carbon footprint. While he talked, Georgia noticed his lips. Not too thin—she wasn't a fan of thin lips. Maybe this wasn't a bad idea.

He grinned as if he knew what she was thinking and it was fine with him. "Okay. Your turn. What should I know about you?" Jay said.

"Well." She considered it. "I'm a PI."

"A what?"

"A PI...private investigator." Better to tell him now. It always had an effect. Men who were intimidated or had something to hide drifted away.

He didn't seem concerned. "So, you're like...what...that woman on *Castle*?"

"She's a cop. I'm private."

"Wow...I wouldn't have taken you for a dick."

She sighed inwardly. So he was trite. Most men were. "Actually, I was just telling Sam I spend most of my day hunched over a computer."

Georgia stole a look at Sam. She and Noel were now chatting, leaving the impression they didn't want to be interrupted. She turned back to Jay. He wasn't intimidated by her being a PI. He raised chickens. He was sexy. She rolled a fry in ketchup, put it into her mouth, then decided she wasn't hungry anymore. She was glad she'd worn her hair down. She ran a hand through it so it would fall over her face just right. Ever so slightly she angled her body into his personal space. "So what do you do when you're not raising chickens?"

"I own a plumbing company."

Stable. Responsible. Established. Even better. And his lips were just right. He gazed back at her with an expression that said there was nothing but clear sailing ahead. Her stomach flipped. This could be a good night. Maybe a great one.

He slid closer and picked up one of her fries. "You mind?"

She shook her head. He'd just finished chewing it when his cell trilled. He fished it out, checked the screen, then got up from the booth and moved out of earshot to answer it.

She stiffened.

She watched him, talking softly, his back to her, shoulders hunched. Then he snapped the phone shut, slipped it back in a pocket, and sauntered back to the table, mustering a weak smile.

But the spell was broken. "You're married," she said.

He swallowed and dipped his head. At least he had the decency not to deny it.

Georgia thought about it. "This must be what it looks like to have egg all over your face." She paused. "Thanks for the drink, but it's time for you to go home."

Chapter 13

By the time Georgia left Mickey's, the wind had kicked up, spitting pinpricks of sleet that stung her face. When she got to the car she turned the heat and defroster on high.

Sam jettisoned her guy soon after Georgia. After what happened to Jay, Noel claimed to be "separated." Not good enough, said Sam, who, after the men made a hasty exit, ranted about the nerve of some men who thought—no—expected women to gratefully drop their panties after one drink.

Like Sam, Georgia was irritated too. Not that Jay was dangerous. Deceptive, but probably innocuous. No. Her disappointment was more subtle: she had allowed herself to hope. To expect something good would happen just because she was ready for it. She should have known that anytime she pretended to be a normal person, someone for whom good things happened as a matter of course, God reminded her that wasn't his plan.

She parked around the corner and trudged to her door, trying to shield herself from the sleet. She had more SUVs to check out, but she wasn't optimistic. The odds of finding out why the guy had been tailing her were growing slimmer. This was one of the times she missed being a cop.

She'd call Gutierrez tomorrow. They would have done the autopsy—maybe she'd learn something. Maybe he'd let her read the GPRs. Aside from that, though, there wasn't a lot more she could do. She wasn't hurt, and no one was threatening her. It might be time to let it go.

She entered the vestibule. On the left wall were six mailboxes. Below them was a small table covered with junk mail. One was for a new pizza delivery place. Someone else wanted to clean her carpets. Nothing interesting or even important, except bills. That's why she only checked her mail every few days. She slid in a key and pulled out her mail: ComEd, phone, and cable bills, and a long white envelope with a blue Post-it attached. She read the Post-it:

Found this wedged between the wall and the table. Don't know how long.

It was signed by one of her upstairs neighbors. She turned it over. Stamped, addressed to her in black ink, but scratchy penmanship. No return address. The envelope was so light she wasn't sure anything was inside. She held it up. Maybe a sheet of paper.

She climbed up to her apartment. Inside she peeled off her coat, gloves, and hat and took the mail into the kitchen. She didn't like unidentified mail. She considered not opening it. She considered putting on gloves in case it contained a toxic substance. No. She was being paranoid. She shook it lightly. The contents didn't move. If it was powder, there was only a trace amount. She was reasonably confident whatever was inside wouldn't explode. She considered asking her neighbor upstairs what he knew about it, but it was already after ten. Too late.

She took a breath and opened it. A small scrap of paper drifted to the floor. She picked it up. Thin, opaque, as scratchy as tissue paper, it had skinny red and yellow stripes on one side. It looked like a fast-food wrapper. She smelled it. A faint odor of grease. She noticed a brown smudge in one corner. Ketchup? There was also the black bleed-through of writing from the other side. She turned it over. Written in the same jagged penmanship as the envelope was a note.

Georgia, I am your half sister, Savannah. I'm in Chicago and I'm pregnant.

I need your help. Please find me.

Chapter 14

Georgia wandered around her apartment, the note in her hand. She didn't have a sister. It was a hoax. A crude, tasteless joke. You just don't barge into someone's life and turn it upside down like that. Sure, there were people who didn't like her. She probably had an enemy or two. But she didn't know anyone with the nerve to do this. It had to be a lie.

She padded into the kitchen. Sleep would be impossible. She brewed a pot of coffee. She carefully anchored the note on the counter with an empty mug. The coffeepot beeped. She poured and took a sip. Was this why she'd been tailed? Someone wanted to tell her she had a sister? No. There was no reason to think the tail who'd been gunned down was connected to this note.

The phone call the other night was another matter. Was someone—even "Savannah" herself—calling? If so, why not leave a message? Or text? Unless she couldn't. Maybe she was doing it in secret, contacting her on the sly. Is that why she couldn't talk? Because she got caught? But why *wouldn't* someone want Georgia to know she had a sister? Why force the caller, whoever it was, to hang up? Because it was a lie? Or the truth?

* * *

Georgia had been an only child. Or so she thought. Her father was a cop, her mother, Jobeth, a housewife who abandoned her when Georgia was ten. She knew for a fact that her father never looked at other women afterward. Until the day he died, his liver and heart pickled by booze, he hated women. In fact, as she matured, he began to blame Georgia for his problems.

It didn't help that she had long blond hair, large brown eyes, and a knockout figure that must have reminded him of her mother. Or that she spent most of high school in a blur of backseats, booze, and weed. Until the night she staggered home, lipstick and mascara smeared, and her father pulled out the belt. Shouting that she was just like her mother, a no-good tramp who whored her way out of his life. Two weeks later, when he hit her again, Georgia moved out.

Her mother, on the other hand, was an enigma. She'd been a good mother, but there was something off about her. As if she couldn't let herself be happy for longer than brief moments. They'd be making cookies, laughing and teasing and eating the raw batter despite her mother's warnings that she'd get a tummy ache. But then her mother would suddenly withdraw and behave as if Georgia was invisible.

Georgia would tug on her sleeve and say, "Mommy, did you hear me?" Sometimes it worked, and her mother snapped back. But other times, her mother ignored her and stared into space, her eyes a mix of sorrow, isolation, and fear. As if she was a fragile bird trapped and chained to its roost like that painting and book everyone was talking about. Now, years later, Georgia thought she knew why, but back then, she had no clue that her father was an abusive monster. They—her mother especially—had kept it hidden.

Then came the day Georgia returned home from school and found her mother gone. Her father claimed to have no idea where she'd gone or why. Georgia waited for her to come back, but after a few desperate, soul-crushing months, she persuaded herself she didn't care. Her mother was gone. She didn't love Georgia. Which meant that Georgia was fundamentally unlovable.

That was borne out by the absence of any contact going for-ward. Her mother couldn't be bothered to acknowledge Georgia was still alive. What was wrong with a phone call? Or one of those crappy "Thinking of You" cards? Even an email? It was as if her mother had fallen off a cliff, taking all of Georgia's love and affec-tion with her. And now, if the note was the truth, it seemed as if her mother had replaced her with another daughter, as easily as switching toothpaste.

Georgia took her coffee and the scrap of paper into her bed-room and sat on the bed. The tick of her alarm clock sliced the silence like a blade. She reread the note.

I am your half sister, Savannah.

Her mother, Jobeth Crawford, had been raised in rural Geor-gia. The closest city was Savannah. Her childhood had been the happiest days of her life, her mother always said. That's why she named her Georgia. For her home, and for her baby daughter's peachy-pink skin. Her mother had taken Georgia down south when she was five. Her memories of the trip were hazy, but she did remember a picnic table with slabs of ribs, coleslaw, and fresh peaches. And lots of grown-ups whose perfumed sweat stung her nose and whose lipstick stained her cheeks. Naming another girl "Savannah" wouldn't have been a stretch.

I'm in Chicago and I'm pregnant. I need your help. Please find me.

Chicago was a big place. Why didn't Savannah say where she was? And why didn't she leave a phone number? If the note had really come from her half sister, wouldn't she want Georgia to contact her right away? Unless, for some reason, she couldn't. Was that why she'd asked Georgia to "find" her? But if that was the case, how had she been able to write the note at all? It didn't make sense.

Georgia fired up the computer and Googled "Jobeth Craw-ford," something she hadn't done in years. When she was still on the force, she'd tried to do a background check but came up empty. No "Jobeths" this time either, but she did find a few "J. Crawfords" and even a "JB Crawford" in Minnesota. Still, she doubted her mother would go north. She'd probably headed south. Or west.

She closed up Google and was about to ball the note up and pitch it in the trash when the brown splotch in the corner caught her eye. She examined it. Even though it was on a sandwich wrapper, the smudge didn't look thick enough to be ketchup. A coffee stain? Gravy? Or something else?

She shook her head. She had to stop. Lots of young girls ended up pregnant. Why should she care about one of them? Even if she did claim to be her sister? Her family history wasn't one of intimacy. Or permanence. Why should she care? The chances were that someone was just fucking with her. It wasn't her problem. In fact, when she thought about it, there was no reason for her to give a shit at all about a young girl in trouble. Her mother hadn't.

Chapter 15

"I never thought something like this would happen a block away from us." The woman behind the counter fingered a strand of pearls around her neck.

A second woman in the back of the shop replied. "I know what you mean. It's—it's disturbing."

The next morning was one of those bright, crisp days that made people think winter wasn't so bad. Georgia had stopped into the Susan Hatters art gallery, a relatively new shop not far from the crime scene. It was the type of upscale place Evanston had lured in an effort to distinguish itself from the blight of Rogers Park on one side and the middle-class ennui of Wilmette on the other. Unfortunately, a murder on one of the main thoroughfares wouldn't help its carefully crafted image.

"From what I can tell they don't have many clues." The woman with the pearls was attractive in an over-sixty, Botoxed way. With expensive clothes and even more expensive cosmetics, the only giveaway of her age was her hands, which, despite a perfect manicure, revealed loose, crepey skin speckled with age spots. "Have you heard anything, Susan?"

"Nothing," replied the other woman, who was clearly Susan Hatters, the owner. She looked Georgia up and down, then flashed her a smile.

Georgia smiled back. She briefly considered telling them who she was, but the police hadn't released any information connecting her to the crime. She kept her mouth shut.

Jittery from too much caffeine and not enough sleep, she'd popped into the gallery to take a break from the questions swirling around her brain. She couldn't draw a straight line, and the artwork was way out of her price range, but she was attracted to art. She would study the play of light on a canvas, its shapes and colors. She would admire the composition and speculate about the mood of the painter. Matt used to say it had something to do with left-brain activity—or was it right-brain? He'd tried to interest her in photography, claiming the principles were the same. But photography was too real; it exposed too much. She gazed at a colorful abstract in blues, greens, and violet. She shied away from color in her own life.

"Well, they're saying it was an isolated incident," Pearl Lady went on. "And that there's no danger to the community."

"So what's their theory? Drugs?" Hatters asked. With long brown hair tied back in a ponytail, she was wearing jeans and a flannel shirt and looked more like a hippie than a gallery owner. Maybe that was the point, Georgia thought. Pearl Lady for the older generation, Hippie Sue for the younger. Ingenious.

"Isn't it always?" The older woman gave a shrug and twisted her pearls again.

Georgia turned to a painting of a sailboat being launched off the shore of a rocky beach. She tilted her head. Something about that setting was familiar. She knew this place. She tried to blot out the chatter so she could concentrate, but the women's conversation was relentless.

"I hear there's going to be a press conference this morning," Pearl Lady said.

Georgia's stomach lurched. That was news to her. Had they ID'd the tail? Or was the conference simply to soothe nervous residents? Were they going to reveal her part? Gutierrez had promised not to; then again, he wasn't in charge. Some PR flunky might pull rank on him. Having her name bandied around was not good. It would draw attention to her. And whoever gunned down the tail.

She continued to stare at the sailboat. She knew nothing about technique, but she was drawn to the painting. A lonely beach, cresting waves, a muscular surf. A figure stood on the boat, but it was indistinct, and she couldn't tell if it was male or female. That had to be intentional, Georgia thought. The artist wanted to emphasize the smallness of man versus nature. One lonely sailor against the elements.

"I hear the mayor's speaking," Pearl Lady said.

Georgia's gut loosened. The fact that the mayor was talking meant the press conference was political. The mayor of Evanston, a down-to-earth woman Georgia occasionally saw in the grocery store, needed to calm turbulent waters. She'd gone door to door after a previous murder asking residents for suggestions on how to make the city safer. Georgia turned away from the painting.

"You like that?" Hatters asked. "We just got it in."

"It's powerful," Georgia said. "I feel the passion."

Hatters nodded. "That's what drew me to it."

"Funny, it looks familiar. I keep thinking I've been there before."

"It was done by a woman in Glencoe. She was away for a while and just got back."

"Where was she?"

"I'm not supposed to say." Hatters's voice dropped to a conspiratorial whisper. She leaned over the counter. "But everybody knows. She was in prison."

Georgia sucked in a breath. She turned back to the painting and peered at the artist's initials in the lower right corner. *A.W.* Andrea Walcher. She'd dealt with Walcher and her daughter on a case not long ago. She'd been to their house, a palatial estate that overlooked the lake in Glencoe. The painting was a lake view of the rocky beach below their home. *Small world,* she thought.

Or maybe it wasn't.

Chapter 16

Georgia reached Gutierrez on his cell a few minutes before the press conference. "You were going to keep me in the loop."

"Your point?" No "Hi, how are you." More important, no "I'm sorry." Gutierrez wasn't big on pleasantries. Then again, neither was she.

"How about the mayor's about to hold a press conference, and I heard about it in an art gallery?"

"It's got nothing to do with the investigation. It's just to smooth things over. Remind everyone the mayor is committed to make Evanston safe. I didn't think it was relevant."

He had a point. Still, it rankled.

"You got anything new?" he asked.

She hesitated, then decided to be a good soldier and summarized the review of her cases. She gave him the names of people she thought he should follow up on. Then, "What about the autopsy? It was this morning, right?"

"Not much. Except for one thing."

"What was that?"

"There were some tattoos."

Georgia stiffened. "What kind?"

"The kind they get in Russian prisons."

"What were they? Fire? Stars? A castle? Nazi symbols?"

"How do you know about those?"

She smiled inwardly. "I worked a case years ago where tattoos were important."

"They were on his chest. And his back. And his arms. Stars, military insignias, even a frigging fortress."

"You know that's all code, right? Like how high up they were before they went in, how many years they spent in prison—"

"We're working on it."

Of course they were. She cleared her throat. "What about the owner of the SUV? I seem to recall one or two names that sounded like they were from that part of the world."

"We're on that, too." He was quiet for a minute. "Listen, Davis, we're not planning to release anything about the tattoos. So if it leaks, I'll know who."

"Got it."

"Anything else?"

She debated whether to tell him about the note. She decided not to and clicked off. A few years ago while she was still a cop, someone had dropped off a videotape at Ellie Foreman's home. She still wasn't sure what to call Foreman: a friend, a colleague, a pain in the ass? The tape showed the murder of an unidentified woman. Both she and Ellie had traced the woman, helped in part by a tattoo on the dead woman's wrist. That tattoo, a star rising out of a torch, had been favored by Russian criminals.

She headed down to the coffee shop. A lot of bad guys had slipped into the country after the Soviet Union collapsed. They were called Mafiya, but in truth, they weren't that organized. Russian mobsters had no loyalty. No omertà. Or quid pro quos. They were vicious, soulless thugs who would rather kill than negotiate. For them, murder—the more violent the better—was simply the cost of doing business.

If the vic who'd been shot the other day was Russian Mafiya, it put a new spin on things. Maybe the guy hadn't been tailing her to get or give information. Maybe she was just his mark; maybe he was planning to mug her. Which meant she'd ended up in the crossfire by chance. Her lucky day. Or maybe he was being taught a lesson by someone else. Concepts like loyalty and friendship held no meaning for these scumbags. They'd off each other as easily as they would outsiders.

The coffee shop was crowded for late morning. Machines steamed, belched, and spouted. Georgia waited in line, wondering how many customers were gapers who'd come in to check the crime scene. She looked through the window. The scene had been released, and there were no more reminders of it, no flutter of yellow tape or cast-off evidence bags. Still, people hungered to be part of it. To share the terror of near disaster.

"Hey, peaches." Paul's voice brought her back. "The usual?"

She looked up and smiled. "Sure." She glanced at the row of pastries in a glass-enclosed case. "And a blueberry muffin. To go."

Paul slid the door open, grabbed a white food wrapper, and reached for the muffin. He dropped it in a small bag and handed it over. "On the house."

"Why?"

He waved at the people in line. "It's the least I can do. I'm having the best week ever."

"Homicide's good for business, huh?"

He flipped up his hands.

"You know, I do have a question," she said. "Where do you get those wrappers for the pastries?"

"The wrappers?" He looked confused. She pointed to the box on the counter.

"Oh, those. From the food-service company."

"Do they sell more than one kind?"

"I wouldn't know."

"Do you have the company's name and number?"

"It's in the back. I can check when it's a little quieter. Want me to text you?"

She looked at the line behind her. It wasn't long, and she had no plans for the afternoon. "I'll wait."

Chapter 17

Rosebud Restaurant Supply was about as far south as you could go and still be in Cook County. Once Georgia was on I-57, traffic eased. Downtown skyscrapers were replaced by ten-floor buildings, two-story constructions, and finally one-story boxes. At the same time, the space between them expanded. Soon she was passing snow-covered fields that reflected the sun so intensely her eyes hurt. She opened the glove compartment, took out a pair of shades, and slipped them on. Out here you could see how flat the prairie really was. Every road seemed to stretch to the horizon. Georgia hunched her shoulders. The openness, the lack of a place to hide, was unsettling.

Half way to Kankakee, she reached University Park, which straddles the southern border of Cook County and spills into Will. A small planned city that seemed to spring fully formed from the belly of the prairie, the city was named for Governor's State University, which was designed for working adults.

A few minutes later she pulled up to a low-slung white building, with, of course, a giant rosebud painted on the side. She parked in a small lot and went in. The reception area, if you could call it that, consisted of an interior window with sliding glass panels, behind which was an unoccupied desk. Across the room was a six-foot-square patch of blue carpet and two industrial-looking chairs. An artificial plant and a spread of outdated magazines lay on a small glass table. Someone had made a halfhearted attempt to be welcoming.

Georgia made her way past the sliding glass partition, wondering where the receptionist had gone. She knocked on a door leading off the reception area. No response. She turned the knob. Unlocked. She pushed through into a long hall with cinder-block walls and three doors. One was open.

"Hello? Anyone here?"

She heard the squeak of casters rolling across the floor. A male voice rang out. "In here."

As she walked down the hall, she caught the scent of fresh bread. It was an appealing aroma, except Rosebud was supposed to be a food-service distributor, not a bakery. She reached the open door and peered into a small office. A roly-poly man with salt-and-pepper hair and a full beard was just standing up, an open book and a half-eaten sub on his desk. Case of the bakery aroma closed.

The man was short, but he had the most cheerful blue eyes she'd ever seen. He must be Santa's younger brother. He pushed away the sandwich and book. Though its cover was upside down, she could tell it was a crime novel by a popular Chicago author.

He caught her glance. "You like him? This is his latest. It's good. It's about a PI who—"

She cut him off. "I'm not much of a reader."

A disappointed look came over his face as if he'd been ready for a serious discussion on the merits of the genre. He squared his shoulders. "Well now," he said, his voice all business, "how can I help you?"

"Sorry to barge in, but I'm looking for some information and your company was suggested. My name is Georgia Davis, and—I'm—an investigator."

His eyes widened. "An investigator?" He stole a glance at the book. "Like a PI?"

She swallowed. And nodded.

His jaw dropped. "I don't believe it. All my life I've been waiting for someone like you to come through the front door." He grinned and raised his hands. "And here you are!"

Georgia slid her hands into her pockets. Usually it was her looks that got in the way, and she'd have to waste time fending off come-ons and double entendres before she could get on to business. But little Santa was hot for her career. She tipped her head to the side, amused.

He closed the space between them and stuck out his hand. "I'm Rick Martin. And this is just my day job. I'm a writer. I'm working on a crime novel." He yanked a thumb toward the book. "Reading helps."

Georgia smiled and waved a hand. "So this—this place is just a hobby?"

"I wish." He drew himself up. "I am," he intoned dramatically, "the son of Rosebud."

"Pardon me?"

"What can I say?" Martin rocked back and grinned. "My father loved *Citizen Kane*. Movies, books...Pop was a frustrated story-teller. Probably what got me started."

Martin couldn't be much more than five four. He barely came up to her chin. As if he'd read her mind and wanted to minimize the difference between them, he went back to his desk and waved her into a chair. "So you're really a PI? Where?"

"Mostly Evanston."

His eyes went shiny with awe. It was too much.

"It's not what you think," she said. "It's usually pretty boring."

He flicked his hand. "Yeah, yeah, that's what they all say. But there's a reason you've come all the way down to God's country from Evanston. I bet I'm in for a good story."

She smiled at that. "I have a food wrapper. At least I think it is. I wanted to know if you could identify where it's from. What restaurant."

He rubbed his hands together. "Well now, that's different. Want to tell me how you got it?"

"Not really."

"I didn't think so." He let out a resigned breath. "Okay. Let's see it."

She pulled out the note, which she'd put in a small paper bag. She handled it gingerly.

He read it. "Someone has a long-lost sister?"

"I'm not here for an explanation of the contents," she snapped. "Just the paper."

"Sure. Sure." Frown lines creased his forehead.

Georgia felt guilty. She should apologize for being testy.

He looked up. "Listen. I'm not trying to be a bastard, but I need to touch it. Get a feel for the weight and texture. I'll be careful."

She handed it over. "Edges only. If you can," she added.

Martin took an edge of the note between his thumb and forefinger and massaged the paper. "Seems like standard weight. And texture. Kind of your basic wrapper. Which makes it hard to say where it was produced. There are a lot of possibilities."

"There's no way to be more specific?"

He shrugged "There are so many varieties. Waxed, unwaxed. Foiled or not. On one or both sides."

"And this one?"

"Just your standard deli wrap. It's not coated with anything. They use this kind at places like Subway or Potbelly's."

"What about those yellow and red stripes running down the edge?"

"I was getting to that. You can customize wrappers any way you want. For example, the foiled ones come in silver, gold, even red. Deli wrap can be translucent, have a checkerboard pattern, and be any color. You can even put your logo on it."

"But this isn't customized?"

"Like I said, it's hard to tell. Especially with such a small piece. If I had the whole thing..." He let his voice trail off.

"This is all I've got. Could it be one of yours?"

"Doesn't look like it."

"Is there a catalogue of different wraps and who makes them?"

"It's complicated. Each manufacturer, even each food-service company, has their own."

"Is there a way to check them and see who makes this one? Online, for example?"

"Frankly, if you're not in the business, it would be hard. I mean, you could, but you probably would get frustrated. Too many choices."

Georgia didn't reply.

He straightened. "This a heater case?"

She resisted the impulse to roll her eyes.

"It is, isn't it?" He looked almost gleeful.

He'd misinterpreted her silence. She should correct him. Before she could, though, he jumped in. "I have an idea. Can I keep this?"

Georgia was about to say no when he cut her off. "No, of course I can't. You have to send it in for prints and stuff. Unless you already have..." He paused, his expression as hopeful as a puppy's.

She shook her head. "Sorry. I can't let you keep it." She reached for the wrapper. It was time to head back. It had been a long shot, anyway. She was gathering her things when he raised his palm.

"Hold on." Martin rolled back from his desk, opened a drawer, and pulled out a smartphone. "Let me take a couple of shots." He smoothed out the wrapper, anchored it with the edge of his book to keep it flat, and shot three or four photos. He checked the images on his screen and took a few more. "Just to be safe."

This time it was her turn to be hopeful. "You really think you can identify it?" she asked.

"No promises, but..." He squinted at the back of the phone, where the last image was still displayed. "Hey...did you see this?"

"What?"

"This smudge." He pointed to a darkish area on the image, then looked at the wrapper itself.

"I did. I figured it was probably ketchup or gravy. Maybe a coffee stain."

"I don't think so. Remember, there's no coating on this wrap. Which means whatever that is was easily absorbed. But, you see, ketchup is really thick. Even a little would have congealed and hardened on top. Despite the lack of coating. But that didn't happen. So I doubt it's ketchup. Or gravy."

She looked at him. "What are you saying?"

"It could be meat juice." Martin shrugged. "Or coffee." A gleam came into his eyes. "Then again..."

Georgia finished. "It could be blood."

Chapter 18

The press conference was the lead story on the news that
night. Evanston's mayor said all the right things: the cops
were working hard; anyone with information about the
gunman or victim should come forward; and here's what we're
doing to make Evanston safer. There was no mention of evidence,
the autopsy, or, thankfully, Georgia's role.

She got up and turned off the tube. She was beginning to
think the incident was random. If they'd found any evidence she
was the target, the police would have told her—they were all over
it. But they hadn't. That was good. She made a grilled cheese
sandwich. Halfway through eating it, she realized she wasn't hungry. She pushed the plate away, got up, and retrieved the note
from the paper bag.

She examined the smudge on the wrapper again. If it was
blood, how did it get on the wrapper? Wouldn't someone with a
cut or scrape, or even a bloody nose, use a tissue? Unless there
wasn't one. In that case, someone might well have used whatever
was lying around, including a food wrapper. Still, what were the
chances the blood—if it was—came from the woman who claimed
to be her half sister?

Georgia tried to think it through. If a client had a relative who
was pregnant and in trouble and might have traces of blood on a

food wrapper, what would she advise? Track it down? Ignore it? Wait for more evidence?

But was this wasn't a client. This was personal. She thought about calling Sam to talk it over, but she hadn't told Sam much about her family. There was one person who knew her history, but she wasn't in touch with him. To call just because she had a problem wasn't fair.

On the other hand, they'd always bounced ideas off each other. He was a good problem solver. Despite everything, on a professional level she trusted him. He'd been a cop too. She flicked on her phone and clicked on his name. His voice mail picked up.

"You've reached Matt Singer. Leave a message."

She disconnected.

* * *

The next morning she dialed a number before she changed her mind.

"You've reached the Illinois Crime Lab." A recorded voice told her to dial the extension she wanted. She punched in three numbers.

"Lou Simonelli here."

"Hey, Lou. It's Georgia Davis." Lou, short for Louise, was a criminalist who'd worked a few cases with Georgia when she was on the force.

"Well now. Davis. I haven't heard from you in years. How you be?"

"Good."

"Gone private, I hear."

"For a couple of years now."

"So I hear. Not doing too badly either, baby cakes."

Georgia smiled. She liked Lou. "Listen, Lou. I need a DNA test, and I need a referral."

"What kind of test?"

"Identification and comparison. Possible siblings."

"For a case?"

She didn't answer.

"Does it need to be legally submissible? You know, hold up in court?"

"No," she said. "Can you refer me to a good lab?"

"Are the mothers willing to give samples?"

Georgia blew out a breath. "The mothers? I don't frigging know who the mother is. That's why I need the test."

"Hmm." Lou paused. "I know it sounds crazy, but to get the best results, it's better if you have the mothers' DNA—at least one of them—for comparison."

Georgia went rigid. She couldn't get results unless she knew who the mother was. But the reason she was ordering the test was to figure out who the mother was. She was spinning around a Catch-22. But all she said was, "I don't have the mother's DNA."

"In that case, you may not get conclusive results. Sibling DNA reports are tough. A lot of times you just can't tell."

Georgia thought about it. Too many variables. This was the time to end the call. To thank Lou and put the matter behind her. Then, "Do you know a lab that could do it?"

Lou was quiet for a minute. "Well, there's a place in Lincoln Park we use when we're backlogged."

"Which means you use them a lot."

Lou laughed. "They're good, but they're not cheap. In fact, if I were you—"

"That's okay. Give me the name."

"Hold on."

Georgia heard the rustle of papers and a murmured conversation in the background. When Lou came back, she reeled off a name and number. "Ask for Jim. He knows what he's doing."

"Thanks, Lou."

"I'm ready for a drink anytime."

"Soon." Georgia hoped she sounded sincere.

Lou laughed. "I guess I won't hold my breath. Hey, are you still—oh, never mind."

"What?"

"No. Not important. Call me when you want to get together."

Georgia disconnected. She hadn't talked to Lou in years, and she knew what Lou was going to ask. There was no reason she would know about Matt—they traveled in different worlds. She checked the time. Barely eight thirty. She dialed the number Lou gave her, hoping someone would pick up.

A man's voice answered. "Precision DNA."

"I'm looking for Jim, please."

"You got him."

"Lou Simonelli referred me. I'm an investigator."

"Lou's good people," he said. "What can I do you for?"

Georgia explained.

"We can do that—you'll be giving us samples for comparison, right?"

"I can give you the potential sibling samples. At least I'm pretty sure I can."

"What does that mean?"

"I have a sample that could be blood." She hesitated. "Then again, it might be ketchup."

"Oh." He paused. "Well, I guess we'll find out."

She felt a little less foolish. "But I don't have a sample from the mother."

"You sure you want to do it that way? It would be a lot more accurate if you—"

"I know, I know. But I don't have the mother," she said. "How much are we talking about and how long will it take?"

"Well, if you really want to go ahead, I can ballpark it. Of course, it depends on the quality. What are they? Besides the blood or ketchup?"

"Blood from one sibling if you want it. And hair from—for the other."

"Good. That's relatively easy. I assume they're in good shape?"

"One will be."

He paused. "Well, assuming the other one is too, extracting

DNA and comparing them will run you about five hundred. It can take about twelve working days, give or take a day. Of course, if it's a heater, you can get it in four or five days."

"If I want to pay more."

"Right," Jim said cheerfully.

"How much more?"

"Well, since you're a friend of Lou's, let's say seven fifty."

Seven fifty and five days. Just to follow up on what probably would be a waste of time and money. Not to mention the stress of waiting. She thought it over one more time.

At least they took credit cards.

Chapter 19

⸎

G eorgia read about the dead blond pregnant girl two days later. She'd been reviewing Chicago's crime stats online, a habit she picked up when she was on the force. ChicagoCrime, a quasi-official website, was remarkably accurate when it came to homicides, arsons, and other felony crimes.

The body had been found, according to the website, in the far northwestern suburbs near the town of Harvard, Illinois. Sixty miles northwest of Chicago. Usually ChicagoCrime didn't cover incidents that far out, so Georgia was puzzled until she read the details. The unidentified body had been left on the side of Route 173, which meant it could have come from anywhere, including Chicago. The victim had been severely beaten. A passing trucker called it in. The investigation was ongoing. Georgia checked the time of the report. Barely an hour ago.

She got up and started to pace. This was just a coincidence. Had to be. Savannah was in Chicago. Not sixty miles away in Harvard, Illinois. On the other hand plenty of people say they live in Chicago when they really come from Glencoe, Franklin Park, or Hinsdale. Georgia kept pacing, and with each step her irritation grew. Why was she allowing herself to get sucked in? Why spend money, time, and emotion on what would likely be a case of mistaken identity? Was she that desperate for a family connection, however flimsy?

She went to the kitchen window and looked out. Another storm had dumped a few inches of snow, but it was a pure, crystalline morning, and the kids across the street were building a snowman. Their squeals and laughter carried across the street. Their mother was outside too, and all three were rolling a ball of snow across the yard, tamping it down as they did. They'd already built the base.

Georgia lowered the blinds. Harvard, less than ten miles from the Wisconsin state line, had been mostly farmland, but over time, many of the farms had failed. A Motorola plant was supposed to save the town, but it failed too and was shuttered in 2003. Harvard's biggest claim to fame was its Milk Days Festival, held every June to honor farmers who boosted milk production during World War Two. In fact, a giant cow named Harmilda stood in the middle of the town square.

It was Saturday, but she went to her phone and punched in a number. She got lucky.

"O'Malley."

"Hey there," Georgia said. "I hear I owe you one."

"For what?"

"You talked to Gutierrez the other day."

"Oh yeah," he said in a clipped tone. Dan O'Malley was not one for rambling.

"It's been noted. And appreciated."

He chuckled. "So what's going on? You mixed up in that homicide?"

"Not really. I thought the vic was tailing me, but now I don't know. Not sure it matters anymore. The trail seems to have gone cold."

"Yeah, well. You never know." He cleared his throat. "How's business? You getting by?"

"Crime is recession-proof, remember?"

"Tell me about it."

"That's why I'm calling. I just read about a body turning up in Harvard earlier this morning. A young woman. Pregnant. Blond. Can you get me some 411?"

"Tell me you're not working a case that involves her."

"I'm not working a case that involves her."

His snort told her what he thought of her answer. "I guess it would be useless for me to ask why."

"It would."

A sigh. Then, "Let me see what I can do. You'll be at this number?"

"All the time."

He called back a few minutes later. "They'll email me the police report when it comes in."

"Hey, Dan. You're the best."

"Okay. Enough with the flattery. You should know that they actually found her about five miles west of the Harvard city limits on Route 173, in Boone County, so Harvard PD handed it off to the sheriff's office."

"Why am I not surprised?"

"And since it's less than ten miles from the state line, they've got Walworth County involved too."

"Wisconsin cops?"

"Yup." O'Malley's voice was stern. "Davis, you know the drill, right? If anyone ever finds out we talked, I deny it 'til the cows come home."

"Interesting choice of words, given that Harvard used to be the dairy capital of the Midwest. But you're the frigging deputy superintendent. What kind of trouble would you be in?"

He ignored her question. "Of course we could remedy that anytime."

"How?"

"Come back on the force, and we'll be kosher."

"You're dreaming, rabbi."

"I'm trying." He paused, and when she didn't add anything, he cleared his throat. "Okay. Another thing. The dicks working the case will know I requested the report. I'm gonna have to give them something."

"There's no chance I could talk to them?"

"You just keep pushing, don't you?"

"It's my job."

"No, you can't speak to them. And you can't use my name. I'll get you the report after I get it. And after you take a look, you'll tell me why you wanted it."

"Sure," she said brightly.

"Oh, and by the way. I don't want to hear about a PI up in McHenry County who just happened to run into the detectives working the crime scene."

"No way, Chief."

Chapter 20

I t took more than an hour to get to Harvard. The day had clouded over, and layers of dirty gray sky threatened to match her mood. She drove west on Route 173 through the center of Harvard, then to its outskirts, where she passed farms and snow-covered fields. She almost missed the crime scene, which appeared like a Hollywood set that had materialized on the prairie.

Three patrol cars, all different colors except for their flashing red and blue Mars lights, two vans, yards of police tape strung on one side of the road, and about a dozen people in padded coats and gloves, all looking important. She drove past the scene, then turned around and inched back. She wasn't making herself scarce, she rationalized. She just didn't want to attract attention. She parked a hundred yards away and headed over, making sure she stood far enough away for the cops to think she was a gaper.

One of the cruisers was black and white and was emblazoned with the Harvard, Illinois, PD logo. The Boone County Sheriff's Department cruiser was black with a yellow stripe, and the third, a black cruiser with both yellow and red stripes, looked like a lame version of the Batmobile. She could just make out "Walworth County Sheriff's Department" on the side. She tried to figure out which officer belonged to which force, but in their winter gear they all looked the same. One of the vans said "Illinois State

Police" on it, and the other was from the Walworth County Coroner's Office. They had to be tussling over jurisdiction. Whoever had the body would have the power. She craned her neck trying to see if the corpse was still on the road, but the crowd of officers obscured her view.

She stamped her feet and rubbed her hands in the bitter cold, remembering O'Malley's warning not to cause trouble. Finally, after about twenty minutes, the coroner's van drove off, passing her on the road. The body must be inside. Shit. She'd really wanted a glimpse of it up close. Not that she'd know who she was looking at. But she could have taken a photo unobtrusively with her iPhone. A few minutes after the coroner's van left, the Walworth County Sheriff's cruiser pulled out, also passing her. Two officers sat in the front. She was about to go back to her car when the cruiser slowed, stopped, and backed up.

When it was abreast of her, the passenger window rolled down, and a male voice called out. "Aren't you Georgia Davis?"

Georgia reeled back, surprised. She hunched her shoulders against the cold. "Who—who wants to know?"

A chuckle. The cop was smiling. "You don't recognize me?"

She squinted. He looked familiar but she couldn't place him. He was wearing shades. Straight dark hair, receding from his forehead. Pale skin. Thin face. Bundled up in a down coat. She shook her head.

"I'm Jimmy Saclarides, Lake Geneva police chief. You were here a couple years ago at Luke Sutton's house. We met."

A wave of memories washed over her. Molly Messenger's kidnapping. Her mother's fatal highway "accident." Georgia had tracked a witness to Wisconsin's Castle Rock Lake, then brought her to a safe house in Lake Geneva. Except the house belonged to one of the town's richest families, the Suttons, a fact she hadn't known until she got there.

Now she vaguely remembered meeting Saclarides on the driveway leading to the Sutton estate. But she wasn't focused on him then; she was involved in her case. Plus, it was the middle of summer. In his winter gear, he was practically unrecognizable.

"Yeah, I remember." She hoped it sounded like she really did.

Saclarides checked his watch. "Look...uh...have you had lunch?"

Georgia recognized an opportunity when it knocked, and this one was practically breaking down the door. She shook her head.

"Great. Why don't you meet me in twenty minutes at Saclarides in Lake Geneva? My family owns the place."

Chapter 21

Georgia made her way into Lake Geneva, turned on Broad, then drove down a short alley that opened into a parking lot. At the edge of the lot was a cheerful white-brick building with blue shutters and door. A sign on the door said, "Welcome to Saclarides."

As she opened the door, a tantalizing mix of aromas greeted her: lemon, garlic, rosemary, and other spices she didn't recognize. Her appetite revved up as if she hadn't eaten in weeks. Saclarides was already there, standing at the back of the restaurant talking to an older, dark-haired woman.

Without his coat, she could see he had a great body: tall, muscular, slim hipped. A great butt, too. His nose was thin and long, his eyes widely spaced and brown. Despite living in a summer resort town, those eyes had seen their fill of trouble, she could tell. Right now, though, they radiated warmth and humor. She felt suddenly shy.

He waved her over. "Georgia, this is my aunt Ava. She and my mother run the place, but Mom's not here today."

Georgia smiled and shook the woman's hand. "Pleased to meet you, Mrs. Saclarides."

"It's Aunt Ava, sweetheart. Everyone calls me that." The woman beamed and led them to their number one booth, as she called it. A blue tablecloth covered the table, and a small vase with artificial flowers sat on top. She launched into a rapid-fire discourse of what Georgia assumed was Greek. Jimmy answered her.

The woman folded her hands and smiled. "*Kalos.*"

"What was that?" Georgia asked after she'd left.

"Ava says she knows what you want to eat."

"She does?" She'd been wondering why there were no menus on the table.

"It's her little ritual. She tells everyone what they want so that when she brings out whatever it is she's cooked, they'll think she made it especially for them."

Georgia sat down.

Saclarides smiled. "You still have no clue who I am, do you?"

"We met in front of the house, wasn't it? Luke Sutton's?"

His eyebrows arched. "You do remember."

She felt her cheeks heat up. "How did you recognize me?"

"You're not easy to forget."

Her cheeks were on fire.

He must have caught it. He cleared his throat. "I'm a cop, remember? Got the third eye. You were trying to hide a woman who worked in a bank."

"That's right."

"Heard you ended up in Arizona."

She nodded.

"And almost got yourself killed."

Mentally, she made a note to call Ellie Foreman when she got home. Ellie and Luke Sutton, the owner of the safe house, were a couple. What had she told Saclarides about her? Foreman knew Georgia didn't like her business spread far and wide.

As if he knew what she was thinking, he said, "Don't worry. Luke is one of my closest friends. It stayed between us."

Aunt Ava interrupted with two bowls of steaming soup. After she set them down and left, he said, "We're Greek, but this place has the best chicken noodle soup east of the Mississippi. I recommend it."

She dipped her spoon into the bowl, blew on it, and took a sip. She felt her eyes widen. "This is good!"

He looked pleased and started in on his. She watched. He didn't slurp. Two points.

After a few mouthfuls, she put her spoon down. "So what were you doing at a crime scene in Illinois?"

"And you know it's a crime scene because..."

Shit. Her stomach tightened. She wasn't supposed to know that. Or was she? She couldn't remember what the ChicagoCrime website report said. "I...I—"

"It's okay. I know you're a PI."

She felt herself relax.

"To answer your question, it was basically professional courtesy. Lake Geneva attracts a lot of people, but we don't get a lot of murders. So when something happens nearby, we try to cooperate. Especially when it's someone we don't know."

"So..." She tried to be casual. "You don't have an ID on the woman?"

"Not yet."

"Where was she found?"

"At the edge of Route 173 just east of Capron. Outside Harvard city limits."

"Cause of death?"

He shook his head. "Don't know for sure. She was partially frozen." He spooned more soup into his mouth. "But she had multiple stab wounds on her neck and torso. Lacerations on her arms and legs too." He paused. "And tracks on her wrists."

Georgia picked up her spoon, wondering why he was so generous with information. "Were they fresh? The tracks?"

"Not particularly."

"So she stopped when she got pregnant."

He shrugged. "Maybe."

"You think she's from around here?"

"Don't know."

A busboy collected their bowls, and Aunt Ava brought two

plates heaped with what looked like moussaka, grape leaves stuffed with rice, and some kind of fish. Enough food for five people.

He gave her time to sample everything. Which, of course, was delicious. Then, "Okay. You pumped me pretty good. My turn now. Why are *you* here?"

She'd been waiting for it. "Would you believe 'professional courtesy'?"

"Not good enough."

She hesitated. "Okay. It's personal."

He chewed and swallowed, then looked up. "Still not good enough."

She bit her lip. "Look, I'm not here in any official capacity. But you can call Ellie. She'll vouch for me."

"What makes you think I don't believe you?" He broke off a piece of bread.

She met his eyes. They were honest and direct. Unflinching. She looked down.

"Georgia..."

She looked up.

"Are you in some kind of trouble?"

"No. Nothing like that."

He chewed the bread, then inclined his head. "So then, you won't mind giving me your contact information. When I find out who the victim is, I could let you know."

She wondered what he was really asking. She swallowed. Whatever his motive, she had to decide whether to let a cop back into her life, however peripherally. Still, she understood cops. She'd been one herself. And this cop seemed to get *her*. And despite the dance they were doing, there was a chance he might have solid information for her.

She gave him her number.

Chapter 22

Savannah—Ten Months Earlier

Vanna knew by the "yeahs" and "uh-huhs" that her mother was talking to the school. School officials waited until evening to call when there was a problem, figuring there would be a better chance of finding a parent at home. In her case, however, it didn't matter. Her mother had been fired—again—and was home all day.

Rather than wait for the storm she knew was brewing, Vanna went outside for a smoke. The truth was she had cut school. She'd spent the day getting high with Dex. Then his friend Freed came over, and, well, they were all high on meth, and she let them tear her clothes off and fuck her. It was only the three of them; you couldn't really call it a party. But it beat school. She just didn't see the point of sitting in class wondering where her next hit was coming from.

She stubbed out her butt and squared her shoulders, ready to go back into the shabby garden apartment they rented. Opening the door, she was greeted by a frigid silence that pummeled the air and filled the cracks in the walls. Vanna repressed a shiver. She wished her mother would just let it out. Confront her with a torrent of screams and yells. But that wasn't her style. When she was upset with Vanna, which seemed to be all the time now, her mother would withdraw. Act as if she wasn't there. She'd been that way as long as Vanna could remember; in fact, everyone had called Vanna a daddy's girl when she was little. With good reason. It was her father who gave her affection and love. But after he was mowed down by the eighteen-wheeler, her mother grew even more remote. Her body was present; her shadow, too. But her heart and soul had frozen into tiny bits of ice. Vanna started to call her the Snow Queen.

Vanna heard the oven door squeak. Dinner—if you could call TV dinners that. Her mother claimed she bought the good stuff, but it all tasted like shit, and they put enough chemicals in the crap to give you cancer. She remembered as a kid watching some inane TV commercial about the guy who said he'd be over by five to help the family eat their lasagna. At the time she'd actually believed he would show up on their doorstep. Now, though, she couldn't imagine anyone coming to visit them voluntarily.

She wanted to avoid her mother, but she had to pass through the kitchen to get to the bathroom, and she needed to pee. She hunkered down in the front room—the parlor as her mother called it, as if they were rich, cultured people who said such things with an offhand shrug. She sprawled on the pullout couch they'd rescued from somebody's front yard and fished out her cell. Another metallic squeak from the oven door. Then,

"Savannah, we need to talk." Her mother's voice wasn't loud, but its dead, icy tone made it sound like a shriek.

"I'm in here."

"And you need to be in *here*. Right now."

Vanna hesitated. She always pushed it. She couldn't help it. Her defiance controlled her. She knew it was just to elicit a reaction from her mother. Any reaction, even an angry one. Supply heat and light and maybe the icy shell would melt. But it never worked. Her mother ignored her rage, refusing to deal with it head-on. It was as if Vanna, in all her purple self-righteous fury, was invisible.

Why couldn't she just be yelled at and grounded like other kids who whined about losing the car keys and missing a party at Joe's? As if being grounded in a house with cable, Internet, and a fridge full of food was cruel and unusual punishment. Not like this arctic reality, all endless dark nights with no morning sun. A life sentence with no parole.

She edged into the kitchen.

Two tinfoil pans containing pasty beige-and-green glop sat on the counter. They looked barely defrosted.

Her mother stood at the stove, arms crossed, still holding the cell in one hand. "You know who that was." Her mother's chin jutted out toward the phone.

Vanna didn't reply.

"They said you haven't been in school all week."

Her voice still had a southern lilt, Vanna thought. Even after all these years. She shrugged.

"I suppose you're not going to tell me where you were," her mother said coolly.

Vanna tilted her head. Better to play offense. Strike the first blow. Maybe this time her mother would be different. "What do you care? It's no sweat off your back." Money was tight since her father was gone, and her mother had started to complain how expensive it was to raise a child. Especially a girl. "I wasn't mooching off you."

"No. I guess you weren't," her mother said after a pause. "You were probably in someone's backseat working for your lunch."

Vanna sucked in an unsteady breath. This was different. Was her mother actually putting up a fight? Vanna decided to test it. "Like I said, why do you care?"

"I'll tell you why. We're running out of cities to live in. Why do you think we're always moving?"

"Because ever since Daddy died, you can't keep a job."

"We're not talking about me." Her mother's expression was calm. "You can't seem to keep your legs closed. Or your head clear. Your juvie file is getting pretty thick. I wouldn't be surprised if the cops gave us a personal escort to the edge of town."

She crossed her arms, matching her mother's stance. "Well then, won't you be happy when I turn eighteen? You won't have to deal with me anymore." She paused. "Or me with you. I haven't seen you sober for nearly a year."

Her mother spent her days in a kind of trance, guzzling wine or rum until she passed out on the couch. A good day was when her mother waited until after dinner to start drinking.

"Alcohol is legal," her mother replied.

"So it's okay to be an addict? As long as it's legal?"

Her mother swayed and grabbed the edge of the counter. Was she going to collapse? Vanna almost took a step forward to steady her, but her mother abruptly straightened on her own. A wave of humiliation rolled over Vanna. Why had she even tried? Her mother didn't need her, didn't want her, didn't love her. Vanna was nothing more than a useless appendage.

But she didn't know how to stop pushing. "What are you going to do? Lock me in my room? Then apologize and tell me how sorry you are when you let me out?" She let her arms fall to her sides. "Go ahead. I don't care. I want to die."

Vanna had no time to prepare for the sudden clap, the stinging flesh, the tears that involuntarily welled up when her mother slapped her across the face. Vanna's hand flew to her cheek. "The fuck you do that for?"

"I wish you'd never been born," her mother said.

Vanna massaged her jaw with her fingers. "I've known that for a long time." But inside she was almost elated. She'd forced a reaction. Finally, after how many months, her mother had actually shown some emotion. It briefly occurred to Vanna how low they'd both sunk if provoking her mother gave her pleasure. She pushed the thought away. "Yeah, well, you should have died along with Daddy."

"Maybe you're right."

"You're a shitty mother."

Her mother pressed her lips together. Another show of emotion, Jobeth-style. This was a big night. Vanna shot her mother a defiant look.

"At least Georgia never talked back."

Something registered. This was new information.

"Georgia? Who the fuck is Georgia?"

Her mother blinked. Then she bit her lip, as if she knew she'd said too much.

Vanna caught it. "Who the fuck is Georgia?"

"No one." Her mother's voice went flat. She turned away.

But Vanna was in no mood to let her mother skate. She closed in, grasped her mother's shoulders, and shook her. Actually shook her. "Who is Georgia?"

Her mother didn't flinch, and she didn't turn around. "Pack your things. We'll leave tomorrow. We'll go to New Mexico."

Vanna dropped her hands and tried to steady her breathing. "No. Not this time. I'm not going."

Her mother shrugged. "Suit yourself."

Vanna spun around to the kitchen drawer where her mother kept the cooking stuff. She slid the drawer open, grabbed the biggest knife inside, raised it, and went back to her mother. "Turn around, bitch. Who is Georgia?"

This time her mother did turn around. When she saw the knife, she blanched. Fear shot across her face, but her voice remained chilly and dispassionate. "Put it down."

"Who's Georgia?" Vanna said sharply.

Her mother kept her mouth shut.

Vanna aimed the knife at her mother. "*Who is she?*"

Her mother kept her eyes on the knife for what seemed like forever. Then, as if she knew she had lost the battle, her entire body sagged. She averted her gaze, dropped into a kitchen chair, and covered her eyes with her hands. Vanna heard a long exhalation.

"Georgia—Georgia is your sister."

"What?"

"Your half sister." Her mother wouldn't meet her gaze.

"I have a sister?"

Jobeth didn't reply.

"*Look* at me." Vanna brandished the knife.

Her mother raised her eyes to Vanna. Vanna didn't know whether it was because Vanna had a weapon or because she had forced a confession. Still clutching the knife, she moved in. "Where is she?"

Still no reply.

"*Where?*"

Her mother swallowed. "I think she lives in Chicago."

Vanna's mother had lived in Chicago. She'd been married to a cop. Charlie Davis. But he'd been a drunk, and a mean one, her mother had admitted. He beat her regularly. But now there was a daughter. "You have another daughter and you never told me?"

"What difference would it have made? Do you think our lives would be any better?" Her mother's lips curled up, but it wasn't a smile. "Your father saved me. He made my life worth living. And now he's gone and I'm back where I was years ago."

"Why haven't you talked to her? Called her? Had her come out and visit?"

"It wouldn't make any difference. I haven't spoken to her in twenty years. I don't know where she is..." She shrugged. "She won't want to hear from me, anyway. I walked out on her."

And now you have *me*, Vanna wanted to say. It's just you and me. But she didn't. It wasn't true anymore. There was someone else. Her sister. Even if she was just a ghost. Vanna would never have her mother to herself. The old familiar rage bubbled up. "I should kill you."

Again her mother's lips formed that weird imitation of a smile. "I wish you would. Neither of us has anything worth living for."

But Vanna didn't kill her mother. She did something worse. She decided to sever the cycle of hot rage and icy distance that ricocheted between them. It had given them both nothing but pain and grief. And now it would be finished. Vanna had an out. Another chance.

After her mother passed out, an empty bottle of wine on the floor, Vanna put a change of clothes into her backpack and lifted fifty bucks from her mother's purse. She hoped it was enough for a bus ticket. If not, she'd have to work it off. She slipped the bills into her pocket and crept out of the apartment. Then she went back inside, opened her mother's closet, and took out her peacoat. It would be cold in Chicago. She took one last look. Her mother was still sprawled on the sofa, unmoving. She wouldn't wake up for hours. And when she did, Vanna would be a thousand miles away.

Chapter 23

Georgia picked up the phone Monday morning.

"Is Georgia Davis there?"

"Speaking."

"Hi, Miss Davis. This is Rick Martin."

Georgia frowned. "Who?"

"Rosebud Restaurant Supply?"

Comprehension dawned. The roly-poly guy she'd visited down in God's country. "Sure. How are you?"

"Good, good." He giggled. Actually giggled. "Hey, I hope you don't mind, but I've been doing a little sleuthing."

She groaned inwardly. When a civilian got involved in an investigation, it usually blew up. They thought everything worked the way it did on TV. The evidence would be clear. The bad guys would be caught. Justice would be served. Then she reminded herself that, technically, as a PI, *she* was a civilian.

"I'm not sure that was a great idea," she began. "You could do more harm than good."

"I figured that's what you'd say. But I couldn't help myself. You know."

She didn't, and his presumed intimacy grated. She'd met the guy only once.

"You wanted to track down that sandwich wrap," he said. "Right?"

"I still do."

"Well then, I think we're good."

"We?"

"Well, you know what I mean. *You*."

"Uh-huh."

He cleared his throat. "I checked through my catalogues, and I found a couple of companies that were in the ballpark. They had paper and a design that was similar. I was about to call them when I found the exact wrap."

"You're kidding." Georgia figured it was a long shot.

"Nope," he chirped. "It's a company right here in the Midwest. In Michigan."

"You're sure it's the same?"

"Absolutely. It wasn't in the catalogue. I found it online in a little corner of cyberspace."

"Impressive." She had to give him that. "Thanks, Rick. What's the name of the company? I'll give them a call."

"Macomb Paper. But—um—you don't have to call them."

Her stomach tightened. "Why not?"

"I already did."

"Why the hell did you do that?" She knew her tone was sharp.

Suddenly he sounded tentative. "I—er—I just knew you'd be looking for restaurants in Chicagoland that used their paper and I wanted to save you the trouble."

That's what you get when you deal with amateurs. Georgia ran a hand through her hair, unsure whether to laugh or cry. She forced herself to breathe. To center herself.

"So what did you find out?" Her tone, however, veered toward acid.

"There were—are three."

"Three what?"

"Three restaurants in the area that use the wrap from

Macomb's. Or did." He paused. "I thought you'd want to know which ones."

"You thought right." She took a pen from an empty can of beer on her desk where she kept pens, pencils, scissors, and a matt knife.

"One is Tony's, a joint in Joliet. But they closed six months ago. The economy, you know."

"Go on."

"The other is in Oakbrook. Susie's Sandwich Café." He paused again. "And the third is downtown. Just off Roosevelt Road. Benny's Deli."

"Benny's? Really?"

Benny's was a well-known lunch place, popular with Chicago power brokers as well as truck drivers. The owners claimed to have the best corned beef in town, and they were right. She'd been there.

"Yup." She heard the pride in Martin's voice. "'Course the wrap could be different than the scrap you saw. Place like Benny's probably customizes theirs."

She didn't have the heart to scold him. Instead she thanked him. "But, Rick, don't meddle anymore. It could be dangerous."

"I guess that means you don't want me to go with you to Benny's."

"That would be a good guess."

He sighed theatrically. "Okay. But when they publish the book, I want to be in the acknowledgments. Okay?"

Chapter 24

Although Benny's had been around since the 1940s, they'd moved several times and their present incarnation was in the South Loop. The place wasn't much more than a one-story shack with a red sign outside; inside were two rooms with a lot of tables crammed together. There was no pretense at decoration, and the food was served cafeteria-style. Still, by the time Georgia pushed through the door at lunchtime the next day, the place was teeming with cops, aldermen, lawyers, and other Chicago VIPS, all of whom jostled each other good-naturedly.

The staff at Benny's were notorious for a smart-ass attitude, but customers gave as good as they got, and the hot, steamy air was filled with cheerful put-downs, one-liners, and verbal jabs. The best part, though, were the smells. Part garlic, part corned beef, grease, and soup, nothing was better than the aromas wafting through a good deli, Georgia thought. She'd inhale them all day.

She approached a counter that ran the length of the room where about a dozen people stood in line. Three men behind the counter were making up sandwiches, dishing out latkes, coleslaw, and soup. At the end of the counter was a neon "Carry-Out" sign, below which two Hispanic women assembled meals and slid them into paper bags. On the counter between the two women lay a box of wrappers with the familiar red and yellow stripes down one edge. She watched as one of the women drew out a wrapper. Now that she could see the whole piece, she noticed the name "Benny's" printed in red letters in the center of the paper. Rick Martin had been on the mark. They'd customized their wrap.

Even so, she couldn't loiter too long; the place was geared for a speedy turnover. She waited near the carry-out sign, and when it was her turn she ordered a corned beef on rye to go. She watched as they layered more than three inches of meat on the bread. Enough for a week. She asked for extra coleslaw and Russian dressing, and one of the women snapped, "Why you not ask for a Reuben?"

She apologized with a smile and said, "Don't forget the latke and pickle."

The woman shot her a look. "Whaddya wanna drink?"

"Diet Coke."

The woman retrieved a small plastic container with coleslaw, another with Russian dressing. Then she wrapped the sandwich, latke, and pickle, put everything and the drink into a white bag, and handed Georgia a yellow receipt. Georgia took everything up front to pay, winding around a couple of aldermen she regularly saw on TV. She also passed a man who looked remarkably like Senator Dick Durbin.

Back in her car, she unwrapped the sandwich, latke, and pickle but made sure to save the wrap. She bit into the sandwich. It was just as good as she remembered. It was a clear but frigid day, and she'd almost ordered matzoh-ball soup too, but the sandwich alone was so hearty she could eat only half. She had no room for soup. She finished the pickle, took a bite of the latke, then slipped everything else back into the bag. Dinner.

She'd snagged a space across the street from the restaurant on Jefferson where she could watch people going in and out. She fished out her camera and took pictures of anyone exiting with a take-out bag, although she didn't expect any leads. Still, she had to be thorough.

The sun was slanting toward the horizon when a gray Hyundai with a placard on the roof that said "Benny's" pulled up in front of the restaurant. Georgia straightened. A delivery guy.

An average-sized man in a down jacket and a wool Bears hat climbed out of the Hyundai and went inside. Georgia got out of her car and stationed herself in back of the Hyundai, shivering in the arctic chill. The guy came out ten minutes later, carrying two cardboard boxes filled with bags with tickets stapled to them. He looked to be somewhere in his twenties. His face was pale, his eyes bloodshot, and he needed a shave. Guy had a rough night. He got in his car and drove away.

Ten minutes later another car, a Corolla like Georgia's, also with a placard on the top, pulled up. She watched a young African American man trot into the restaurant, emerging a few minutes later with a box of white bags. He stowed the food in his backseat and pulled out.

She went back to her car and watched him pull away, but not before she'd scrawled down his license plate, just as she'd done with the first guy. She'd wanted to question both about their deliveries over the past few weeks, but they had no incentive to talk to her. Even if they did, they might tell those customers that a detective had been nosing around asking questions. Plus, she didn't know which delivery guy knew what. She had a fifty-fifty chance of picking the right guy. Which meant a fifty-fifty chance of choosing the wrong one too. It was time to go home and start digging.

Chapter 25

Two hours later Georgia knew enough about one of Benny's delivery guys to make a return visit. Kroll's and FindersKeepers revealed that Bruce Kreisman, the owner of the Hyundai, had fled the state of Florida six months earlier for kiting checks. Overdrawing on accounts at several banks, he'd made off with twelve grand. Miami still had a warrant out for his arrest. She was surprised Benny's hadn't picked it up during a background check. Unless they didn't do one.

She wolfed down the rest of her corned beef sandwich. The guy in the Corolla was clean. Dropped out of high school but was taking a correspondence course online. Worked as a night janitor downtown. The car was registered to Selma Hunter, who could have been his mother, aunt, or girlfriend.

The next morning she was back at Benny's before lunch. The gray Hyundai pulled up around eleven.

"Hey, Bruce!" she called as she slid out of her car. "Is that you?"

The guy whipped around. Even though she was twenty yards away, a look of panic overspread his face.

As she trotted across the street, Kreisman appraised her, and some of the panic faded. He was trying to figure out whether he knew her.

"It *is* you, isn't it?" She pasted on a grin and kept her voice friendly, almost flirty.

But when she was within a few feet of him, his eyes narrowed, and he began to turn away. "Sorry. You've got the wrong guy."

"You're not Bruce Kreisman?"

"I don't know who you're talking about." He headed for Benny's door.

"You sure you're not the Bruce Kreisman with an outstanding arrest warrant in Miami?"

He froze, his back to Georgia. Then he turned around slowly. A cagey look came over him. He had to be thinking that she was "just" a woman. Less of a threat. She was used to it. He back-tracked in her direction, a determined look replacing the fear. The asshole thought he had a plan.

She stood her ground and blew on her hands. The cold, battering wind fell just short of the Hawk.

He stopped. "Who the hell are you?"

"My name is Georgia Davis. I'm an investigator."

"An investigator?" His voice broke on the word.

"I'm private."

Something in his eyes caught. "I told you I'm not Kreisman." His face darkened; he looked like he was going to flip her off. Again he spun around as if to leave. Then he stopped. "But the guy who used to own this car was."

"Excuse me?" Georgia faked a confused expression.

"Yeah. I bought this car off of Craigslist. Guy's name was Kreisman."

"So you are..."

"Josh. Keller."

And I'm Taylor Swift, Georgia thought. She wrapped her muffler tighter around her neck. It was too cold to play games. "Sorry, that won't cut it, Bruce." She fished in her pocket, drew out a sheet of paper, and pointed to a photo. Although the printout was black-and-white and not the best resolution, the similarity to the man standing in front of her was unmistakable.

Kreisman swallowed. He looked like the kid who'd blown off his homework then was called on in class.

"Look, it's too cold to talk out here. Let's go to my car." Once in the Toyota, she asked, "So how long have you been in Chicago?"

His gaze flitted everywhere except toward Georgia.

"About six months, I figure," she said.

No response.

"Well, believe it or not, this is your lucky day, Bruce. I don't want to make trouble for you. In fact, I'm not interested in *you* at all. You help me out, and I go away. Forever."

Now he looked directly at her. "What do you want?"

"Information."

He hesitated, licked his lips, then gave her a brief nod.

"How many delivery guys does Benny's have?"

He was quiet for a minute. Then, "Depends on the day. And shift. There are usually two of us. When it's really busy, they use a messenger service."

"When is your shift?"

"It changes, depending on the day. Nothing routine."

"But you do have regulars, right? Businesses, customers that order a lot?"

He shrugged in mute acknowledgment.

"I'm looking for a young girl. Maybe blond. Definitely pregnant. Do you remember delivering to someone like that?"

"Shit, lady. There are thousands of women like that all over Chicago."

"How about during the past couple of weeks?"

A glint in his eyes told Georgia he knew something, and a smug look came over him. "I might. What's in it for me?"

She volleyed the smug look back. "You really have to ask?"

He glanced around, then nodded.

"Really?" He was testing her. "Okay, well, you can't say I didn't try." She grabbed her car key, still in the ignition, and fired up the engine.

His brow furrowed. "What are you doing?"

"You haven't given me much choice." She pulled out her cell. "You can get out now. Have a nice day."

His worried look intensified, and he raised his voice above the whine of the engine. "Man—I mean lady—you can't do this."

She smiled. "And that's because..."

"Look. I like it here. Got a new girlfriend. Place to live. Steady job. Know what I mean?"

"I do. Like I said, too bad." She flipped up the locks on the door. "Time's up. I gotta make a call."

He blew out a breath. "Wait."

She looked over. His expression deepened from worry to fear. A real fear. She could smell it.

"I'll—I'll tell you. It's just—well—I don't like those people."

For the first time in their conversation, the guy looked like he was telling the truth. In fact, he might have shivered when he said the word "people."

"What people?"

He shook his head. "Don't know who they are. Or what they're doing. And I don't want to."

"Show me, Bruce."

Chapter 26

Georgia followed Kreisman and the Bennymobile into the bowels of the South West Loop. The police academy wasn't far away; as a cadet, she'd come down here every day. But the area had changed since then. Sandwiched between the Loop to the east and the UIC campus to the south, it had been a commercial zone. Now, though, neat, one-story warehouses stood where decaying buildings and the accompanying detritus once were. Cheerful signs for Home Depot, Best Buy, Whole Foods, and even a bank or two loomed overhead.

She followed Kreisman through a warren of industrial streets with so many dead ends, twists, and turns that she wondered whether he was leading her in circles. Eventually, though, he pulled up to a small, tidy warehouse with a large sliding garage door and driveway in front. The door was shut tight, and there were no trucks or cars on the driveway. There weren't even any swirls of graffiti on the walls. No lights inside; no figures moving around. When the wind gusted, a screen door on the side of the building flapped and banged against a door. But the deep silence between the gusts gave it the feel of a place that had been abandoned.

Kreisman parked a few yards down. Georgia did too and climbed out of her Toyota. Kreisman stayed in his Hyundai, his gaze flicking warily from the warehouse to Georgia, then back. She went over and motioned him to roll down his window.

"That's the place." He yanked a thumb toward the warehouse.

She scanned the building's perimeter. "Doesn't look like anyone's here."

"I can't help that," he snapped.

Georgia frowned. Was he setting her up? She was supposed to have the leverage here. "You sure this is where you saw a pregnant woman with blond hair?"

He nodded.

"When?"

"Maybe ten days ago. The last delivery I made."

"Just the one woman? Or were there others?"

He shrugged.

"Come on, Bruce, you've gotta give me more."

"It's—it's none of my business." He hesitated. "Listen, man, I mean lady. I did what you wanted. I gotta split."

Georgia backed off. Something about this place was freaking him out. "How often did you deliver here?"

"Like I said, maybe once or twice a week. Until last week."

"Big orders?"

"They were okay."

"What does that mean?"

"You know, five or six sandwiches. They ordered a lot of soup."

"Drinks?"

"Naw. Just food."

"What else?"

He scowled at her. "What do you mean?"

She leaned into the car. "What else can you tell me about the place and the people?"

"I don't know."

"Well, someone had to give you money when you gave them their food. Who? Describe them."

"I never got a good look." His knee started to pump up and down.

She folded her arms.

He blew out a breath. "Okay, so this guy would meet me outside."

"What guy?"

"I don't know. Kind of stocky. Short hair."

"White?"

He nodded. "Spoke with a thick accent."

"What kind?"

"Russian maybe?"

Georgia arched her eyebrows. "You sure?"

"How the hell—I dunno. Maybe he was a Polack or something?" His knee was pumping furiously.

"So a guy would come outside. He'd take the order. Give you money. You never saw the women, but you know there were some inside. How?"

He shifted from foot to foot. "I really gotta go. My boss is gonna throw a shit fit."

Georgia's eyes narrowed. "Tell me, Bruce."

He winced. "Okay. So once the door on the side opened and this girl in a bathrobe ran out."

"What girl?"

"Christ, lady, I don't know. A girl. Blond. Pregnant. In a pink bathrobe. She ran down to my car."

Georgia stiffened. "What happened?"

"The guy started to yell at her. She yelled back. Then—"

"In English?"

He shook his head. "It was one of them languages I don't know."

"Okay. Then what?"

"Well, then this other guy runs out and drags her back in. She's screaming her lungs out. But then the door slams and it all stops. At least, I couldn't hear her anymore."

"You said girl, not woman. You think she was under twenty-one?"

"I dunno."

"But she didn't want to be there. She obviously wanted to leave."

"Duh." He made a small mewling sound, somewhere between a laugh and a cry.

"And she was pregnant."

"Uh-huh."

"How were you able to tell, if she was wearing a bathrobe?"

He went quiet. But the defiant look in his eyes said he wasn't that stupid.

"Okay." She nodded. "Anything else?"

"No. And I'm done here." He keyed the engine.

She wasn't going to get much more. She leaned in through the open window. "Well, if you think of anything else, give me a call." She dug in her jeans pocket, gave him her card, and straightened up. He took the card, then gunned the engine so forcefully that he burned rubber as the Hyundai sped away.

Chapter 27

After Kreisman left, Georgia trudged up the driveway and jiggled the handle on the garage door. It was securely locked and felt way too heavy to force. She leaned her ear against it. Nothing but the tinny sound of wind blowing through the cracks. She walked around to the side to the banging screen door, the door the girl in the pink bathrobe presumably ran out of. The screen door opened, but a padlock was attached to the door behind it. The door was metal, probably steel. She bent down and peered under the crack at the bottom of the doorjamb. No light.

She circled the building and saw a second metal door in the rear, but it was padlocked as well. A green Dumpster stood a few yards away. She went over and lifted the lid. The stench was unbearable. She held her breath and peered in.

It was filled with broken bottles, Chinese food containers, paper plates, and the remnants of half-eaten sandwiches. She grabbed a stick and poked around the top layer of garbage. She saw tissues with lipstick, an empty tube of toothpaste, and a few other objects she couldn't identify and didn't want to. She levered the stick to reveal more of the Dumpster's contents. Underneath some crumpled newspapers and fast-food wrappers, she caught a glimpse of something pink. She angled the stick trying to expose more. A pink bathrobe. She lowered the lid and threw the stick away.

What was this place? A holding pen? Why was no one around? When had they left? And why was the pink bathrobe in the Dumpster? She thought about canvassing the adjacent warehouses, then reconsidered. What if those buildings were owned by the same people? Or what if they were looking out for the place in the owner's absence? What would happen when they reported that a strange woman was checking it out?

She took a few steps back and glanced up. No second story. Nothing but a flat roof. She walked around to the driveway and headed to her car. It was a bleak day, layers of gunmetal-gray clouds pressing down on their way to earth. No one was hanging around outside. She opened the Toyota's trunk, took out her bolt cutters and a Maglite, and went to the rear of the warehouse.

But when she picked up the padlock to examine it, the lock fell away from the hasp. It was unlocked. She froze. Why? Was someone inside? She backtracked to her car, put away the bolt cutters, and grabbed her baby Glock. Slipping it into her holster, she approached the back of the warehouse again with the Maglite, unsure whether to go in. She waited another minute but heard nothing that indicated a human presence. Cautiously she opened the door and stepped inside.

Right away a peculiar odor, both sweet and rancid, washed over her. She couldn't quite place it. Rotting food? Perfume? Both? She breathed through her mouth. A yawning dark cloaked the place in black. She flicked on her Maglite.

On either side were two rooms, both with doors, both closed. In front of one of the rooms was a bathroom. A center aisle led her to the front part of the warehouse. A light switch hung on the wall nearby. She flipped it. Nothing happened. She swept the Maglite around a room about the size of a six-car garage. Concrete floor. Cinder-block walls. Empty, except for an air mattress, mostly flat, on the floor. In the center of the room a few plastic chairs were grouped around a scuffed TV table. No TV.

Georgia wiped a hand across her brow. She was sweating. Mostly from fear, she knew, but she forced herself to suppress it. She needed to focus. This was a warehouse, but there was nothing to indicate goods were being stored or transported. Unless those goods were human.

She aimed the Maglite into a corner. The familiar white bags, the kind Benny's used, were crumpled up, but that hadn't stopped rats or other rodents from foraging. She frowned. That must be part of the odor. As she moved the beam to the other corner, something glinted in the light. She stepped closer and saw bits of tinfoil, some with scorch marks. She kept probing the light and saw a couple of brown plastic prescription vials.

As she backed up she tripped, and something clattered on the concrete floor. She started and swung the Maglite down. A can of Diet Coke skittered across the floor and was still rocking. She let out her breath. Had this place been the den for a sex-trafficking ring? Women snatched from who knows where, enslaved, and kept docile by hooking them on meth or smack? And was one of these women her half sister?

She retreated to the back of the warehouse and opened the door to the bathroom. Her reflection in the mirror of the medicine cabinet was distorted, making her mouth and chin unnaturally large. She looked into the cabinet. Nothing, not even a bottle of aspirin.

Then she checked out one of the other small rooms in the back. Nothing there either, except trash piled in a corner. She focused the light on the pile and was able to make out a mound of discarded tissues and toilet paper. An empty cardboard box was part of the pile. She took a closer look. A home pregnancy test kit.

The last thing sex traffickers wanted was a girl to become pregnant. They needed working girls. So if one of them did get pregnant, wouldn't they make sure she had an abortion? Georgia thought back to the body of the blond, pregnant girl found on the road near Harvard. But that was fifty miles away.

She fished out her iPhone and was shooting some pictures

when a squeak startled her. Someone was coming through the back door. She snapped off the Maglite. A dark gloom descended. It was impossible to make out objects. She pulled out her Glock and spun around.

Footsteps shuffled on the concrete floor. Just one person. With an uneven tread. The intruder had a limp. Which gave her an advantage. Hell, what was she thinking? *She* was the intruder.

She crouched on the floor of the small room. A dark, hulking shape passed by the open door, then stopped. He'd seen her. He backtracked, his shape filling the door frame.

"Don't come any closer," she said. "I've got a gun."

Chapter 28

T he shape seemed to shift its weight.

"I said, stop where you are. Right now."

The movement ceased. A moment passed. Then a phlegmy cough broke the silence. "I hear yuh."

A southern drawl. Georgia felt her breath catch. "Who are you? What are you doing here?"

"This be where I live. Who is you?"

Relief surged through her. Suddenly, she was terribly tired. She stood up. "How long have you lived here?"

"Few nights. Maybe more."

"Sit on the floor."

The figure did.

"Okay, I'm going to turn a light on."

"No. No light."

"I need to make sure you're not armed."

"You the police?" His accent was on the first syllable.

She didn't answer. She snapped on the Maglite with one hand, still aiming her Glock with the other.

A black man in sweatpants and cowboy boots. Some kind of jacket, but no gloves or hat. Salt-and-pepper hair, a ragged face, plenty of stubble. The guy was shivering, but he tried to smile. "Hey, you shine that light somewhere else? I can't see shit."

She angled the light to the side.

"You 'bout scared the living piss out of me. But I got a bottle in my jacket. And I could really use a drink right about now." He started to reach toward his pocket.

Georgia moved the light back to his face. "Don't even think about it."

His hand stopped. He tried to block the glare with it. "Ain't no gun; I don't have none. Why you here? Ain't no one supposed to be here no more."

"What do you mean?"

"I seen 'em leave."

"Who?"

I don't know who. But they all pack up and left."

"When?"

"I told you. About a week ago."

"Who were they?" Georgia repeated.

"Lady...I keep telling you. I don't know. Now, you wanna let me get my bottle?"

"In a minute." He was probably out of range, all the way across the room, but better to be careful.

"You said you didn't know much about the people who were here."

"That's right."

"Were they mostly women?"

"There be men too."

"Could you tell what they were doing?"

"Figured they was hos and pimps."

"What made you think that?"

"When I get here, there's perfume, hair stuff, makeup too. I cleaned up some, but you know..." His voice trailed off. "Guess they was in a hurry."

"What else?"

He shook his head. "Nothin.' I be staying here now. It ain't half-bad." He stopped. "Hey, I told you what I know. You wanna help me?"

"How?"

"You wanna blow some air into that air mattress yonder? My breathing ain't so great."

Georgia crept closer and shone the light into bloodshot eyes. She could see he was breathing hard. Emphysema? He gazed at her with such a beseeching look that she couldn't turn away. The guy hardly had breath enough to live. Much less come after her.

"Okay." She holstered her gun, lowered the light, and walked past him into the other room where the air mattress was. She hoped there were no bedbugs or roaches nesting in it. "You can get your bottle now."

Chapter 29

The homeless man raised questions for which Georgia had no answers, so she swung back to Benny's to wait for Bruce Kreisman. An hour later he hadn't shown up, so she went inside. It was midafternoon but business was still brisk. She ordered a bowl of matzoh-ball soup to go, and when they handed her the white bag at the take-out counter, she asked about Kreisman.

"Oh, he no here," one of the Hispanic women said, her accent thick.

Georgia frowned. "Your delivery guy just left?"

"Sí. Almost *una hora*, one hour now."

"Did he say where he was going? Or when he'd be back?"

The woman shook her head. "He say he have important business. But you know, boss is no happy. He could fire." She clucked her tongue. "You wan' I tell him you come?"

It was Georgia's turn to shake her head. "It's not important." She carried her soup back to the car, not liking the fact that he was doing some "business." Especially since she'd given him her card.

She ate her soup in the car, then headed to the Eisenhower. She figured she could make it to Oakbrook where Susie's Café was before rush hour. But traffic was building and progress was slow, which gave her time to eye the billboards on the side of the freeway. Signs for McDonald's, a gambling casino, and a car dealer flashed by, but after those was a black billboard with a photo of a pregnant African American girl who couldn't have been more than twelve. Fuchsia letters blasted the words "People who have sex with children are criminals. Stop teen pregnancy."

Georgia gripped the wheel. She wasn't a proponent of unmarried pregnancy without a damn good reason. Despite her Catholic upbringing, she used to recommend abortions for the pregnant hookers she busted when she was on patrol. Until the day she'd been downtown at a museum and wandered into a shamelessly pro-life exhibit. She mentally prepared herself not to be swayed, but one of the display cases showed actual three-dimensional models of what fetuses looked like at various stages of pregnancy. Even at twelve weeks, the model looked remarkably like a tiny baby. When she realized those tiny beings were alive, she'd had to flee the museum. Once in a while, images of those babies still came unbidden.

She snapped on the radio. The all-news station was predicting four to five new inches of snow, and a few errant snowflakes were already landing on her windshield. She would be caught in traffic after all.

Chapter 30

Susie's Café occupied the corner of a shopping center in Oakbrook between Chico's and a jewelry store. Red and blue signs promised a Euro cheerfulness, which was enhanced by blue-checked plastic tablecloths inside, replicas of windmills on the walls, and lots of travel posters. The place was nearly empty, and only one woman was behind the counter, but the meager offerings of pastries and sandwiches in the display case indicated either that lunch had been successful or that the place was on its last legs.

Georgia approached the woman, who was wearing a blue-checked gingham dress with an apron tied around her waist. She looked ridiculous.

"Hi," she said, trying to sound pleasant.

The woman gave her a curt nod. Not the warmest of welcomes. Did she feel as foolish as she looked?

"I'm in the mood for something sweet." Georgia smiled.

"Well"—the woman waved her hand toward a line of pastries—"we only have these left."

Georgia pretended to study them but tried to peer through the display case to see if there was any wrap on the counter. Nothing. She glanced up. "Glad business is so good."

The woman's gave her a blank look. Maybe it wasn't.

"I can't decide. Why don't you recommend something? Oh, and it's to go. I need to get home before the snow starts."

The woman studied her for a moment, then slid the display case open and removed a small apple crumb cake. "How about this?"

"Perfect. How much?"

"Four fifty-nine."

"Okay. Could you wrap it for me?"

The woman disappeared into the back with the crumb cake.

Georgia shifted her weight. A moment later the woman reappeared with a small white bag. Did every restaurant use white bags? Georgia dug out a five from her wallet and peeked into the bag while the woman rang it up. It had been wrapped, but the wrapper was very different from Benny's. It was a tissue decorated with blue and white checks, not the red and yellow stripes Benny's used. Georgia pulled out the pastry. "Oh, what a nice wrapping," she said.

The woman scowled as if Georgia had just said the lamest thing in the world. Which she had.

"It matches the tablecloths," the woman said in a dull voice.

Georgia glanced at a table. "It sure does." Then she said, "You know, when I was here before, I thought I remembered the wrapping being red and yellow. Or at least it had those colors in it."

The woman's expression seemed to imply "What kind of idiot focuses on the wrap?" But Georgia was the customer. "We haven't used those in six months. We upgraded." Her listless emphasis on the word "upgraded" made Georgia think the woman didn't give a damn about wraps one way or the other.

"Six months? It's been that long since I've been here?" She paused. "I guess time really does fly." *Oh God. Couldn't she do better than that?*

The woman tilted her head, but her scowl deepened. "Will there be anything else?"

"No. You've been very helpful."

Chapter 31

Back in her car Georgia unwrapped the pastry and took a huge bite. The baked apple, tart and gooey, combined with the crisp, sweet topping was delicious. She savored the taste and mulled over what she'd learned. It wasn't a sure bet, but it was looking like Benny's was the only restaurant using the wrap that "Savannah" had written on. Which meant, assuming the note was genuine, that Savannah might be connected to the warehouse in the West Loop.

She took another bite of pastry. She could trace the owner of the warehouse when she got home, see who popped up. Now, though, she needed to concentrate on her driving. The snow had intensified and was falling at a steady rate. Visibility was practically nil. Traffic was at a standstill on I-294, so she tried going east on surface streets. Still, the drive from Oakbrook to Evanston took more than two hours. By the time she pulled into a parking spot near her apartment, the apple crumb cake was long gone and the snow was dancing horizontally across the streetlights.

She pulled up her collar, braced herself, and slogged to the door of her building. She stopped to retrieve her mail. A few bills, but also an unfamiliar white envelope. She turned it over. The return address was "Precision Labs." She sucked in a breath. The

DNA results. She fingered the envelope. Thicker than one page, but not much more.

Inside she put the envelope on her desk. She carefully took off her coat, hat, and gloves and hung them up, as if she might need to remember exactly what she did and when she did it. Then she started to pace around her apartment.

The truth could hide—she'd known that as a cop and knew it now as a PI—but eventually it worked its way to the surface. It might take years. Even a lifetime. But what would she do if she did know the truth? If Savannah and she were related, it would require a fundamental rearrangement of her emotional life. Her mother had borne another daughter. She had a sister she'd never known.

But did that mean she was supposed to be her sister's savior? And if so, for how long? What if she couldn't stand the girl? Where were the rules for that? And who the hell wrote the handbook?

She let out a long breath, stopped pacing, and went back to her desk. She picked up the envelope and ripped it open. Two pages fell out. She scanned the first page, a chart titled "Sibling Report (Half vs Unrelated)—Legal Test." On the left were a series of incomprehensible letters and numbers under the heading "Genetic Markers." Across from each marker were two columns headed by the words "Allele A" and "Allele B." Underneath those columns were more numbers. Finally on the right was a column titled "Likelihood Ratio" with yet more numbers, although they were smaller than the others.

She had no idea what all the numbers meant and skipped to the second page, which included the interpretation. She read through a paragraph of qualifications, which basically said the absence of the birth mother's DNA prevented them from drawing a more definitive conclusion. She bit her lip. The report went on to say that a ninety-one percent probability was considered the lowest possible level for which one could say two individuals were related.

"Okay, okay," she muttered. "What's the bottom line?"

The last two lines told her. "Based on the genetic results, the alleged half siblings are 23,780 times more likely to be related as half siblings than to be unrelated. The Probability of Relatedness as Half Siblings is ninety-five point five percent."

Chapter 32

leep wouldn't come and Georgia lay in bed listening to the swish of the wind. She finally dozed off before dawn, but the growl of a snowplow woke her. She went to the window, raised the shade, then lowered it again. The new blanket of snow was glazed with an unapologetic sun, as if it was mocking her for her lack of sleep.

She brewed a pot of coffee and took a mug to her computer. She clicked onto the Cook County Assessor's website, clicked "Search by address," typed in the address of the warehouse, and pushed enter. Seconds later she had the warehouse's property index number, or PIN, a unique fourteen-digit number assigned to every piece of real estate in Cook County. Armed with that, she went to the Cook County Treasurer's Office website, pulled down the "Property search" portal, and entered the PIN. Less than a minute later, the tax payments for the warehouse popped up. Along with the payments was the most recent owner of record, a corporation named Executives Unlimited. The contact for the corporation, which, according to the website, had purchased the property a year earlier, was attorney Chad G. Coe.

She smiled. A property search used to take an entire day. She would have to drive downtown to the Assessor's Office, wait, fill out a form, then wait some more. Then she'd go to the Treasurer's

Office and do it all over again. Today that process could be accomplished in less than five minutes. She wished she could high-five her computer. Instead, she Googled Chad G. Coe.

There weren't a lot of mentions. He had no website, but he was on LinkedIn. She clicked on the URL. His profile was thin. He was listed as an attorney in the Greater Chicago area. But it didn't include any previous employment history, education, or specialty areas. She tapped a finger. Every attorney had a specialty, even if it was more fantasy than reality. She looked for the last update he'd made on LinkedIn. Nothing within the past three years.

She sipped her coffee. Chad Coe wasn't advertising or promoting himself. No "All inquiries welcome." No mention of clients. And no references. He looked to be flying under the radar. Why? She went to the Illinois Attorney Registration and Disciplinary Commission's website and discovered why. After she entered his name, she saw he'd been suspended from the bar for stealing his clients' money three years earlier. The legal wording was "Not authorized to practice law as an attorney." But the suspension was only temporary. He had been reinstated a year ago.

There was an address for him somewhere in Riverwoods, a small but affluent suburb west of Deerfield. She wrote it down. Then she checked one of her private databases and found a phone number at the Riverwoods address. She called the number, making sure to first block her caller ID, but discovered it had been disconnected. Which made her wonder if the address would lead to a dead end, too.

Chapter 33

⌘

Twenty minutes later Georgia pulled up to a building in Rogers Park with a sign proclaiming, "Paul Kelly: Lawyer & Insurance Agent." Kelly was a lawyer she'd worked with during her first big homicide case. His office consisted of two large but sparsely furnished rooms on Morse Street. She stopped in the coffee shop three doors down and bought two coffees. She tried to remember how he took his; one sugar, no cream, she thought. Armed with steaming cups, she pushed through the door.

The light was on in the front room, but the door to his office was partially closed. Even so, she could hear him on the phone. "Yes, rates are going up. They're trying to jack 'em up before ACA is fully implemented." There was a pause. "Of course it is. But you ever known an altruistic insurance company? They're not charitable institutions, you know." A few more words, then she heard the sound of the phone being slipped into the cradle.

She walked in. "Hey, Kelly, how's the insurance biz?" She used to tease him he was hedging his bets—if he couldn't make it as a lawyer, he had a fallback. In reality he was an excellent lawyer.

"Don't let it get around," he'd shot back. "I make good money from insurance."

Now he swiveled around in his chair where he'd been gazing out the window. "Davis. What a surprise!" He gave her a broad smile, which the deep frown lines on his sixtysomething forehead said he didn't do often. "What brings you down here?"

"I thought you could use some coffee." She handed it to him. He nodded, took the coffee with one hand, and motioned her into a chair with the other. He wasn't a big man, and he always wore the same thing: a shabby navy jacket, khaki pants, and a blue shirt. Fluorescent light bounced off his shiny bald head.

He doctored his coffee methodically, throwing the sugar packet in the trash before he stirred his drink with a wooden stick. Satisfied, he brought the coffee to his lips.

"So what's up? I have a feeling this isn't a social call."

"I was hoping you could get me some information about a lawyer."

"What about him?"

"He was suspended from the bar two years, according to ARDC."

"Dipped into the client's trust account, did he?"

Georgia tilted her head. "How did you know?"

"That's the most common reason lawyers get suspended."

"I didn't know." She paused. "Paul, I need to know more, but I don't want to work my way through the hearing transcripts." She could get them if she went online, but she didn't want to admit she was dyslexic. Plowing through them would take hours. "Can you run down the case for me? Don't you have a friend on the board or something?"

"She's a clerk. But it's the same thing." He grinned. "You want I should give her a call?"

"That would be great."

"For you, Davis. Only for you."

He put on a pair of reading glasses, spun his circular black Rolodex—the old-fashioned kind with white cards you don't see much these days—found what he was looking for, and picked up the phone. He paused, took a sip of coffee, then punched in the numbers.

"Jamie? Hi, Paul Kelly here. Hey, I need a favor. Yeah. Suspended by the Supreme Court." He covered the phone. "Who and when?"

"Chad Coe. About three years ago."

Kelly repeated the information, then laughed. "I'd wait for you until the clock strikes thirteen, sweetheart." He sipped his coffee, played with the telephone cord, and whispered to Georgia. "She's checking. Got everything all computerized. Easy, peasy."

Georgia nodded.

He waved her off, then sat up straighter. "Yeah, uh-huh. Hold on. Lemme get some paper." He grabbed a sheet and a pen. "Okay. When? Uh-huh. Really? How? Okay. I got it. Thanks."

He hung up and studied his notes. "Well, I don't know what your dealings are with this guy, but I hope you got—or get—your money's worth."

"Because..."

"Chad Coe apparently has or had a gambling habit. Sports mostly. Bookies, racetrack, casinos. Was in over his head and got caught with his hand in the cookie jar. To the tune of a hundred grand."

Georgia folded her arms.

"His firm fired him, of course, and a couple of his clients filed a complaint with ARDC."

"And?"

"He didn't contest it. Admitted he was a gambler, showed remorse. Said he was going to GA. Therapy too. So they only gave him twenty-four months. He was reinstated," Kelly said. "By the way, he paid the money back right away."

"If he was losing his shirt, how did he suddenly get a hundred grand?"

"That's what I asked." Kelly shrugged. "Jamie doesn't know."

"You think he went to a shark?" In which case whoever fronted him the money owned him.

"Who knows? Could have been family. Or a bank loan. But it's clear he found another source of income."

Georgia thought she knew who that source was.

He picked up his coffee. "Why are you interested in this creep?"

"His name came up in a case I'm working."

He peered at her over his glasses. "I don't have to tell you that a law degree doesn't make someone a good guy, right?"

"*You* are."

He colored all the way up to his shiny bald scalp.

Chapter 34

The chirp of her cell phone woke her from a nap two hours later.

"Davis..."

"Georgia?" A man's voice. "It's Jimmy Saclarides."

She blinked herself awake. "Oh, hi." She sat up.

"Sounds like I woke you."

"No," she lied. "I was—uh—reading."

"Oh. Well. Hey, I'm down in your neck of the woods visiting Luke. He's at Ellie's."

"Oh."

"And I was wondering whether you'd like to grab some dinner."

"Did you get an ID on the body?"

He cleared his throat, and when he replied, she heard his disappointment. "I may have some information."

Georgia realized she'd screwed up. "You know what? That doesn't matter. I'd love to have dinner."

"Oh." His tone grew decidedly more cheerful. "Great."

They met at Hole in the Wall, a tiny Italian place in Northbrook where the menu was posted on a large chalkboard. Despite its being a weeknight, there wasn't an empty table, and waitresses carrying garlic-scented pastas wound carefully around customers' elbows, knees, and winter coats draped over the backs of chairs.

"It smells heavenly," Georgia said as they waited for a table. "How did you know about this place?"

"State secret." He smiled and drew his fingers across his lips to indicate they were sealed.

Georgia smiled back. "Oh. Of course. Ellie."

He was wearing a green sweater, collared shirt, and jeans that emphasized his best physical asset. When he smiled, the crow's-feet in the corners of his eyes crinkled nicely. He caught her checking him out and his smile broadened, deepening the crow's-feet. She looked down, suddenly self-conscious.

"You look great too, Georgia."

Her lips parted. How did he—? Of course. He was a cop. A trained observer. She felt herself color. She was also in jeans but wore a black sweater with a bright-blue scarf. Her blond hair was down, and she had even put on makeup.

The maître d' led them to a table against the wall.

"I forgot," she said as they sat down.

"What?"

"That you're a cop."

He laughed. "Don't hold it against me." It was a cheerful laugh. Genuine. She couldn't help smiling.

"You think it will last? Ellie and Luke?"

He inclined his head, as if he thought it was an odd thing for her to ask. "Actually, I do. They fit well together. You know what I mean?"

I'm glad someone does, she thought.

The conversation through hors d'oeuvres and wine was light. Georgia peppered him with questions about being a cop in Lake Geneva, how he and Luke became friends, his family. But when their entrées came—pasta for him, veal for her—he held up a warning finger.

"Tread carefully, Georgia. I know your MO."

She jerked her head up. "What do you mean?"

"You keep asking me questions so you won't have to reveal anything about yourself." But his expression was warm and welcoming, and for the second time in less than an hour, she felt her cheeks burn. "I'm not falling for it," he went on. "Your turn."

"There's not much to tell." She shrugged. "And this veal is wonderful."

"Why don't you let me be the judge of that?" He extended his fork toward her plate. She cut a piece of veal, which he speared and put in his mouth. "You're right." He nodded and looped a forkful of pasta from his plate and offered it to her.

She took it, chewed, and smiled. "Wonderful."

"But you're not off the hook."

She lowered her fork to her plate. "I'm from a lace-curtain Irish family on the West side. My mother left when I was about ten. I lived with my father. He was a cop. Then I became one. That's about it."

He let a moment go by. When she didn't add anything, he said, "I don't think I've ever met a woman with less to say."

She swallowed. *When would she figure out the rules?*

Her self-criticism was cut short when he reached across the table where her hand lay and covered it with his own. "It's okay." He smiled. "I've got time."

Now her face was on fire.

A moment later she slowly pulled her hand from his. "So tell me about the body of the pregnant woman."

He leaned back and laced his hands together. "She was a runaway."

"How did you trace her?"

"Dental records."

"She was American?"

Jimmy nodded. "Kansas City."

She tensed. "Was—was she in the trade?"

"It would seem so. There were tracks on her arms. Faded, but you could see them."

"What was her name?"

"Jennifer Madden."

Georgia relaxed. "How old?"

"Sixteen."

Georgia remembered the billboards on the Ike. "Why didn't she get an abortion? Why go through with the pregnancy?"

He looked like he was considering her questions. "It was getting close. The autopsy said she was about six months at the time of death." He hesitated. "I'm just speculating here, but it's possible she didn't have the money, or didn't know where to go. Or maybe she wanted to have the baby."

"Maybe," Georgia said. She wasn't convinced.

"You seem surprised she was American," he said.

She blinked. She'd forgotten about his cop's observational skills. Again. "Um, well. I...I guess I expected something else."

"You mean girls brought in from other countries?"

She nodded.

"No one has a monopoly on sex trafficking these days." He finished his pasta. "So. You want to tell me why you drove all the way out to Harvard on a cold Saturday morning to eyeball a pregnant corpse?"

The waitress took their plates. Jimmy ordered coffee. Georgia studied him. It would feel good to talk it through. But not with a cop. She knew what he'd say. Still, if there was a chance he could shed some light on the situation and her sister, it might be worth it. So she told him about the note, the Russian guy who'd been killed in the drive-by, the DNA results, Benny's, Bruce Kreisman, the warehouse. Jimmy listened without interrupting. She told him about the home pregnancy kit she'd found. "I know it's a long shot, but I keep thinking maybe it was hers. Savannah's."

Jimmy was quiet. Then, "And maybe it wasn't."

"You think I'm trying to connect dots that aren't there."

"I don't know you that well." He picked up his coffee. "But it does sound like you've spent a lot of time and energy on something that—well, you *hope* will be real."

"She's my sister."

"Your half sister. Who you've never met. And didn't even know about ten days ago."

Georgia bristled. "Are you saying it's not my sister? What about the DNA?"

"What about it?"

"There's a better than ninety-five percent chance we're related."

He tipped his head to the side. "By the way, what was the sample they used to extract DNA from your—sister?"

"A drop of blood on a sandwich wrapper."

"A sandwich wrapper?"

"Yeah." Georgia mirrored his head movement. Why?"

"Did you ever wonder how that blood got there? It's not every day that you find blood on a sandwich wrapper."

She shook her head. "I don't know, Jimmy. Maybe she bit her tongue. Cut her finger slicing the sandwich. Pricked her finger on a fucking needle."

"Maybe."

"What are you getting at?"

"I'm not getting at anything, Georgia. Except to suggest that you step back for a day or two and slow down. Look at it rationally. Is this something you really should pursue on your own? Why don't you hand it over to the police? You used to be a cop. You know they'll do the job."

"Yeah, but they're not going to be looking out for my sister."

"I get that. But when sex trafficking is involved...and the Russian mob..." His voice softened. "You may not like what you find."

Chapter 35

They shared a dessert and dawdled over coffee, both of them seemingly reluctant to see the evening end. Eventually, though, they left the warmth of the restaurant and stepped outside into a night so bitter that Georgia's nose and throat felt peppery when she breathed. Jimmy walked her to her car.

"Thank you," she said softly. "This was really nice."

Jimmy leaned over, cupped her cheeks in his hands, and kissed her lightly on the lips. "Yes. It was."

She opened the door and slid into her car. He held up his hand and waited until she'd reversed out of the parking lot and turned onto Skokie Highway. As she cruised south on Frontage Road, she smiled. Jimmy *got* her. She was pretty sure she got him, too. It was the first time in—well—a long time. She blasted the heat, turned on the oldies radio station, and started singing along with the Four Tops. She hadn't done that in a long time.

It wasn't until she was on the Edens heading south that she noticed the headlights in her rearview were a little too close. How long had they been there? She snapped off the radio and accelerated. The vehicle behind her did too. She slowed down and shifted lanes. So did the headlights. She was being tailed.

It was a clear night, a half-moon bathing everything in silver. Back in the middle lane she peered into the rearview again, trying to make out the vehicle, but the headlights were blinding. They rode high, though, so she suspected it was an SUV or van. The fatal drive-by in Evanston a few weeks earlier had involved an SUV. She pulled out her cell and her baby Glock and laid them both on the passenger seat.

It wasn't until they were south of Willow that the tail made his move. The car sped up and pulled into the left lane as if to pass her. It *was* an SUV. But she knew the trick. The driver was trying to come abreast of her. She pulled into the far right lane, narrowly avoiding a collision with a truck, whose driver blasted his horn. She let the truck pass and settled in close behind, hoping it would move into the middle lane and block her from the SUV. Unfortunately the truck flashed its turn signal and exited on Dempster. Georgia followed suit, still hoping to use it for cover. The SUV careened up the exit behind them. But the truck suddenly slowed and pulled into a gas station just beyond the cloverleaf. Georgia didn't have enough time to turn and follow the truck. She was in the open. Despite the cold night, droplets of sweat trickled down the back of her neck.

She flew east on Dempster. Although it was heavily traveled, there were only two lanes in each direction. There wasn't much traffic, and no snow, so Georgia tried to serpentine between the lanes, but the SUV mirrored her. Her only advantage was that the road was well lit, and in the glow of the streetlights she thought she could see two figures inside.

She had to lose them.

She was planning her next move when the SUV suddenly appeared on the shoulder to her right. She stiffened. The rear window rolled down, and the barrel of a long gun emerged. She floored her Toyota, unable to tell whether it was a shotgun or assault rifle. But Toyotas weren't great on acceleration, and a second later she saw the flash of a muzzle and heard a cannon-like blast. Her car veered wildly and fishtailed into the oncoming lane, which, thankfully, was free of traffic. At the same time she realized she hadn't been hit. But her tire was. The SUV peeled off at the next corner and headed south. She wrestled the Toyota to the shoulder and plowed into a snowbank.

Chapter 36

Georgia thought about calling the cops, then reconsidered. There was nothing they could do now except file a report, and she didn't want to spend hours repeating the same thing to a beat cop or surly detective who'd been rousted out of bed. Instead she called AAA and waited for them in a twenty-four-hour coffee shop—she was too flustered, and it was too damn cold to change the tire herself—when her cell chirped. It was probably the mechanic who'd been tapped for the job. They were always late. Without checking the incoming number, she picked up.

"Davis."

"Saclarides."

She was momentarily distracted. "Oh, hi."

"I won't keep you. I just wanted to say what a good time I had tonight."

She wanted to smile, but it didn't come. "Me too." Her voice broke.

"Hey," Jimmy said. "Is everything okay? You sound...strange."

She blew out a breath. "Someone just shot out my rear tire."

"What?"

"It sounded like a shotgun."

"Where are you?"

"On Dempster. East of Lincoln. The car's on the shoulder. I'm in a coffee shop."

"I'm on my way."

* * *

An hour later, she was on her way home, Jimmy following in his Accord. He'd insisted on changing the tire himself. She canceled AAA and when she got home, she started a pot of coffee. She joined Jimmy in the living room.

"Thanks again for changing the tire."

He waved it off. "You didn't call the cops." It was a statement.

She explained why.

He shrugged. "Does that mean you have his plate and you're going rogue?"

She shook her head. "No plate. No ID. All I know is that it was a dark-colored SUV." She stopped.

He looked over. "What?"

"I told you about the drive-by in Evanston, right? The Russian or Eastern European guy who got popped?"

He nodded.

"The shooter was in a dark SUV."

The coffeepot dinged. Jimmy rose and headed toward the kitchen.

"I'll get it," she said.

"Sit. Just tell me where the cups are. And sugar."

She did.

He returned a minute later with two steaming mugs. "Someone who takes potshots at your tires is not good. You need to report this."

"Yeah, but here's the thing. They were directly across from me in the next lane. They had a clear shot at my head, but they shot out the tire instead. Why?"

"You tell me."

She shrugged. "No clue."

"Georgia, for a smart PI, you're not acting like one."

"You think it has to do with Savannah?"

"Do things like this happen to you on a regular basis?"

"The drive-by in Evanston happened before I heard about Savannah. And there's no reason to think the two events are connected. For all I know, this was just some asshole with a gun on a power trip."

Jimmy shot her a look. "Tell me something. If this happened to one of your clients, what would you tell them?"

"That someone was trying to warn them. Or send them a message. That next time they might not be so lucky. That they needed to protect—"

"Hell, Georgia," Jimmy cut in. "This was no warning. You don't shoot out a tire in the middle of the night with snow on the ground and not expect the driver to lose control and get hurt. Or worse. Maybe you should stop what you're doing. Reassess. Go to Plan B."

"I can't. I have a sister I didn't know I had. She's in Chicago and she needs me. I have to find her."

"Not if you're going to have your head blown off in the process."

She wanted to tell him the rest, to pour it all out. That she was alone in this world. And that the mere suggestion she had a sibling had triggered a flicker of hope that maybe she wasn't as alone as she'd thought. That maybe there was *someone* she could call family. That the chance to end the curse of being nobody's child was so seductive that she couldn't abandon it. But she kept her mouth shut.

Jimmy leaned toward her, elbows on his knees. "Plus, there's the fact that I've just started to know you, and I want to know you better. A lot better."

A tiny smile lifted the corners of her mouth. "Thank you."

"For what?"

"For caring." She put her coffee cup down, reached out, and stroked his cheek.

He went very still, as if anything he did or said would break the spell.

She dropped her hand. "You know something?" she said softly. "I don't want to be alone tonight."

He broke into a smile. "Neither do I."

Chapter 37

Savannah—Nine Months Earlier

Savannah thought she was entering the Emerald City. The lights weren't entirely green, but there were plenty of them, and despite the dark—it had to be after midnight—the city sparkled. Cars glided down streets, bright headlights chased the night away, and a steady hum seemed to pulse through the air. A hazy memory of her childhood kicked in, and she recalled her mother calling Chicago the promised land. Vanna smiled to herself. She'd made the right decision.

The bus entered a tunnel, then lurched to a stop. The sleeping woman beside her, who smelled so vile Vanna had to breathe through her mouth, snorted and blinked awake. Vanna hoped the woman's body odor wasn't contagious. As people shuffled off the bus, most of them still sleepy and slow, she grabbed her backpack and climbed down.

Her fellow passengers scattered, some heading through an arch with a sign that led to public transportation. Others, greeted by friends or family, proceeded out to the street. Vanna hadn't considered what she would do when she arrived; she never thought she'd actually make it to Chicago. But here she was.

She followed some of the passengers out to the street. Huge

skyscrapers were illuminated, their lit windows sparkling like stars. A hazy glow suffused the sky, lightening it from black to grayish orange. The Loop, she recalled. It wasn't that she hadn't been in big cities before. They'd lived in Tucson, Houston, and Albuquerque, but there was something different about Chicago. She could feel it.

It was late March, and flowers were blooming in Colorado. Here, though, the frigid air had a bite; she was glad she'd "borrowed" her mother's jacket. She hurried back inside.

The interior of the terminal was as big as a train station, with arcades and shops, now closed, leading off a main hall. The walls were white and spruced up with gaily colored murals; this was not the tiled wall, concrete floor, and shabby ticket booth of the bus depots she knew. The place was well lit, and if you didn't know what time it was, you couldn't tell it was the middle of the night. Still, the fluorescent lights gave everyone a slightly green cast. Emerald City—a place where magic dust was dispensed by fairies who never slept. She giggled.

"What's so funny, sweetheart?" a male voice said behind her.

The giggle died in her throat. Startled, she spun around. A man was checking her out. He had thick dark hair and dark eyes. He wasn't bad looking and was probably somewhere between thirty and forty. But he was nicely dressed in a white shirt, brown leather jacket, and khakis. Her gaze went to his shoes. Her mother always said to check a stranger's shoes. If they were in good shape, the person cared about their appearance. His were shiny black loafers that looked almost new. A good sign.

"Well?" he said, a smile on his face. He had the trace of an accent. She couldn't place it.

Vanna hesitated. She wasn't an idiot. She knew she wasn't supposed to talk to strangers. But this guy wasn't the sort of bum who lurked around bus depots looking for a handout or a drink. In fact, she wondered why he was at the bus station at all. He looked like the type who should have been flying. Then again, she wasn't in Kansas anymore. Did all the men in Chicago look like this? If so, this hadn't just been a good decision—it was a fucking awesome one. And who knew? Maybe he had some blow.

So she gave him that "maybe I'd like to know you better" smile and answered his question. "What's funny? Nothing. I'm just so fucking glad to be in a real city."

The man's grin widened, and he nodded. "I know what you mean. Where are you from?"

"Colorado. What about you?"

"Originally? Poland. Kraków. But I live here a lot of years."

"Why Chicago?"

He waved his hand. "Look around. You can do anything you want. Get anything you want. Even in the bus terminal."

"Anything?" She ran her hand up her arm.

He folded his arms. "What do you want?"

She favored him with the smile that made the boys back in Colorado get hard. "What are you offering?"

When he smiled back, she could tell from his expression that she'd roped a winner.

Chapter 38

Savannah

Vanna realized later she never had a chance. Men like Lazlo were vultures waiting to swoop down to snatch their prey. At the time, though, she thought it was luck. She was due for a break. She kept flirting with him, and he flirted right back, making veiled references to a party and the fun they could have. Finally he came in for the kill, although she didn't know it then. She was only fifteen, for Christ's sake.

"So what is your name, sweetheart?"

"Vanna."

"Ha! Like the TV show, eh?"

She grinned. "Don't I look like her?" She twirled in a circle, letting him get a good look.

"Better." His gaze turned calculating. "You must be hungry."

She smiled seductively. "Starving. How did you know?"

He laughed. "Come with me. I buy you food." His arm went around her shoulder.

She shrugged. "Okay." Just like that. She was on her way. In a new city. Not hard at all.

They left the bus station and started walking toward the skyscrapers. Despite the frigid air and dark sky, the city threw off a throbbing, pulsing energy just waiting for Vanna to own it. No wonder her mother and sister—it still sounded weird to say that word—loved the place. A block into the walk, though, even with her mother's jacket, she started to shiver. She'd have to get warmer clothes. Maybe Lazlo would spring for them.

In a few blocks they came to a twenty-four-hour greasy spoon. Lazlo led her inside and bought her a hot dog and a Coke. She'd been hoping for something more substantial, maybe steak. At least pizza. But this was better than nothing. She wolfed down the food.

"Ah. You were hungry," he said.

She peered at him from under her eyelashes. Some fashion magazine said it made a woman look sexy. "What's for dessert?" She made her voice sound throaty and suggestive, another trick the magazine advised.

He looked at her and smiled. "We have dessert someplace else."

"Good." She settled back in the booth. "But you should know...I only like certain flavors."

His brow creased as if he didn't understand.

She was trying to telegraph that she did blow. Not smack, not angel dust, not Ecstacy. Just blow. "You know, the white stuff."

He still looked puzzled but spoke as if he understood. "Yes, white. You will see. Only white."

He led her out of the hot dog place. She still wasn't sure if he got it. "So. You got any wine?"

"Wine?" He frowned again.

"I like white. They go together. White and white," she said.

"Oh yes. We have white."

"Great." She looped her arm through his. They kept walking toward the skyscrapers. They were getting so close she imagined she could reach out and touch them.

"Is your place nearby?"

"Of course." He patted her arm.

They turned right and started down the street. This street

wasn't so well lit, and the sidewalk was cracked. Vanna had to keep her head down so she didn't trip. After a couple of blocks, she said,

"How far away are we? I'm cold."

"We almost there."

"So, Lazlo, why were you at the bus station? Did you just get into town yourself?"

He answered two beats later. "I come from Milwaukee."

"What were you doing there?"

Again a hesitation. "Business." His tone grew less charming. Even gruff. Vanna stole a glance at him. He was looking straight ahead, not at her.

Two blocks later they came to a shabby door front above which a neon sign flashed, "Hotel Leon. Rooms by the Week."

Vanna swallowed. This wasn't the kind of place she was expecting. Where was the penthouse? The spacious condo? He opened the door and guided her in.

"This is where you live?"

"Sometimes."

They walked into a narrow lobby with a small elevator at the back. The front desk occupied one side of the room, but no one was behind it. A warren of tiny cubbyholes held keys with plastic labels attached. An occasional pink message slip peeked out. Lazlo already had a key, so they took the elevator to the third floor.

The room, small and musty, was one step up from a fleabag. A queen bed with a floral spread sat against the wall, and there was a desk with a chipped surface that was marred by several circular white rings. The bathroom flooring consisted of tiny tiles, the kind they used before she was born. She'd been in worse places, but she was disappointed. She thought Chicago hotels would be bigger, better, more upscale. She flopped down on the bed.

"So. Here we are. The party begins." His smile was cold, almost a sneer.

Vanna forced herself not to recoil. She knew what he wanted.

It would be no big deal after he gave her the blow. "I thought we were having dessert," she said.

"We do."

She tried to smile. "Hmm. You said you had my flavor."

He started to unzip his pants.

"Hey. Wait a minute. Where's the blow?"

He looked over, the smirk still on his lips. "Yes. You will."

She stood and planted her hands on her hips. "I don't think you understand." She frowned. "First the coke. You said you had coke."

He laughed. "Coca-Cola. Sure, I get you one. After."

Was he being stupid on purpose? "That's not the kind of coke I mean. You know that."

"You're not choose. I will." His English suddenly deteriorated, and his accent grew thicker. What was going on?

"Lazlo, I want to score some blow. Cocaine. That's why I came with you. I thought you knew."

His expression turned grim. "Come here, Vanna."

A ripple of fear streaked up her spine. She covered it with bravado and pointed her finger at him. "Listen up, dude. Unless you have what I want, this party is over." She tried to head toward the door, but he was faster and got there first, blocking her way.

She scowled at him. "Get away from that door."

"Take your clothes off."

"What the fuck for? You welshed on our deal."

His face took on a malicious leer. "Deal? I tell you deal. You take off clothes. Right now." He stepped out of his pants. He wasn't wearing underwear. Fondling his cock, he lifted it up for her to see. Engorged and throbbing and huge, it wasn't circumcised. Again, no big deal. In any other situation, she'd be thrilled with his erection. She'd made it happen. She was in control. The little blond fuck angel.

Not this time.

She tried once more to shift the balance of power. "First, you give me what I want." She ran her fingers lightly across his dick. "Then I'll give you what you want."

Vanna wasn't prepared for what happened next. Lazlo belted her across her face. She staggered back, her head exploding into a mass of pain. She felt her eyes roll up, and she listed to one side. Her arms involuntarily flailed out, as if hoping he would steady her. But he just stood there. She covered her mouth with her hand. When she pulled it away, her palm was bloody. A tooth felt loose.

"Now!" Lazlo crossed his arms. "Take off your clothes."

His eyes gleamed with a frenzy that frightened her. She tried to back away, but his hands shot out and grabbed her shoulders, squeezing so hard she almost sank to the floor. She tried to shake them off, but he had her pinned.

"Fuck off. That hurts!"

He slapped her again. The pain reverberated around her skull. Her cheeks stung, and her heartbeat thudded through her temples. She groaned, too dizzy to focus.

"You do what I want."

She tried to struggle, but she was no match for him. With his hands still gripping her shoulders, he shoved her back onto the bed. He tore her clothes off. Then, making sure his weight was on top of her, he slipped off his shirt. He had a lot more hair on his chest than the boys in Colorado. Too much. An oily, sweet smell oozed from his skin, as if he'd overdosed on cologne to mask the odor of not bathing. She squirmed, but he pressed down on her with enough weight to make her efforts useless. She had no choice.

"Okay. All right." She panted. "What do you want?"

He grunted, straddled her with his knees and elbows, and shoved his cock in her mouth.

Chapter 39

T he light in the alley slanted toward the house across the street where the kids lived with their mother. They needed it more than she did, Georgia figured. But enough light seeped through her bedroom shade, producing a filmy glow that highlighted Jimmy's face as he slept. One of his arms was stretched over his head. The other lay by his side. A peaceful expression, even the hint of a smile, was on his lips.

She gazed at him, a jumble of emotions roiling her brain. Who was this man who'd made such sweet love to her? Who explored her body but allowed her to explore his, too? Who let her think she was the aggressor but then took control exactly when she wanted? He'd brought her to a place she thought was long dead. Where had he learned to do that? Should she trust it?

He was a cop, but there was something different about him. Police work breeds a darkness in a cop's soul, a darkness so vast that even the most perfect day is marred by its shadow. Some cops come to terms with it; others bury it in a bottle or drugs. Still others, like Matt, her former lover, never did settle their account. Managing requires a delicate balance. Becoming a PI was no guarantee of basking in the light, either. The only difference was that now she could choose how much to take on.

But Jimmy didn't seem to have those demons. Granted, she

didn't know him well, but she had the sense that he had made peace with the dark side. Either he'd never faced evil, which, despite the fact that Lake Geneva was a lazy resort town where DUIs and drug busts were more the norm than murder, she doubted; or he had not allowed it to consume him. Which would make him a special cop. And an even finer man.

As if sensing she was awake, he turned onto his side and smiled, sleep dusting his eyes. She smiled back and lightly traced a patch of light that fell across his chest. Then he gathered her in his arms, and she stopped thinking.

Chapter 40

Morning sun poured through the shade, waking her. Jimmy's hand was cupping her breast. It felt right, she thought drowsily. The way it was supposed to be. As she came fully awake, though, she scooted away and rolled over. He grumbled in his sleep and reached for her, as if trying to recapture their intimacy. When she didn't respond, he slowly opened his eyes. His disheveled hair and welcoming expression made him look sexy, and she thought about making love again, but something stopped her. She threw the covers off her side of the bed and went into the bathroom.

When she came out he was on his back, hands behind his head, watching her. She saw approval in his eyes. Still, she felt exposed and dove back under the covers. She propped her head on her hand.

"Good morning," he said.

"I'd say so," she replied.

He smiled at that and started to stretch. "Do we have to get up?"

"I'll take you out for waffles."

"Is that a bribe?"

"Payback."

"Payback?" He paused, then narrowed his eyes. "You're a hard woman, Georgia."

She shrugged, which was difficult while she was naked and in bed, but she tried.

"I get it, you know," he said.

"Get what?"

"It's morning and you're not sure what happened last night. So it's safer to describe it as a mutual give-and-take. I take you to dinner and change your tire. You let me sleep with you and buy me breakfast. We're even. All paid up."

She let out a breath. Damn him.

"It's okay." He paused. "Except for one thing."

"What's that?"

"You can't get rid of me that easily."

* * *

It was almost noon by the time they finally did get up, which had to be the latest she'd risen in years. They took showers together, which made them even later, and it wasn't until early afternoon that they were seated in a booth at the pancake house in Wilmette. The only reason to go to Walker Brothers was for the apple pancake, a delicious creation of apples, cinnamon, sugar, and dough that was known all over Chicago, if not the country. Georgia rarely allowed herself the luxury of all the calories, but Jimmy admitted never having had one. After it arrived with steaming mugs of coffee, Georgia cut a slice for Jimmy and one for herself. She watched as he chewed. His eyes went wide.

"I've never tasted anything like this." He shoveled another huge forkful into his mouth. "This has got to be the eighth wonder of the world."

"We think so." She stopped. When had she become so proprietary about Chicago food? She sounded like a preening idiot. She cleared her throat. "Don't you have to get back to Lake Geneva?"

"I told you you're not getting rid of me that easily." He cut himself another slice of pancake and grinned. "Especially after a kickback like this. I knew there were perks to being chief of police."

His response confused her, and her expression must have shown it, because his grin suddenly faded. "I called in on my cell. Everything's quiet." He picked up his coffee mug and took a sip. Then, "I've been thinking about last night."

"Me too," Georgia said softly.

"Actually, I was thinking about the assholes who shot out your tire."

Georgia felt a spurt of disappointment. "Oh." She switched into PI mode.

"You made a good point. They had a chance to kill you, but they didn't. The question is why."

"I still think it's a warning or—"

"Or what? Why, given the chance to eliminate a target, do you not take it out?"

She thought about it. "Retaliation, maybe? Force the target to reveal themselves? Send a message?"

"Or scare you."

"I don't scare easily."

"Maybe you should."

She sat back. He was going cop on her, recycling the conversation they'd already had. She knew why. If they kept going over the same ground, maybe she'd remember something new. Some key fragment or scrap of information that would make sense of last night's attack. Jimmy the cop was different from Jimmy the lover. A lover whose warmth and passion she'd wanted to bask in just a while longer.

But he obviously didn't. Was he taking a cue from her—what had he said? That this was payback. They were even. Is that what he thought? She was simply trying to be careful. Keep her feelings in check. She wanted to restart the conversation, but she didn't know how. Reluctantly she focused on what he was saying.

"Lets assume for a minute it's not related to Savannah."

"Why?"

"Just run with me for a second. Brainstorming, they call it."

"Okay."

You've been a PI how long now?"

"About five years."

"You've obviously worked a lot of cases. More if you include the years you were a cop."

"I was just a beat cop. I dealt with simple stuff. Especially on the North Shore. House burglaries, stolen cars, that kind of thing."

"No angry offenders?"

"Most are dead or in jail."

"What if they did their time, got out, and decided to get revenge for something you did to them?"

She shrugged. "Comes with the territory. But you know as well as me they usually don't go after us. They go for the stoolies. Anyway, there's no way I can track them all."

"That's my point. No matter who's targeting you, we're back where we started. Somebody doesn't want to you to do what you've been doing. But you keep trying to find out who. Georgia, today is a new day. Let the police handle it."

Seizing an opportunity to reconnect, she reached out and covered his hand with hers. "I love that you're concerned about me. I'll be careful. But I can't back off. Not yet."

He didn't reply, and a moment later he withdrew his hand. He left soon after.

She paid the check, then trudged to her car. She'd done it again. Made sure to keep a man she liked at a distance. What did they call them—self-fulfilling prophecies? Well, she'd likely made one happen. So why did she feel more alone now than before?

Chapter 41

Georgia had a choice. She could drive to Riverwoods to stake out Chad Coe or head back to Benny's to pump Bruce Kreisman again. She might pick up new information, perhaps even a name that would lead to the assholes who had messed with her car.

It was no contest. It would be much more pleasant to sip a bowl of matzoh-ball soup in a clean, bright place like Benny's than to slump over the wheel in an overheated car waiting for someone who might not appear for hours, if at all. What would she say to the lawyer anyway? Did he know the warehouse he owned was being used as sex-trafficking den? Did he know a pregnant blond girl named Savannah?

She headed downtown under a leaden sky. Thirty minutes later she pulled up to the restaurant and parked half a block away. A light snow fell, no more than flurries, but her boots squeaked on the layer of snow already packing the sidewalk. She stamped her feet as she pushed through the door.

Benny's steamy warmth cascaded over her. She headed to the take-out counter and ordered soup. She wasn't hungry but figured she would save it for dinner. It was after three and the lunch rush was over. The servers behind the counter chatted with each other and the few customers still in line. When her soup was ready, she picked up the white bag along with her receipt.

"By the way, is Bruce Kreisman around?" she asked the African American woman behind the counter.

The woman who'd handed her the soup frowned. "What are you, a comedian?"

Georgia was taken aback. "Sorry. Is he out on a run?"

The woman took in a breath, then let it out through her nose. "Where you been, child?"

"I'm clearly missing something. Was he fired?"

The woman planted her hands on her hips. "No, he ain't been fired."

A second woman came out of the kitchen, wiping her hands on her apron, then crossed them over her chest. She'd obviously been eavesdropping. Both women stared at Georgia as if she was an intruder.

"What's going on? What happened?"

"I'll tell you what happened," the second woman said. "They found him in his car two nights ago. With a bullet hole in his head."

Chapter 42

N ausea climbed up her throat, and Georgia barely made it back to her Toyota. The soup, which had seemed so welcoming moments earlier, was now a bleak reminder of what she'd just heard. She got out of the car, ran to a trash bin, and pitched it. Back in the car she sucked in deep breaths of air.

Georgia didn't believe in coincidence. Last Monday a man tailed her down Sherman Avenue in Evanston. A dark SUV barreled around the corner and someone inside shot him. The next day she got the note from Savannah, which, according to DNA testing, was legit. After tracking the wrapper to Benny's a few days later, she interviewed Bruce Kreisman, who led her to what looked like a sex-trafficking den. Little more than twenty-four hours after that, someone in a dark SUV shot out her tire. Now Bruce Kreisman had turned up dead.

Even an idiot could connect the dots. Who did Bruce Kreisman talk to after he took her to the warehouse? What was that person's connection to her sister? And what was so important that he was killed for it? She supposed his deadbeat pals back in Florida might have tracked him to Chicago, but unless he'd done more than was on his rap sheet, his crimes down there didn't warrant an execution-style murder. Then again, if the Russian mob was involved, they didn't need a reason to kill. It was part of their MO.

Someone didn't want her poking around and was going to lengths to let her know. They could have killed her along with Kreisman. But they didn't. Why? Why shoot out her tire instead? And where did Chad Coe fit in? Was he the head honcho? Or just a soldier in the chain of command?

She started the engine and punched in the address of the warehouse on her GPS. After a number of twists and turns, she pulled up to the curb. The building was dark, all the doors closed. It looked deserted, with no sign of the homeless squatter. She wondered if the Dumpsters were still full of the detritus from the women, but even if they were, it wouldn't tell her anything. Except that they'd canceled their garbage service. But she ought to check. She went around to the back and lifted the Dumpster's lid. The trash was still there: pink bathrobe, food wrappers, empty pregnancy test kit.

The flurries intensified as she drove home, snowflakes whizzing and zooming every which way. Her wipers groaned and scraped across the windshield. She should spring for new blades. It would make things clearer. Not like this case, if you could call it that. Like the snowflakes, all she had were maddening bits and pieces.

She was at a distinct disadvantage. She knew nothing about the other side except that they might have Savannah and they might have killed Bruce Kreisman. They, on the other hand, knew her, where she lived, and who she was talking to.

Chapter 43

T hat evening Georgia cleaned her apartment. When she was younger and living with her father, she'd been in charge of housekeeping. It was a two-story bungalow with curtains that needed washing, rugs that needed vacuuming, and dust bunnies that needed to be swept up.

She'd taken to the job enthusiastically—she wanted the house to be ready when her mother came home. For months the young Georgia assumed her mother would return; she was just taking a break. On vacation. Not gone for good. So every time she vacuumed or dusted or threw in a load of laundry, she tallied her chores on a mental scorecard, thinking that when she got to the magic number, whatever it was, the front door would open, and her mother would be there. She would drop her suitcase and open her arms to Georgia.

It never happened.

Now she had her own place. But her furnishings were Spartan, and there wasn't much to clean. Was her minimalist lifestyle in some way connected to her unresolved feelings about her mother? Perhaps, in some subconscious way, even though her mother had abandoned her, and even though Georgia understood why, she still expected her to come back. Which was why she kept everything neat and orderly. Just in case.

She finished and stowed the vacuum in the broom closet. Something was nagging at her while she worked and had been since she drove back from downtown. It wasn't about her mother, and it wasn't about Kreisman—although she'd decided to take Jimmy's advice and call O'Malley in the morning to let him know what was going on. Hopefully, he'd snag the police report for her.

Whatever was bothering her was at the outer edges of her awareness, but she couldn't force it. It would surface when it was ready. So she fixed dinner, wishing now she hadn't thrown the soup away. She opened a can of tomato soup and made a grilled cheese sandwich. She took the sandwich out of the toaster oven . Jimmy was probably right. She was investing too much in the situation. Better to stop before it got out of control. She wolfed down the sandwich and swallowed her soup.

Maybe it was time for a movie. She took her tablet into the bedroom. She was in the mood for something light and funny. She hadn't made the bed that morning, and the rumpled sheets still smelled of sex and Jimmy. As she scrolled through the offerings on Netflix, she debated whether to call him. For the second night in a row she didn't want to be alone. She didn't want to dwell on the fact that someone was probably holding her sister hostage. And that Bruce Kreisman was dead.

Death. The opposite of birth. Kreisman had been alive but now he wasn't. Babies weren't alive and then they were. A sudden memory of the display in the museum washed over her. Tiny three-dimensional fetuses at twelve weeks, then twenty, then thirty-five. The real things moved their limbs and kicked. Some even sucked their thumbs in the womb.

She sat up. Savannah was involved in a sex-trafficking operation. But she was pregnant. It didn't make sense. The first thing traffickers would do, after hooking girls on the narcotic of the month, was put them on the pill. They wouldn't want the girls to get pregnant.

But Savannah was.

Georgia recalled the empty pregnancy test kit at the warehouse. If Savannah was pregnant, another girl might be too. Which meant that the ringleaders had been sloppy about giving the girls their pills. It didn't add up. Pregnancies just wouldn't be on the agenda of a sex-trafficking ring.

Unless they were.

Chapter 44

Georgia bolted from her bedroom, so much adrenaline pumping through her that she wasn't sure what to do first. She hurried to her desktop and began to search online. It wasn't something people talked about much, but illegal baby-breeding rings, also called baby factories or baby farms, were a burgeoning industry. They catered to couples who'd been rejected from legitimate adoption agencies or were so desperate for a child they elected not to go through the system.

She pored through the references on Google. Most couples who did go through the system adopted from Africa, Central America, or China. White couples who wanted their babies to resemble them biologically got babies from Russia and Eastern Europe. But Russia closed its doors at the end of 2012, and adoptions from Eastern European countries had dropped sixty percent in the past few years.

Was that what Savannah was caught up in? Not a sex-trafficking ring, but a baby-breeding operation? Actually, it might be both, she realized as she read on. Once the babies had been born and sold, the girls who birthed them were often thrown into forced prostitution. She ran a hand through her hair.

Most of the baby rings were overseas and run by organized crime. But those were the rings that had been busted. What about those that hadn't been? There was no reason why a ring couldn't be operating here in the US. Even in Chicago.

Georgia tapped her fingers on the desk: one, two, three, four. That might explain why a lawyer like Chad Coe was involved. Contacts had to be made, buyers found, birth certificates forged, documents prepared. Money needed to change hands. And it all had to appear legal. Was that what Chad Coe was doing? Applying a brush coat to the paperwork so it looked authentic? Most of his "clients" probably wouldn't check to see that everything was legal. He was a lawyer; they'd assume it was.

How much would it cost to buy a baby? The girls had to be housed and fed for nine months. They had to have medical care and checkups. The babies couldn't be delivered in a hospital, so the ringleaders had to have either their own facility or access to one. They would need a doctor or a midwife. Then, of course, there were the legal fees. And that was before any profit.

She pored through legitimate adoption websites, but the dollar figure was hard to ballpark; there were too many variables: whether the adoption was open, closed, local, domestic, or intercountry, private, licensed, or unlicensed. She went back to the baby-farm articles. One estimated that adoptions could cost up to fifty thousand dollars. But the article was written eight years ago. She mentally added twenty-five grand to the price. Which meant if the ringleaders had fifteen or more girls delivering babies, they could be grossing more than a million a year.

Not too shabby.

She tapped her fingers on the desk again. She wouldn't be surprised if some couples paid more than a hundred thousand for a baby.

By the time she finished reading, it was nearly three in the morning. She printed out the articles. She would go through them again tomorrow. As she got ready for bed, it occurred to her she hadn't heard from Jimmy.

Chapter 45

"Ellie Foreman."

"Georgia Davis." It was barely eight in the morning, but Georgia was too wired to sleep. She had already downed two cups of coffee.

"Hey, Georgia. Good morning. Everything okay?"

"Yeah, you?" She forced herself to engage in the necessary conversational niceties. They were important to Foreman. "How's Rachel?"

"When I hear from her, which is about once a quarter, she's fine." Ellie's daughter was now in college, but Georgia had known Rachel before Foreman. Georgia had been the youth officer on the force, and Ellie's teen daughter had needed some "guidance."

"So how is he?" Ellie asked.

"How is who?"

"Don't play coy. Jimmy told us he was taking you to dinner the other night."

Georgia blinked. "He did." An awkward silence followed.

"Well," Ellie said after a few beats, "I guess that's all I'm going to hear."

Georgia kept her mouth shut.

Ellie cleared her throat. "So what can I do for you?"

"Ellie, I'm working on...a case, and I need to talk to a lawyer who handles adoptions. For couples who—live around here."

"Around here?"

"You know, on the North Shore."

"You mean couples who have money."

"Would you happen to know someone like that?"

She laughed. "It would be hard not to. Know people with money, I mean." She paused. "As for a lawyer, you're in luck. The lawyer who handled my divorce handles adoptions too."

"Really?"

"Yeah. She gets them coming and going." Another chuckle. "Actually, that's not fair. She's a good lawyer. I like her."

"Can I call her?"

"Of course. Her name is Pam Huddleston. She has an office downtown, near the Daley Center. Plus a satellite office in Winnetka."

"That's convenient."

"She thought so too. Oh—be prepared."

"For what?"

"Pam doesn't mince words. She'll tell it to you straight. And she swears like a sailor."

"I think I can handle it." Georgia wrote down the number Foreman gave her. "Hey, thanks, Ellie. I owe you."

"Okay. How about this?"

"Excuse me?"

Ellie's voice went flat. "How about you remember that Jimmy Saclarides is one of Luke's best friends?"

It sounded like a warning. Georgia ended the call.

Chapter 46

Pam Huddleston's Winnetka law office occupied the first floor of a small building on Green Bay Road near Elm. In the waiting room Georgia took in the thick oriental rug, a coffee table with a fan of today's papers, and a wall of floor-to-ceiling bookcases. Except for the vacant receptionist's desk—their concession to the weekend, no doubt—it could have been someone's living room.

She sat on an upholstered chair, listening to muted conversations floating out from two offices. The office door nearest the waiting room was open, revealing the profile of a man in a sweater-vest, sleeves on his blue shirt rolled up. He was on the phone, his feet kicked up on his desk. The door to the other office was open only a crack, but Georgia could hear a woman murmuring in hushed tones. She couldn't hear the conversation, but she assumed it was Huddleston and that she was delivering bad news, until the mood was abruptly shattered by a raucous laugh.

Never assume.

The woman who emerged from the office five minutes later had short curly dark hair and ruby-red lipstick. She wore a beautifully tailored pants suit, subtle but expensive-looking jewelry, and stylish boots. Ellie hadn't told her Pam Huddleston was so attractive. Georgia felt underdressed in her jeans and blazer.

"Hi, Georgia." The lawyer extended her hand. "So nice to meet you."

"Thanks for squeezing me in, Ms. Huddleston. Especially on a Saturday."

"It's Pam. Don't mention it. I was up here." She smiled. "Anyway, Ellie said I needed to see you ASAP."

Georgia returned a cautious smile. The lawyer led her into her office.

The office matched her style, subtle but expensive. Oak desk. Executive chair, another oriental rug, nice bookcases, and two sculptures of women that looked vaguely African.

"So," Huddleston said after she settled behind her desk. "Ellie said you were interested in adopting?"

"Well, not me personally."

"Good. Because I don't do them anymore." She paused. "But I can refer you to someone who does."

"That's all right. I'm just looking for information." Georgia tipped her head to the side. "Why did you stop?"

Huddleston shrugged. "The laws governing adoptions in Illinois changed a few years ago. I haven't kept up."

"How did you get into it?"

"It's funny. I kind of fell into it. I would hear about someone who was looking for a baby. Then, as if by serendipity, a young pregnant woman would pop up."

"Pop up? From where?"

Huddleston smiled. "You'd be surprised...housekeepers...daughters of friends who get into trouble, people who wanted to know their babies, or their daughters', or their nieces' would be placed in a good home. Sometimes, a priest or rabbi would call me about one of his flock. It happens."

"So you'd be the agent—the broker?"

"I was the lawyer who put the parties together."

"And you'd do the paperwork?"

"Such that it was."

"What do you mean?"

"Well, as you know, selling babies is against the law. So there was never any contract. It was usually done on a handshake."

"But money changed hands."

"The would-be parents typically paid for the birth mother's maternity expenses. Sometimes it even worked out."

"What do you mean?"

"It means that the girl—the birth mother—could change her mind at any time. Happens a lot after a baby is born. Mom decides she wants to keep it."

"Then what?"

Huddleston flashed her a rueful smile. "Then everyone is up shit creek. There's really nothing anyone can do. That's one of the reasons I don't do them anymore. It's too fucking emotional. But, like I said, I can refer you to someone who does."

"That's okay," Georgia said. "I thought there were some bureaucratic procedures, too. Doesn't Cook County get involved?"

"Sure. In every adoption, the parents file a petition. The birth mother has to consent; then the court does a cursory investigation. They appoint a guardian *ad litem* to make sure the baby is going to a good home. If everything's kosher, an order of adoption is entered."

"What if a couple was—or knew they would be—turned down?"

Huddleston frowned. "Meaning?"

"What if the couple was older, or same sex, or in some way more desperate for a baby than others? What if they were turned down from legally adopting?"

Huddleston sat up straighter, her face a cloud of suspicion. "What are you getting at?"

"Well..." Georgia cleared her throat. "What if—hypothetically, of course—there was a service that took all comers? Even though it's against the law?"

"Are you talking black market babies?"

Georgia nodded.

Huddleston didn't answer for a minute. Then she laced her fingers together on the desk. "I'm not gonna lie to you. The thing you have to realize is that children are considered a commodity these days. There is a growing, almost frantic need to parent. At the same time there's a dwindling number of healthy babies available."

"So I hear."

"And there will always be people with a blank check. A rich trader...an elderly man with a younger wife...a—"

"So it's possible," Georgia said.

Huddleston nodded. "That's another reason I got out of the business."

"Ethics?"

"If it's an illegal adoption, someone has to forge the papers—the birth certificates, adoption papers, and such."

"Presumably a lawyer."

Huddleston nodded. "They'd have to show receipts for payments—I mean expenses—time spent on the arrangements, crap like that." She flipped up her palm. "Too risky."

"So, basically, what you're saying is whether it's a legal adoption or illegal, chances are the parties would benefit from having a lawyer."

"You bet."

Georgia hesitated. Then, "Have you ever heard of a lawyer named Chad Coe? From Riverwoods?"

"No, but like I said, I'm out of the loop. Did you check ARDC?"

"All I could find out was that he's active." She paused, then dug out a business card. "If you hear anything, could you let me know?"

Huddleston took the card, then shifted in her chair. "Georgia, you seem like a straight shooter to me. And I know Ellie is. So I have to ask. Why are you chasing this down? Why not turn it over to the police?"

Georgia didn't answer.

"If it turns out to be a black market baby ring, you could end up tangling with some very nasty people."

Georgia hesitated. "I have a sister who is pregnant and might be involved with them."

Huddleston kept her mouth shut. For a lawyer it was a rarity.

Chapter 47

Georgia drove to Riverwoods the next morning. Her route took her past the forest preserve, where sparkling trees were frosted with a dusting of white. Further on, the sun poured through a stand of elms, creating a halo effect that made her think God approved of her mission. He should only know the evil that clung to the dirt underneath.

Chad Coe lived on Portwine, a street with houses so rustic they could have been carved out of the forest around them. Coe's house was recessed from the road, with a long driveway in front. The lot itself must have covered several acres and was so thickly wooded that it gave the feel of a retreat. Georgia slowed and peered up the driveway. A black Beemer was parked at the far end, next to one of those monster SUVs that North Shore mothers liked to drive. A quick glimpse of the house revealed a redwood exterior that blended well with the surroundings.

She turned around and parked about fifty yards north of the house. As she peeled the lid off her coffee, steam fogged the windshield. She cupped her hands around it, grateful for its warmth. Stakeouts were always a crapshoot, and this was Sunday, so she figured she'd familiarize herself with Coe and his family, then come back on Monday. Of course, she might luck out. This was the North Shore and work was king, even on weekends.

She ran the heater intermittently, trying to stay warm while she checked out the neighborhood. With the woods a natural barrier between homes, the giant lots, and the rustic setting, this seemed like a wonderful place to live. Quiet, tranquil, and soothing. A lone bird took flight and climbed high in the sky. She didn't know whether it was a hawk or a vulture, but she watched it soar until it was just a black speck against bright blue. She was so captivated she almost missed the monster SUV backing out of the driveway. Dark red. Illinois plates. A female driver. Someone in back.

She started up the Toyota. The van turned and headed back toward Deerfield Road. She followed and stopped in back at the light. She could just make out a little person in a car seat.

For some reason, she hadn't envisioned Chad Coe having a child. It struck a discordant note. How could the father of a toddler be involved in a black market baby ring? Didn't the man have any scruples? Or maybe she was wrong about him. Maybe Chad Coe was simply working divorces and real estate deals.

She let the SUV pull a few cars ahead. No sense calling attention to herself. She tried to square the thought of Chad Coe, baby dealer, with the image of Chad Coe, father. Her former boyfriend, Matt, had been an observant Jew. He'd also been a homicide detective. Somehow he'd been able to separate the strands of his life and compartmentalize his values so they never clashed. For all she knew, Jimmy was the same way. Maybe most people were. She could work through how a man might rape a woman, then help a lost child find its mother without missing a beat.

She was a mile from Riverwoods when she decided to stop tailing the wife and kid. They weren't her targets. She headed back to the house and waited. Two hours later the SUV returned, only the wife in the car. Was the child at a play date? A class? Georgia didn't have time to ponder it because a few minutes later the Beemer appeared at the end of the driveway. Georgia straightened. A man was behind the wheel. She started her engine.

Coe drove south on Waukegan Road, then west on Shermer into Northbrook. Georgia followed a discreet distance behind. He wove around a couple of residential streets and stopped at a ranch house that was identical to every other house on the block except for the side to which the garage was attached. Georgia drove past the house, turned around, and backtracked. By then, the front door was just closing. She aimed her binoculars at a large front window, but the curtains were drawn. She jotted down the number of the house and plugged it into the Assessor's Office website on her tablet.

The house was owned by Dr. Richard Lotwin. She quickly opened up FindersKeepers. Lotwin was a general surgeon. He'd been affiliated with Newfield Hospital for nearly twenty years, 1988 through 2007. Did that mean he wasn't there any longer? If so, where was he? She started to Google him but had to stop when Chad Coe emerged from the house and headed back to his Beemer.

It was her first chance to take a good look at him. He had tight, curly dark hair, a thick nose, and bug eyes that flitted everywhere, never lighting on one spot for more than a second. He looked soft and round, not buff, and was casually dressed in a leather jacket and jeans. His only concession to the frigid weather was a muffler around his neck. Probably cashmere. He didn't carry a briefcase; instead he had a combination backpack and satchel that trendy professionals carried.

Georgia slouched down in the driver's seat. Coe pulled out of the doctor's driveway and turned in her direction. When he passed, she averted her face as if she was rummaging in the glove compartment. She wasn't sure if he'd seen her.

Once he reached the end of the block, she tailed him again. What business did Chad Coe have with a surgeon? If he was running a baby-breeding ring, shouldn't he be dealing with an ob-gyn? Of course, he might be, and his visit to Lotwin was a different matter altogether. She checked the time. Whatever its objective, the meeting didn't take a lot of time—less than twenty minutes.

Coe drove southeast to Skokie, a village in which Indians, Vietnamese, Jews, Hispanics, African Americans, and Middle

Easterners elbowed one another in apparent harmony. It hadn't always been that way. Thirty years earlier, a group of neo-Nazis were given a permit to march through what was then primarily a Jewish neighborhood. The sight of men in uniform goose-stepping past Holocaust survivors made for tense moments, which, of course, was what the marchers wanted. Long since ended, the marches were now part of the lore of Chicago history.

She tailed Coe to a block of small apartment buildings whose front yards were surrounded by chain-link fences. It was a utilitarian rather than pretty neighborhood, the faded yellow-brick buildings no taller than three stories, and their lawns littered with children's tricycles, cars, and toys. Coe parked across from one of the buildings.

Georgia watched him go inside and swore softly. This wasn't a single-family dwelling, which meant she couldn't check out the occupants online. They were renters and wouldn't be listed on any property records. She'd have to nose around the old-fashioned way. She realized how dependent she'd become on technology for sleuthing. Then she unwrapped a PB and J sandwich she'd slapped together before she left and wondered whom Chad Coe was visiting.

Her cell vibrated, startling her. The caller ID said Jimmy Saclarides. Her stomach flipped.

"Hey." She smiled in spite of herself.

"It's Jimmy."

"I know."

"Sorry I haven't been in touch."

She wanted to tell him she was sorry for pushing him away. That she hoped he'd give her another chance. Instead, she said, "It's okay. I know you must be busy." She winced at how trite she sounded.

"Always…" He paused. "But I'm about to check out for the day. I know it's late, but do you want to get together tonight? I can drive down."

Chapter 48

C had Coe spent an hour in the Skokie apartment. When he came out, he didn't seem to notice Georgia's red Toyota, or if he did, it didn't bother him. Georgia tailed him back to Portwine, where he turned into his driveway. Then she raced back to Skokie, got out of the car, and wrote down the names on the mailboxes of the building. There were six boxes, but only four names, one of which looked Hispanic, another Asian. She frowned. Did the person Coe visited live in one of the unidentified apartments? She hunched her shoulders. She'd have to come back and talk to someone. More time. More effort. She couldn't help wondering whether this was taking her closer to her sister or farther away. It would be easier just to interview Chad Coe in person. But that wasn't going to happen. Not until she had more.

She drove home, showered, threw on a black sweater and jeans, and started in on the names on the mailbox. She'd identified only one of the four, a freelance building contractor, by the time her buzzer sounded.

She buzzed Jimmy in and opened the door. As he climbed the steps, a wave of anticipation rolled through her. He caught it, smiled, and took her in his arms.

* * *

They never made it out that night. A few hours later, she ordered a pizza.

"What do you like on yours?" she asked.

"Anything except anchovies."

"Chicken."

"Oh yeah? Try me."

She grinned, ordered anchovies, and rolled over.

When the pizza arrived, she carried the box into the bedroom. She retrieved a towel from her tiny linen closet, spread it over the quilt, and placed the box on top. They didn't bother to get dressed, and as she watched him chew and loop strands of cheese over his fingers, she remembered what those fingers could do. After one slice, she wasn't hungry. Neither, apparently was Jimmy, because they found other activities to occupy them. The pizza lay abandoned on the floor.

Chapter 49

Sunday morning stretched into Sunday afternoon, and Georgia decided it was her favorite day of the week. They snuck into an early movie, and she felt a wave of pleasure at how protected she felt when he placed his hand on her back to guide her through the door. She caught a glimpse of herself in a mirror and saw a silly smile on her face that she couldn't wipe off. The good thing was that she saw a similar smile on his.

Halfway through the movie, he took her hand and brought it to his lips. She thought she might tear his clothes off right there in the theater. Instead, she took him to Mickey's for a burger after the movie. Owen was behind the bar, back from Florida, and he raised his eyebrows when he saw them. She wasn't surprised; this had to be the first man she'd brought to Mickey's since Matt. Fortunately, Owen was on his good behavior, and aside from a few sly glances, he kept his mouth shut.

It was about five by the time they finished eating. Darkness was closing in.

"Georgia," Jimmy said, "I don't want to, believe me. But I have to go back."

Her smiled faded. She looked down. She needed to slow down. Her heart was way ahead of her brain.

"I promised I'd cover for a guy who just had a baby." He paused. "But what about Wednesday? I can take the day off."

She looked up. Her smile was back. "What are people going to say?"

"About what?" he asked.

"About you taking so much time off?"

He thought about it and grinned. "Let them complain to the chief of police."

Chapter 50

Monday morning Georgia headed back to Skokie. She'd spent last night trying to trace the four names on the vestibule of the apartment building Chad Coe visited, but she'd had no luck. Three had just an initial and a last name, and even if she were able to tie them to the address, she wouldn't get far on her databases. Plus, they were renters, not owners, which often meant a patchy financial history. Millions of people were like that. Technology was a godsend, but it took time—and legal documents—to make a digital footprint.

After a weekend of winter sunshine, which produced a thaw of sorts, a swollen gray overcast ushered in another cold front. Georgia pulled on gloves as she climbed out of the Toyota. She noticed a child's wagon and ball on the front lawn. They hadn't been there Saturday. Someone in the building had kids.

She walked up to the door and studied the names in the vestibule again. The name on one of the first-floor apartments was G. McCune, with the ink-scrawled letters "Bldg Mgr" next to it. May as well. She pushed the buzzer. No response. She pushed again, heard a return buzz unlocking the door, and grabbed the door before it stopped. There was no intercom, and she proceeded into a small, square hall with two apartment doors opposite each other, and a set of stairs at the back. The door on one side squeaked open a crack, and an overweight woman in pink work-out sweats, her hair in old-fashioned rollers, squinted through the gap.

"Yeah?"

"Are you the building manager?'

The woman looked Georgia up and down, not an easy task given the narrow slit of the door. "Who wants to know?"

"I'm—looking for an apartment to rent. I saw empty slots next to two of the buzzers, so I thought I'd ask."

"I have one apartment. One bedroom. Seven fifty a month. Air-conditioning and heat extra."

"That sounds great. Can I see it?"

The woman shrugged. "Gimme a minute." Georgia heard a TV talk show blaring somewhere in the depths of the apartment. The woman closed the door. The TV noise grew muffled.

It was chilly in the hall, not much warmer than outside. Georgia heard the clank of keys. The door opened again.

"I'm showing an apartment, Joe," she called out over the TV, then lumbered out and closed the door. She headed toward the stairs, glancing back at Georgia. "It's on the third floor. But you're young." She paused. "What's your name?"

"Samantha Mandor," Georgia replied quickly, not exactly sure why she felt compelled to use an alias. She just had a feeling. "You're Mrs. McCune?"

"Me and Joe live on the first floor. He's the maintenance manager," she said importantly.

They climbed up to the second floor. Mrs. McCune was already breathing hard. "You just move here?" she huffed.

"I did." Georgia smiled. "From Kansas."

"Got a job?"

McCune was checking her out. She rounded the second-floor landing and, leaning her hand on the banister, trudged up to the third floor.

Georgia decided to play the pity card. "I—I just broke up with my boyfriend. We were living together back in Lawrence. Over three years. But I have a good friend here, and she convinced me to move. You know, to start over." The woman's expression hardened. "Oh, don't worry. I have savings. I can pay the rent."

"Yeah, but for how long?"

"I have good typing and computer skills. I'll work temp until I get a full-time job."

McCune stopped at one of the doors on the third floor. The hall was well lit, Georgia thought, but the faded carpet gave off a musty smell. McCune exhaled into a harrumph. "Computers. Everybody's high-tech these days."

McCune fumbled with the key ring, found the right one, and unlocked the door. They walked in. It was empty and cleaner than Georgia expected, but the faint residue of a foreign scent drifted over her. She couldn't place it. "Who lived here?" she asked.

McCune scratched her head, which was difficult to do with her hair full of rollers. "An Indian man. Engineering student. Don't know where he went."

Curry and saffron. That's what the scent was. "Was he a good cook?"

"I wouldn't know."

Georgia nodded. What kind of building manager doesn't know their tenants? Unless she didn't want to say.

McCune turned around. "You're looking for a job? I might know one."

"Really?" Georgia feigned interest.

"Yeah...got a friend who runs a hair salon. You good with hair?"

Georgia smiled. "Not really. I was sort of thinking of a business job." Hadn't the woman been listening?

"Good luck with that." McCune looked her over again. "What kind of skills you got?"

Georgia hesitated. She'd already told the woman. She decided not to remind her. "I am pretty good with a computer. Word processing. Dictation. I'm organized, too."

McCune harrumphed as if this was the first time she'd heard it. "Everybody's high-tech these days."

This did not bode well. Was the woman senile? Early Alzheimer's? Georgia pretended to inspect the apartment. "You said there was AC. Just out of curiosity, what kind of heat does the place have?"

"Gas forced air. One of the only buildings on the block to have it. We're lucky. The owner takes care of the place."

"Who owns it?"

"A lawyer. Lives in Wisconsin. Retired."

Georgia peeked into a closet, looked into the bathroom, and stood in front of the living room window. The view was of a similar building across the street, barely concealed by the branches of an elm or ash. She turned around.

"You said there was only one apartment available, but I couldn't help noticing there were two empty slots next to the buzzers in the vestibule."

McCune folded her arms. "Yes, well." She went quiet.

Georgia picked up on it. "Well, what?"

McCune's lips tightened. Then she cleared her throat. "We got a nice Mexican couple on the lease, but they have another place in Prospect Heights." McCune paused. "So every once in a while, some of their cousins stay here for a few days. You know what I mean?"

Georgia knew. The unidentified apartment was a crash pad for illegals. She gazed at McCune.

McCune shrugged. "What am I gonna do? We need the income."

Georgia frowned.

"Don't worry," McCune cut in. "This is a safe place. I ain't never had no trouble. Me and Joey make sure of that."

Georgia doubted that a woman who couldn't remember who said what when could know trouble if it hit her in the face.

"Any hint of it, in fact, they're out," McCune was saying.

Georgia ran a hand across her forehead.

McCune took it as disapproval. "Look, we even have a kid here... her mom wouldn't be here if she didn't think it was safe. I babysit her sometimes."

At some point during their conversation, McCune must have decided Georgia would be a good tenant. She was selling *her* now.

"A single mother?" Georgia asked. "Which apartment?"

"Second floor. Claudia Nyquist. Single woman." McCune flashed her a smile. "Works at a hospital."

"Oh?"

"Yeah, Evanston Hospital. Think she's in the computer department." She motioned toward Georgia. "Just like you. I can put you in touch with her if you want." McCune looked hopeful.

"That might be a good idea," Georgia said.

"And there's a contractor here too...you know, a remodeler. Nice single man. I keep thinking he and Claudia ought to go out. But she don't seem interested. Maybe you?"

"What's his name?"

"Bill Tuttle." McCune proceeded to tell her all sorts of things that made Tuttle sound like the most boring man in the world.

"Who's the fourth tenant? I thought I saw an Asian name."

"Oh. They're a Chinese couple. Just got here. Mr. and Mrs. Wong. Nice people. Not much English, though." McCune smiled. "So what do you think? You like it?"

Georgia made sure to be slow to reply. "I'm not sure."

"Well, better make up your mind. The place will go fast. Let me get you an application."

"Sure."

They went back downstairs, where McCune retrieved an application from her apartment and handed it to Georgia. She stuffed it into her jeans pocket and headed to the front door. As she was just about out, McCune asked, "How did you come to hear about this place?"

Georgia pretended she hadn't heard. She waved as she jogged to her car.

Chapter 51

At home Georgia started in on some due diligence. Organizations had such vanilla names for spying. "Due diligence" sounded way more respectable than "surveillance" or "intel." It was professional, nonjudgmental. Even though they were all the same activity.

She disqualified the Mexican couple whose names weren't on the nameplate, as well as the Chinese couple whose names were. She hoped she wasn't profiling, but the Mexicans didn't live there, and the Chinese had just arrived. She didn't think they would have business with Chad Coe. But she did make a note to try to identify the names of the Mexican couple's "cousins." Who knows what they were using the apartment for? It could be worth a return visit.

Then she started in on Claudia Nyquist, who did have a paper trail. Divorced for two years, she'd been upside down on her mortgage in Des Plaines and had to move when the bank took it back. She was currently a data administrator at Evanston Hospital. Had Chad Coe handled her divorce? Helped her with the fallout from the house? Or was she working with him on the baby ring?

The contractor, Bill Tuttle, was as boring on paper as Mrs. McCune made him sound in person. No debts. Only two credit cards. Two bank accounts, one personal, one business. A pickup truck, used. Unmarried. In his forties. Not much else. She decided to skip him for now.

Then she Googled the Northbrook doctor Chad Coe visited before he drove down to Skokie. Dr. Richard Lotwin was from Long Island and had gone to NYU for his undergraduate degree, Chicago Medical School for his MD. He had a wife and two kids. Nothing out of the ordinary. Until eight years ago. He'd been operating on a patient who died at Newfield Hospital while on the table. Lotwin, the anesthesiologist, and the hospital were all sued for malpractice. The case was determined to be a "bad outcome" rather than negligence, and the insurance companies settled it.

But a few years later it happened again, this time to a young boy of twelve who was in for a routine appendectomy. Something went terribly wrong, and the boy, Antonin Tunick, died. Lotwin's medical license was suspended, and he was fired.

Georgia went to the Illinois Clerk of the Circuit Court's website, entered the boy's name, and searched the full docket file. Nothing came up. There was no mention of any lawsuit connected to Antonin Tunick, no settlement, no reprisals.

Odd.

She Googled the boy's name. His mother came to the US from Russia when the boy was a baby. A single mother, she lived in Northbrook. Georgia couldn't help but think the woman had bad karma. If she'd stayed in Russia, her son might still be alive. Not because Russian doctors were so great, but at least she wouldn't have run into Richard Lotwin.

So why didn't the mother file a malpractice suit? Georgia was surprised an ambulance-chasing lawyer hadn't contacted her; the story triggered some media attention. Surely a lawyer would have taken the case on contingency, especially with Lotwin's prior history. But there was nothing.

What's more, she couldn't find anything about a relationship between Lotwin and Chad Coe. She rocked back in her chair. Both Lotwin and Coe had been rejected from their respective professions. Did they meet at some twelve-step program? Or one of those "second-life" programs for people who needed a fresh start?

Whatever their relationship, Georgia needed more. But searching for those connections seemed to be taking her farther away from Savannah, not closer. Then again, what had she expected? A map with neon signs that led directly to her? PI work could be slow going and murky. What would she advise a client in her situation? She'd promise to keep digging until she'd exhausted all leads or tied up loose ends.

She leaned forward and rubbed her palm across her forehead. She thought about tracing Chad Coe's phone records, but she didn't have his cell. And if he was involved in sex trafficking or black market babies, the calls she'd want to trace would likely have been made from burners. She'd have to find another way forward.

Chapter 52

Savannah—Nine Months Earlier

A week after she got off the bus in Chicago, Vanna didn't care where she was or what she was doing. The first three days—at least she guessed that's how long it was—Lazlo made her do things, some of which she'd never done before. She tried to resist and even bit him once or twice, but he retaliated by slapping her so hard her ears rang. At least he took a shower once in a while and made her do the same. When he wasn't raping her, he was on his cell talking in what she learned was Russian.

At some point another woman and man showed up. The woman was rail thin and had short, spiky blond hair; the man was tall and skinny, with a buzz cut and stubble. Vanna started to tell them she was a prisoner, that she was hungry and exhausted and wanted to go home, and that Lazlo ought to be behind bars. But the man clapped his hand across her mouth as soon as she started and shook his head.

"Soon you happy," he said in broken English.

Vanna wanted to bite his hand, but she couldn't reach it with her teeth. After trying unsuccessfully a few times, her cries diminished to whimpers.

Meanwhile the woman rummaged inside a leather bag that

looked like a Marc Jacobs rip-off and fished out a small makeup kit. After unzipping it, she took out a packet of tinfoil, a syringe, and a butane lighter. She barked out an order to Lazlo in Russian, and he brought over an empty glass. She unwrapped the packet, tapped some white powder into the glass, mixed it with water, and put the flame underneath the glass.

Vanna knew what it was. She'd snorted heroin back in Colorado, even smoked it once. But she'd never shot up, even though Dex had told her it was a whole different trip. Her expression must have indicated that she knew what was happening, because the man with his hand across her mouth arched his eyebrows.

"You stop cry now?"

She nodded. He removed his hand. She stayed quiet.

Once the mixture bubbled, the woman picked up a syringe. Vanna swallowed. Was this for her? The woman gazed at her, appraising. Then she drew the mixture into the syringe and motioned with her other hand. It smelled like a box of Band-Aids.

Vanna scooted across the bed. The woman turned to Lazlo, who nodded. Then she took Vanna's hand, turned it over so her palm was up, and rubbed the vein that went from her wrist to her elbow. When it popped up, swollen and blue, she smiled. "Okay." The woman held her wrist and plunged the syringe into Vanna's vein.

It took only a few seconds. First came a rush that flooded her body, spreading into every crevice and pore. But it was different from meth or ecstasy. Instead of energy, intensity, and speed, Vanna felt an overpowering warmth and looseness and calm. Then a feeling of weightlessness. She was no longer on the bed. She was flying above Lazlo, the man, and the woman. Seconds later, a euphoric gravity pushed her gently back on the bed, but Vanna didn't mind. She was perfectly content, a warm blanket protecting her. She wasn't asleep and yet she was in a dream, a dream that numbed all pain. She didn't have a care in the world.

She was aware of what happened next, but it was all mellow and warm and loving. First she fucked the man; then the woman fucked her. Then Lazlo fucked her; then all of them were fucking one another. Her world ended at the edge of the bed, but it was okay. She might have been a prisoner, but if this was how it felt, she'd stay a prisoner forever. Never before had she felt so loved, so cherished.

Chapter 53

Savannah

After that Vanna didn't care about anything except junk. Lazlo and the couple were generous, allowing her to shoot up whenever she wanted. Each time she went to that place, it was bliss. The world was rosy, and she had her rightful place in it. She even wished happiness for her mother. Her poor mother, who would never know the joy that could be hers.

A couple of weeks later the blonde showed her how to shoot up between her toes. Better, the woman said. More hygienic. No one wanted to see tracks on a girl's arm. There was plenty of skin down there, and she told Vanna she could alternate toes. By the time she got through the skin between them, the punctures on the other foot would have healed and she could start over again. Vanna giggled.

It was sometime during the third week, about the middle of April, that things changed. Still holed up in the fleabag hotel, Vanna hadn't been outside in weeks. Sometimes she forgot she was in Chicago. Lazlo was gone most of the time now, but he left her with a goon, though not the man who brought her dope. This was a guy with a gun, who reeked of body odor and foul-smelling cigars, and banged her whenever he could tear himself away from the TV.

He'd grunt when he came and fall asleep afterward, but mostly he ignored her, as if she was nothing more than a lump of flesh, there to service him. Once in a while he brought her a sandwich or fries, but between the junk and the lack of regular food, Vanna could feel her ribs sticking out. When Turdball napped—of course he snored—she thought about calling room service or ordering a pizza, but they'd disconnected the phone, and the door was double locked. Once in a while, when she was coming down, she thought about taking his gun and turning the tables on him. But he slept with it holstered around his middle, and there was no way she could get it without waking him.

The periods between shooting up were getting longer, and she needed dope more often. But the couple came only once a day. Sometimes they left her an extra hit, which the goon used as a reward after he screwed her. They wouldn't let her shoot herself up, even though she'd watched how they prepared it and knew she could. But as long as she could get to that warm, loving place, she didn't much care who did it or how she got there.

Between the highs, though, she began to feel a gnawing, empty sensation. Sometimes she was restless and broke out in a sweat. She began to lift the shade and peer out the window. The view was limited: a dreary brick building across the alley with a Dumpster against the wall. But if she angled herself at the edge of the window, she could see a scrawny tree in the backyard and a fire escape leading from the window to the ground.

She wheedled and pleaded with Turdball. "Isn't there a park nearby?" she asked. "Can we go out for a walk? It's boring here." But he pretended he didn't understand English and raised the volume on the TV. Which started to piss her off. Vanna didn't like to rely on anyone. And yet she was dependent on the couple who brought her dope, and when they didn't show up, she had to fuck Turdball to get it. She began to plan an escape.

The logistics would be tricky. The woman had taken her

clothes, even her mother's jacket. Vanna usually lay around in a bra and panties, sometimes one of the men's dirty T-shirts. Assuming she could escape, how to score was another problem. Although not as thorny. She was in Chicago; there was H all over the place. She knew what to do—it wouldn't be much different from what she'd done back home. The biggest challenge would be getting away and finding some clothes.

She convinced herself that once she was out on the street, someone would help her. She knew how to repay them, and once that happened, she'd be on her way. She went to the window, raised the shade, and looked out. The tree in the backyard across the alley was budding. Which meant it was spring, and warmer. She studied the fire escape, trying to calculate how much time it would take her to climb down.

She lowered the shade, went back to the bed, and pretended to shiver. "My feet are cold. You got any socks?"

When he returned a blank stare, she pantomimed putting on socks.

He gazed at her as if considering it. His hand crept to the gun. Then he shook his head.

Shit. Did he know what she was planning? She lay back against the pillow, if that's what you could call the hard lumpy material, oily and smelly from so many heads resting on it. Turd-ball glanced at his watch. He was probably figuring out if he had enough time to fuck her again before the couple showed up. For the first time since, she welcomed his interest. Maybe he'd fall asleep afterward. She smiled in what she hoped was a seductive way. He got off his chair.

Luck was with her. Afterward he did fall asleep. Once he started snoring, Vanna sprang into action. She slid off the bed and quietly opened the closet door. A thin, dusty blanket lay on a shelf. She draped it around her and tried not to think about how many men had come on it. She crept to the window and unlocked it, but as soon as she started to raise it, it squeaked.

Even though the TV was still on, Vanna froze. Turdball

snorted and shifted but didn't wake. Carefully, slowly, she raised the window. The subsequent squeaks weren't as loud, and the noise from the TV muffled them. Once it was open wide enough, she scrambled onto the fire escape. The first thing she did was fling the blanket to the ground. Then she started down. She knew she should have closed the window but didn't want to waste time. She just prayed she would be fast enough to get away.

At the bottom of the fire escape was a gap of about ten feet between the last rung and the ground. She climbed down and let go. She fell, twisting her foot, but forced herself to get up. Her ankle hurt like hell, but she kept going. She snatched the blanket, threw it over her, and limped toward the back of the hotel. Even though the sun was shining, it wasn't as warm as she'd hoped. She wouldn't be able to stay outside for long. She needed shelter. Someplace to hide.

She remembered the Dumpster alongside the building in the alley. That would be the last place anyone would think to search. And while the idea was, on its surface, disgusting, the truth was she probably wouldn't smell much worse than she already did. She hobbled along the fence line of the hotel's property. She was sure she'd seen a gate to the alley, but now that she needed it, she couldn't find it. Where was it? Panic rolled through her. She didn't have much time. Turdball must be awake by now.

She gazed up and down the length of the fence. No gate. She'd been so sure it was there. Was it just something she'd imagined? A heroin dream to give her the illusion of freedom? She had to find another hiding place. Maybe in the basement of the hotel. Every building had a basement. She shuffled to the back door of the hotel, thinking she would slip inside and take the stairs down.

Instead she ran into Turdball. He was aiming his gun at her chest.

Chapter 54

Tuesday morning blew in a deep azure sky painted with fluffy white clouds that seemed to augur spring, but the air was still frigid enough to numb Georgia's fingers. She was back at Chad Coe's house in Riverwoods, cupping her hands around a thermos filled with coffee. Coe was beginning to irritate her; she had plenty of suspicions about the guy but nothing concrete—except that he owned a warehouse that had housed a trafficking ring, at least temporarily. Even if he didn't know what the place was being used for, he had to know the people he rented it to weren't your fine, upstanding citizens.

His wife pulled out in the SUV around nine with their child—Georgia thought it was a girl—in the car seat. Another hour went by before Coe followed in the Beemer. Georgia tailed him, this time to a large A-frame house on Greenwood Avenue in Glencoe. She parked, jotted down the house number, then fired up her tablet. Nothing happened. Crap. She'd forgotten to charge it last night. Her tablet had become as critical a tool as her Glock. More so, in fact, when she considered how much she used it. She'd have to check the owners later. She bit her lip. Another annoyance.

Coe stayed at the house for more than an hour. Was he seeing a client? Finally he emerged and walked briskly to the Beemer.

Looking almost jaunty, he rubbed his hands together as if he'd scored big. He fired up the car, then headed west to Waukegan Road. The man was more than an irritation, she decided; he was making her crazy: driving here and there, popping in and out of places. Did he work out of his car like that lawyer in the crime novels?

At Waukegan Road he turned south to a small strip mall between Dundee and Shermer that included a gas station, a driving school, a liquor store, and a nail salon. Coe parked in back of the Le Nail Spa and went inside.

Georgia turned into a strip mall across the street and parked facing out. She knew this salon. Ellie Foreman had told her about it. Years ago they'd been involved in the same case, Georgia as a cop, Ellie as a video producer. Foreman had discovered the place was a mecca for Russian immigrants; almost all the women who worked at the salon hailed from the former Soviet Union.

When Georgia looked into it, she discovered why. Apparently a popular magazine in the Soviet Union had featured Northbrook, Illinois, in an article ten years earlier, calling it an ideal place for Russians planning to emigrate to the States. She wasn't able to get her hands on the article itself, but she'd been told it hyped Northbrook's schools, low crime rate, reasonable cost of living, and resources that helped immigrants learn English and American customs.

Whatever it said, it had worked. Over the years thousands of Eastern Europeans had moved to Northbrook, and the village developed a reputation as a Russian émigré's paradise. Unfortunately, the crime rate was no longer low. Wherever Russians went, they brought crime, and the Russian Mafiya were all over Northbrook.

Still, there was no reason to think that a place that offered manicures and pedicures was coddling a nest of gangsters. More likely they were just hardworking women struggling to make ends meet. Georgia got out of the car and pulled on her gloves. She didn't want them to see the sorry state of her nails. Bitten to the quick. A manicure would be wasted on her. The few times she'd had one, the polish chipped in hours, and a day later, her nails looked like they'd gone through the spin cycle of a washing machine. She slowed her pace and crossed the street, as if she had all the time in the world. As she sauntered past the salon's window, she peered in, pretending she'd just noticed the place.

Two rows of manicure tables, twelve in all, filled the room. Women in pink, blue, or green smocks sat at the tables. Five or six customers, their nails in various stages of decoration, sat across from the girls. The girls with no customers paged through magazines, watched a TV mounted on the wall at the far end, or chattered on their cells. She didn't see Chad Coe.

Georgia pulled the front door open and walked in. A list of prices was taped to the wall. She pretended to study it until a slim woman in a blue uniform approached her.

"May I help you?" Her English was heavily accented.

Georgia whipped around and pasted on a wide smile. "Good morning. How long have you been here? The salon, I mean?"

The woman furrowed her brow. "Oh, about ten years, I think."

"That long? Wonderful. I'm so happy to find you. I just moved here."

"You want mani-pedi?" the woman asked.

"I sure do. May I take a quick look around?"

"Course." The woman flashed her a toothy smile.

Georgia strolled between the tables to the back of the room. She hoped she looked like she was inspecting the place. At the back of the room underneath the TV was a table with a coffee machine, cups and condiments. Beside it was a back door that presumably led outside. On the other side was an alcove leading to a smaller space. She poured herself a cup of coffee, hearing a low murmur coming from that direction. She took her time doctoring the coffee, although she usually drank it black. Then she turned around and casually glanced toward the alcove.

Chad Coe was in earnest conversation with a middle-aged blowsy woman whose red lipstick dominated a face with birdlike eyes, painted-on eyebrows, and the faint shadow of a mustache. Unlike the other women in the shop, she wore a long flowing skirt and white blouse. Was she the owner?

Neither Coe or the woman appeared to take any notice of Georgia, so she retraced her steps to the front, thanked the woman who'd greeted her, promised to call for an appointment, and ducked out.

Georgia went back to her Toyota, threw out the coffee, and climbed in. She pulled out, crossed the street, and parked in the lot of the first strip mall. The Beemer was in front of the salon's back door. Georgia was at the other end.

Chad Coe came out a few minutes later. So did the woman he'd been talking to. Both got in their respective cars. The woman drove an older Chevy Impala. There were two exits from the lot; Coe turned one way, the woman the other. Georgia decided to stick with Coe. She would check out the woman another time.

But Coe must have finished his business, because he drove back to Riverwoods. She headed back to Evanston.

Chapter 55

By the time Georgia was home, she was famished. She took out the leftover pizza from the weekend—she'd frozen it—and reheated it. She wolfed down four slices. Mushy but edible. She was washing dishes when she recalled Pam Huddleston, Ellie Foreman's lawyer, mentioning how integral lawyers were to the adoption process and how it was all perfectly legal. It reminded Georgia she hadn't checked out the couple from Glencoe yet.

She pulled out her tablet, plugged it into the charger, then dug out the couple's house number on Greenwood and went to her desktop. She went online to the Assessor's Office, then the Cook County Treasurer's website.

John and Monica Purcell had bought their house thirty-two years ago. Which meant they—or at least the husband wasn't a young man. She Googled their names, not expecting to find anything. But she did. She clicked on a URL that took her to, of all things, the website of St. Peter's Episcopal Church in Highland Park. Another click took her to the church newsletter, where she read the following:

Church members John and Monica Purcell are looking for a kidney transplant for John, who is suffering from polycystic kidney disease. Unfortunately his advanced age makes him an undesirable transplant candidate.

John is currently on dialysis, but the family asks anyone with information that might facilitate a transplant to contact them through St. Peter's church office.

Confusion swam through her. What couple thinks about adopting when one of the parties is ill? Georgia looked up polycystic kidney disease. PKD was a genetic disorder in which people, usually in their thirties or forties, developed fluid-filled cysts that could grow to the point where the kidneys failed. While some cases could be treated with diet and medication, in others, dialysis or a kidney transplant was necessary. Fifty percent of people with PKD progressed to kidney failure, also called end-stage renal disease. Which could lead to death. Purcell's senior citizen status didn't help his chances for a transplant.

She closed the website and stood. Chad Coe had visited a couple who were looking for an organ transplant, not a baby. He'd stayed for more than an hour. Afterward he'd gone to the nail salon. Chad Coe owned a warehouse where pregnant girls were staying. What was the link between the two? Suddenly Georgia felt queasy.

Chapter 56

The next morning Georgia called Le Nail Spa for an appointment.

"Le Nail Spa. Hello?" The voice on the phone stretched the word into three syllables.

"Good morning. I came in yesterday to look around. Are you the woman who I talked to?"

"Yah. I remember. You want appointment?"

"I would. I'd like the lady who had on the long skirt."

"She only work 'til two."

"I can come in at one. What is her name?"

"Zoya."

Of course.

At twelve thirty Georgia drove to the salon and parked in back. She considered how to play it. She had to be subtle, work around the edges. She didn't want to raise any alarms. But she wanted to see if the woman would bite.

Inside were the same women in the same smocks in the same spots, as if they were part of a frozen tableau. Georgia grabbed some coffee and headed to the alcove. Zoya, wearing the same red lipstick, painted eyebrows, and implacable expression, sat behind a manicure table. Today, though, instead of a long skirt, she wore a multicolored caftan with a turban on her head.

Georgia smiled.

Zoya returned a cool nod.

"Thank you for taking me."

"How you know to ask for me?" she asked, a trace of suspicion on her face. Her voice was as low-pitched as a man's.

"It's clear you are an important person—you have your own room. I figured why not start at the top?"

Zoya straightened, as if Georgia was paying homage and she was acknowledging it.

"Sit." Her voice was gruff, like sandpaper.

Georgia sat. For an awkward moment, nothing happened. Then she realized Zoya was waiting for her. She placed her hands on the manicure table. Zoya took one, then the other in her hands, turned them over, and inspected them. Then she sniffed. "Not good. You bite."

Georgia gave her an embarrassed shrug. "I get nervous."

"You grown woman. Not be nervous. You stop."

"I wish it was that easy."

Zoya flashed her an indifferent look. "You choose color." She motioned to a shelf behind her full of nail polish.

"Um...maybe a pale pink." She wondered if Jimmy would notice. It occurred to her he hadn't called. Today was Wednesday. Wasn't he supposed to come down today?

Zoya got up, turned around, rummaged on the shelf. She selected three bottles, all different shades of pink, and set them down. "'Which one?"

Georgia picked up Pink Taffeta. Zoya got up, went to a sink, filled a bowl with water, and squirted dishwashing liquid in it. Then she brought it back to the table, sat down, and nodded for Georgia to dip her fingers in.

While her nails were soaking, Zoya examined Georgia's left hand. "You not married?"

Crap. She'd forgotten to wear the band she kept at home for exactly this purpose. "Oh no...I mean, yes, I am married. I took the ring off because I was coming here. You know, I didn't want..."

"I see no ring."

For a moment Georgia was puzzled. Then she realized Zoya meant the impression of the ring on her bare finger. "It's always been a little big," she said sheepishly. "I keep meaning to have it sized, but..." She let her voice trail off.

A cell phone buzzed. Zoya's expression didn't change, but she stood. "You stay. I back." She grabbed a bag off the floor, pulled out a cell, and retreated into a small closet. She left the door open, and from her deferential tone and one-word responses, it sounded like she was receiving orders. Georgia wondered who was on the other end.

Five minutes later she came back. "Okay." She gestured for Georgia to lift her fingers and took the bowl away. She dried Georgia's hands with a small towel, inspected them again, and went to work with an emery board. There was practically no nail to file, but the sensation was pleasant, despite the sound of scratching. It was soothing to have someone care for her, even if it was just a manicure.

"You have kids?" Zoya asked, not looking up.

Georgia noticed a whisker on her chin. "No kids."

Zoya looked up.

A good sign, Georgia thought.

"We've been trying, but so far no luck. Jimmy...my husband...would love it if we did, but..."

"You go doctor?"

"Over a year now. Fertility treatments. Pills. The works."

Zoya nodded but kept her mouth shut. She put down the emery board and picked up an orange stick. She started pushing back the tiny cuticle on Georgia's nails. "You really stop bite. Okay?"

"Okay."

Georgia waited. *Let her bring it up*, she thought. *Then I'll know.*

But the woman was quiet. She finished Georgia's cuticles, picked up Pink Taffeta, and gave it a shake. Georgia deflated. She wasn't going to get anything out of the woman. She'd resigned herself to failure when Zoya said,

"So you adopt, yes?"

Georgia jerked her head up. "Excuse me?"

"You can't have baby, you adopt?"

Bingo.

Aloud she said, "We haven't really thought about it. Yet. Do you think we should?"

Zoya shrugged. "Many people yes. Is gut. You have family." She opened the nail polish and started in on Georgia's left hand, all the while shaking her head, presumably at Georgia's minuscule nails.

Georgia shook her head too. "I know. I'm sorry."

Zoya looked up. "Sorry what about?"

"My nails."

"Ahh."

Georgia let some time go by. "My husband, well, I don't know if he wants to adopt. He still thinks we can do it on our own."

Zoya nodded. "And you?"

"Oh yes. In a heartbeat." At Zoya's bewildered expression, she explained. "I'd do it tomorrow if I could. If Jimmy"—she paused—"agreed."

Zoya finished the first coat. "I do another coat one minute."

Five minutes later, the second coat was done. Zoya snapped on a heat lamp and said, "You wait 'til dry."

Georgia smiled. "Thank you."

Zoya nodded. Then her expression changed. She actually looked engaged, as if she wanted to tell Georgia something.

"What?" Georgia prodded, making sure she was still smiling.

"You come back, tell Zoya when you ready for baby adopt."

"Really? Do you know someplace?"

Zoya waved a dismissive hand, then smoothed her fingers down the side of her face. Georgia had the impression she was reticent to say more. "You come. We talk."

"Thanks. What's your last name?"

"Tunick."

"Well, thanks, Mrs. Tunick. I'll be back."

Chapter 57

It wasn't until Georgia paid for her nails, left a generous tip, and exited the salon that she realized she'd heard the name "Tunick" before. But where? She tried to dig it out of her memory, but it wouldn't come. She'd have to wait for it to bubble up from her subconscious. Nonetheless, it was apparent Zoya was caught up with Chad Coe in some kind of operation that involved black market babies, adoptions, and maybe more, although Georgia didn't want to think about the "more." She was making progress.

She slipped into her car and ran her palms around the steering wheel. It was almost two, the time that Zoya got off. She slouched in the front seat, trying to be invisible, but angled the rearview mirror so she could see the salon's back door. A minute later Zoya emerged, talking into her cell. She got into her dark red Impala. She didn't appear to notice Georgia.

Georgia let her drive around to the street, then started up her Toyota. When Zoya turned right out of the lot, Georgia waited a moment before following her. Zoya headed to the Tri-State and swung down the ramp to the highway. Georgia did the same, making sure to keep a couple of car lengths behind. As they headed north a few snowflakes drifted down. Georgia felt a spit of annoyance. She didn't need snow now. But God, or Mother Nature, or whoever, wasn't listening, and lazy, fat, wet flakes kept drifting down. She switched on her wipers and hunched over the wheel. She also turned on her GPS so she'd know where she was in case visibility worsened.

Just north of Libertyville Zoya turned off the expressway and headed northwest on Route 173. Route 173 was where the body of the pregnant girl from Kansas City was found, albeit forty miles farther west. A burst of energy kicked up Georgia's spine.

The snow escalated into a full-fledged storm. The wind picked up too, swirling the snow in irregular eddies across her windshield, reducing visibility to nearly nothing. In a way, that was good—Zoya would be so focused on her driving she might not notice Georgia behind her. Georgia blasted her front and rear defrosters. Trucks coughed up slush as they passed in the other direction, making the drive more miserable. Only a couple of weeks had passed since she drove up and ran into Jimmy, but it seemed longer. Winter had a way of distorting time, elongating the minutes, hours, and days.

When Zoya continued past McHenry, perhaps the most far-flung town from which people still commuted into Chicago, Georgia almost turned back. Traffic was already sluggish and would be snarled soon. She could tail Zoya another time. The gloom from the storm cast a faux purple twilight over everything, and she was weary of driving.

Then she spotted a road sign that said Harvard was only thirty miles ahead. Georgia sat up, all thoughts of abandoning the surveillance banished. She was now directly behind Zoya, but the woman still didn't seem to notice. She'd made no moves to elude Georgia, although in this weather, who would?

It took almost an hour to get to Harvard. Georgia checked her GPS as they entered the town. They were less than a mile from where the girl had been found. As they reached the center of town, Georgia expected Zoya to turn off the main road, but the woman surprised her and kept heading west. Georgia squinted through her windshield. Did Zoya know Georgia was pursuing her? Was she leading Georgia on a wild-goose chase through the snow?

Georgia drew back and let Zoya get so far ahead that she almost missed the turn. They had just driven through the small town of Chemung and then Capron, ten miles west of Harvard, when Zoya made a left. The snow obliterated the street signs, and the road was unidentified on the GPS. The only thing Georgia knew was that she had crossed from McHenry into Boone County. She followed, barely able to make out the car's taillights in the distance. A mile or so later, Zoya made another turn into what appeared to be deep farm country, although the blanket of snow hid the remnants of what was likely soy beans, hay, or corn.

Zoya drove faster, as if she was tethered to a homing device. Georgia momentarily lost sight of her. She sped up too, although her Toyota was not good in snow and she was nervous about plowing into a tree or fence post. The road deteriorated; underneath it seemed to be pitted with stones. She passed a field littered with rusted farm equipment, now partially covered in white. Finally she picked up Zoya's taillights in time to watch her make a left. Georgia reached the spot a moment later and was about to follow her when she realized she'd be turning onto a private driveway. Trees bowed under snow lined both sides of the drive, their stripped and wiry branches swinging in gusts of wind. A weak light shone at the other end of the drive, maybe a hundred yards away. A farmhouse. Or a barn. Or both. And this driveway was the only way in.

Georgia put the Toyota in park and watched the sedan pull all the way up to the light. The Impala stopped; its red taillights winked out. She heard the faint thump of a car door closing. Georgia got out and snapped some photos with her smartphone to mark the location.

Chapter 58

She was close. She knew it. She backtracked to the tiny village of Capron. It was after four, dusk deepening into purple shadows, but she wasn't ready for the trek back to Evanston.

She stopped at the Village Café, a diner that, happily, was still open. The place, small but tidy, gave off the scents of bacon, fried food, and onions. Overriding those smells was the aroma of freshly made coffee, and she ordered some from a round, pleasant woman. Seated at a table, Georgia checked the photos on her phone. In the eerie winter light, the location looked spooky yet nondescript—just snow, trees, and the expanse that was the driveway. She closed the camera app and was surprised to find she had a wireless signal, especially in the storm. She checked her email. Nothing important. And no word from Jimmy.

That was when it came to her. Zoya Tunick. Holy shit. Tunick was the name of the boy who'd died on the table while being operated on by Richard Lotwin. Was Zoya his mother? She Googled his name again; the same articles came up, but there was no mention of the mother's first name. Still, how many Tunicks could there be in Northbrook?

Now it made sense. Zoya hadn't filed a malpractice suit because she didn't have to. The Russian Mafiya was known to exact vengeance of the eye-for-an-eye variety; they held a grudge for generations. She imagined how it could have happened: a couple of thugs visited Lotwin. Let him know that if he didn't want *his* kids to end up like Antonin Tunick, he'd do what they wanted. Which was to deliver babies for the baby-breeding ring. And Zoya was a powerful part of the organization. Georgia wondered if that in some way made up for the death of her son. No. Unless the woman was an unfeeling bitch, how could it?

She was buoyed by the connection. She finally had a working hypothesis about the baby-breeding farm. Still, she needed proof. She checked the time; it was early. She went back online to try to suss out the farm's owner. She wasn't sure if Boone County's property records were online, like Cook's. She went to the Boone County gov site. The answer was maybe, if she had a pin number. But she didn't.

She scanned the web for information about Capron. It was a tiny town, fewer than two thousand people. That was both good and bad. Good, because only a few people knew about the place; bad, because people in small towns all knew one another's business. Unless that business was kept well out of view. Plus, she reminded herself, the population count was probably limited to the town, not necessarily the farmland surrounding it.

She mulled it over. Capron was small; it was unlikely to have any law enforcement of its own. It probably relied on the Boone County Sheriff's Department, unlike Harvard, which was large enough to support its own department.

She sipped her coffee, thinking about the Harvard police and Jimmy and the day they'd met, or, to be accurate, met again. That had been a good day. A very good day. She checked her messages. She should have heard from him by now. They had a date. Was there a problem? Of course, now that the snow was flying, there was no way he would want to drive down, and she didn't want him to. The irony was she was only twenty-five miles from Lake Geneva. If she drove over, she could surprise him. He could fill her in on Capron. Maybe they'd research the property records together. She smiled. Who was she kidding? Capron wasn't even on the list of reasons she wanted to see him.

Chapter 59

Georgia finished her coffee and called Jimmy. She got his voice mail. She used the facilities and climbed back into the Toyota for the drive into Lake Geneva. Jimmy usually had dinner at his mother's restaurant, so she headed there, remembering the lunch they'd shared only a couple of weeks ago. She pulled into the driveway. Three inches of snow already covered the gravel-packed parking lot, but the lights from the restaurant beckoned. She parked. She didn't see his car, but it was early.

A sudden shyness came over her. She didn't want to go into the restaurant unless he was there. So she stayed in her car and fired up her tablet and went over her notes, which were in the Cloud no matter what device she used.

She was trying to figure out her next step when a car pulled into the parking lot. It was a dark Accord. Jimmy's car. Her heart caromed around her chest. Jesus. She had it bad if just the sight of his car could make her lose it. She opened the car door, ready to get out and jog over, snow be damned. But then she spotted someone in the front seat beside him.

Georgia closed her car door and made sure the dome light was out. She watched as Jimmy parked, got out, and went to the passenger side. A woman slid out. Georgia caught a glimpse of a pale face framed by long dark hair and a saucy wool hat. Jimmy smiled at her, cupped her cheeks in his hands, just the way he did with Georgia. Then pulled her to him in a tight embrace.

Chapter 60

Georgia blasted the heater on the way home. She was ice-cold, but it had nothing to do with the weather. The cold was within, a cold that would fail to go away even if she danced across hot coals. All the old tapes replayed in her head. She'd been rejected again. She was unlovable. She was destined to be alone.

It took nearly three hours to get home, and when she did, she went to bed. She slept late the next morning. A bright, showy sun woke her, and when she raised the shades, she witnessed the magic of Chicagoland politics. The snow had stopped and the streets were clear. While politicians couldn't control the weather—at least yet—they did control its cleanup. They had to; their next election depended on it. Still, the sunlight bouncing off neat piles of snow at the curb and her neighbors' lawns made her want to scream. How dare the day look so cheerful?

When she checked her phone, she found two voice mails from Jimmy. How could he be AWOL all day, then manage to call last night? She figured he was spending the day with Saucy Hat and forgot he had a date with Georgia until he got home. She debated whether to return the calls. She should be mature about it; perhaps it was something else entirely.

No. A crack in their relationship had appeared, and if Jimmy was anything like Matt or Pete, over time that crack would expand into a spiderweb of mistrust and suspicion. On the other hand, if she ignored the calls, she could pretend the crack wasn't there. At least for a while.

She dressed, making sure to grab a muffler and extra socks. The glitter of the sun's rays was deceptive; the thermometer outside her window read eighteen degrees. She opened the door and headed to the coffee shop.

The comforting aroma of fresh coffee wafted over her as she swung through the door, and she decided a latte would be even more comforting, calories be damned. Paul was looking impossibly chipper this morning, and after she placed her order, he grinned.

"Why are you in such a good mood?" she asked.

"Why not? The storm's over, it's a beautiful day, and God is smiling down on us."

"You got laid last night."

"That, too." His smile widened. "Then again, you're not doing too bad in that department."

Her heart skipped. She couldn't help it. "What do you know about it?"

Paul let out a mock sigh. "How soon ye forget. You brought him in here a week ago."

Georgia remembered. She and Jimmy had run in for a quick coffee and Danish over the weekend. Now, though, she kept her mouth shut. Paul's smile thinned, and she sensed he was going to follow up when her phone chirped. She fished it out of her pocket. Jimmy's name flashed on the caller ID. She let it go to voice mail.

Paul saw it and lifted his eyebrows. When the chirping stopped, she could hear the churn of the hot-milk machine, the quiet hum of conversation, the rustle of someone turning a newspaper, the tap of fingers on a keyboard.

She took her latte, sat down, and tried to focus on Chad Coe, Zoya, and the farm in Capron. In the harsh light of day, her hypothesis about the baby farm didn't seem so clear-cut. The farm might simply be the place where Zoya lived. Except that Bruce Kreisman had told her at least one pregnant girl had been in the warehouse downtown, and when she'd showed up, it had been abandoned. A few days later, she learned Kreisman had been killed . Because of his debts in Florida? Or because Kreisman had led her to the warehouse and told someone? Even if he had, why would someone kill him for it? It was a brutal retaliation for loose lips.

She called O'Malley to ask if Chicago had any suspects in Kreisman's murder. When he finally called her back, he said Chicago PD had nothing and wasn't looking too hard. In fact, he said, they probably wouldn't find anything unless it fell from the sky with Chicken Little. Because they had virtually no evidence, CPD might even reclassify his death from homicide to death investigation to keep the city's crime stats in check.

Georgia worried a hand through her hair. Kreisman was a lowlife; he wasn't going to be missed, even by the cops. So how did his death connect to the farm? If the operation really was a black market baby factory, maybe it was based in Capron, and the warehouse was just a convenient spot, the downtown branch, so to speak, where they picked up johns and got the girls pregnant. The farm could be the place they took the girls afterward. It was in the middle of nowhere, which meant few neighbors and no tourists. Assuming the girls were young and healthy, they could spend their pregnancies on the farm, maybe even go into labor and deliver their babies there. Then the infants would be whisked away and sold.

She dug out her tablet. She needed to find out who was in charge of the operation. It wasn't Chad Coe; from his behavior, he was on the logistical side. Arranging. Enabling. But not getting his hands dirty. It wasn't Lotwin either, and she didn't think it was Zoya. Georgia remembered the phone call Zoya took while doing her nails. She'd sounded submissive. Was she talking to the boss? The person who took the money? Recruited the girls? Decided what baby went where? Or was she just talking to a boyfriend or relative?

She reviewed her notes on the people Coe had visited. The doctor. The couple in Glencoe whose husband needed a kidney transplant. The apartment building in Skokie. She went over the tenants in the apartment building. The Mexicans, the construction guy, the Chinese couple, and the woman who worked at Evanston Hospital.

She reread what she had on Claudia Nyquist. Upside-down mortgage. Divorced. Moved from a house in Des Plaines to a cheaper apartment in Skokie. Worked in computers at Evanston Hospital. Some kind of data administrator. In a hospital.

She checked the time. Eleven in the morning. She gathered her drink, tablet, and coat, and waved good-bye to Paul.

Chapter 61

E vanston Hospital was always in a state of renovation. Fifteen years earlier they'd remodeled the first floor and parking lot. Now a sign on the elevator announced they were
working on the upper floors. Georgia didn't get it. The elegant
lobby, with its abstract art, a player piano, and lots of marble,
looked more like an upscale hotel than a hospital. Was the spiffy
décor supposed to cheer up patients? They rarely left their rooms.
Was it for visitors? Did they really expect family members to be
comforted by happy furnishings? Maybe it was for employees, to
lighten the fact that they dealt with illness and death all day.

Inside the elevator Georgia pushed the button for the third
floor. Hospital shift changes usually happened just after lunch,
but that might not be the case for an IT or data employee. With
luck Claudia Nyquist would be at her desk until five.

She found the data administration office in a corner of its
own wing and pushed through the door. A receptionist's booth
was vacant; then again, computer geeks probably weren't inundated with appointments. She smiled, imagining the type of person who would want to meet a nerd. To the right of the booth was
a large room partitioned into cubicles, each with a desk, chair, and
computer monitor. Most of the cubicles were occupied by men

tapping on keyboards, and for an instant, Georgia felt like she'd walked into a video arcade.

She went down one side of the room and found an empty cubicle with a fake purple flower in a tiny vase on the desk. Next to it was a small heart-shaped picture frame with a photo of a rosy-cheeked little girl who couldn't be more than four. This had to be Claudia Nyquist's desk. Georgia remembered the apartment manager saying she babysat for Nyquist. There was no other decoration in the cubicle, but a bright blue quilted parka hung on a hook, and a pair of matching boots lay on the floor. Paper and files were strewn across the desk, and a molded plastic chair was squeezed into a corner. Georgia sucked in a breath; she was a little claustrophobic and imagined the walls closing in. She was examining the cubicle for other clues about the woman when a man poked his head in.

"Can I help you?"

Georgia turned around. The man looked to be in his thirties, unkempt dark hair and scrawny. He looked like a nerd, with glasses, a pocket protector, and flakes of dandruff on his shoulders. Central Casting couldn't have done a better job.

Georgia forced a smile. "Oh, hi. I'm waiting for Claudia. Is she here?"

The man frowned. "I saw her earlier. Maybe she's using the facilities. Can I help you?"

"That's all right. Claudia is—the friend of a friend. I work a few blocks away. At the art gallery. I wanted to see if she was free for lunch."

"Oh." Nerdface managed to look surprised and disappointed at the same time. "Well, have a seat."

Georgia nodded and gingerly maneuvered herself into the chair. Nerdface disappeared.

Five minutes later, the door to the office squeaked open. An undertone of conversation followed. Georgia couldn't be sure, but the male voice sounded like Nerdface. When she heard a whispered "said she was a friend," she knew. He was the office magpie, chatting up everyone so he could keep tabs on them.

Nyquist appeared. Medium height, she was about twenty pounds overweight. Her jeans were tight, her sweater too big, but she had lovely straight blond hair that hung down her back. A black canvas bag, big enough to qualify as a small suitcase, was slung over her shoulder. Her face was pleasant but not pretty, and she wore no makeup. Georgia didn't blame her. If she spent all day in this desperate cubicle, why bother?

A worried frown pinched her face when she saw Georgia. "I'm sorry. Do I know you? Do we have a meeting?"

Georgia spotted Nerdface lurking outside the cubicle. "I know your pal is listening in on our conversation, so just to set the record straight, I did not tell him I was your friend. I said I was a friend of a friend."

Nyquist threw a glance over her shoulder toward Nerdface and shook her head. Georgia heard footsteps recede. Nyquist came in and sat behind her desk. Her bag dropped to the floor. "Who would that be? My friend, that is?"

Georgia waited a beat. "Chad Coe."

Chapter 62

T he woman blanched, then tried to cover it. Her hands, which had been on the desk, disappeared into her lap, and her spine straightened. She cast a furtive glance at Georgia, lifted a hand, and tucked a lock of hair behind her ear.

"Who?"

Georgia inclined her head. This was amateur hour. "You heard."

"What did you say your name was?"

"I didn't."

"Who are you?"

"I told you. A friend of Chad's."

"I don't know anyone named Chad."

Georgia blew out an irritated breath. "Look. We can go around the dance floor as many times as you want, Claudia. I have time. But I know you need to do your work. And your pal with the pocket protector is just bursting to tell your boss about my visit. He's the kind that could make trouble for you, isn't he? And trouble is the last thing you need right now."

Nyquist swallowed.

"So let's cut to the chase, shall we?"

Nyquist squirmed and flashed Georgia a guilty look.

"You're basically in a really bad place. If you're not up shit creek, then you're close. You were underwater on your mortgage. You got divorced. Neither you nor your ex could afford the house. So the bank took it. You moved to a cheaper apartment in Skokie. In fact, this job is your only anchor."

Nyquist played with her hair.

Georgia appraised her, glanced at the photo of the little girl. She decided to take a risk. "But the job doesn't pay enough for you to keep your daughter in day care. So now someone—your husband, maybe your relatives—has threatened to take her from you."

Tears welled in Nyquist's eyes. "How do you know that?" she whispered.

She'd guessed right. Georgia suppressed her satisfaction. "And then you met Chad Coe." She went on. "Where did you meet him? At a bar? In the hospital cafeteria? The nice new parking lot?"

Nyquist bit her lip. "At Dominick's."

"The grocery store." Georgia followed up. "He followed you there, didn't he? From here."

Nyquist looked up at Georgia, astonishment warring with tears.

Georgia felt the warmth of triumph. It wasn't hard to put things together when you knew how people behaved. "And he told you he knew a way for you to make a lot of money. Move to a better house than the one in Des Plaines." She paused. "How am I doing?"

The woman nodded.

"All you had to do was take a peek at the records of infertile couples who came in. Couples who were trying to conceive but couldn't. And give him their names."

Nyquist's brow furrowed.

"How much did he pay you for each lead?"

"Infertile couples? What are you talking about?"

"Oh, come on, Claudia. I thought we were past that."

"No...really. What names? What couples?"

Frustration rolled through Georgia. The day had started out badly and, despite her inroads a moment ago, it was deteriorating. "For the adoption ring."

Nyquist flipped up her hands. "What adoption ring?"

Georgia studied the woman. Nyquist's posture was rigid, all her wriggling and fidgeting and playing with her hair gone. She was telling the truth.

"I have reason to believe that Chad Coe is part of a sex-trafficking ring where the girls are impregnated and forced to give birth. Their babies are then sold to couples who want them. Without going through the hoops of adoption."

Nyquist sat back, a puzzled look on her face.

Georgia pushed. "If you're helping him in any way, what you're doing is illegal. You could be prosecuted. In fact, you could go to prison. Forget about a new home. Keeping your daughter. Even this job. All of that goes up in smoke if I tell the authorities what you're doing."

"Are you with the police?"

"What are you hiding?"

"You didn't answer my question."

"I'm not the one who's breaking the law."

Nyquist leaned forward. "You think I'm mixed up in an illegal adoption ring? One of those baby-breeding farms?"

"Aren't you?"

Nyquist laughed. Actually laughed. Then she slumped in her chair. Defeat washed over her. "If only it was."

A prickly feeling climbed up Georgia's back. She thought back to the church newsletter that described how the couple in Glencoe needed a kidney transplant. The queasiness she'd felt then returned.

Nyquist tilted her head. Relief spread across her face. "You know, I'm glad you're here. Whoever you are. I can't do this anymore."

Georgia ran her tongue around her lips. "My name is Georgia

Davis, and I'm a private investigator. You and I need to go some-where and talk."

Chapter 63

Georgia had to keep a tight rein on her emotions over the next hour. She hadn't wanted to consider the possibility that Chad Coe and the baby-breeding operation included the sale of body organs. Who in their right mind would? The notion that people could profit from selling the parts of a person, dead or alive, was monstrous. People who perpetrated that horror were just pretending to be human.

Still, like a suspicious lump that is undiagnosed, she couldn't ignore it. Georgia and Nyquist took the elevator to the hospital cafeteria in the basement and snagged a table in the back. Nyquist went through the line and brought back vegetable soup, a chopped salad, and three rolls with butter. Georgia had no appetite. Once Nyquist downed a few spoonfuls of soup, she seemed more relaxed.

"Look," she said. "I don't care what happens to me anymore, but Christy—that's my daughter—is in danger. I need help."

"Why don't you start at the beginning," Georgia said.

Nyquist sat back. Her expression was one of embarrassment, even humiliation. "Okay. Here it is. I have a drug problem. They're prescription drugs. Oxy, Vicodin, stuff like that. At first I was getting them from someone in the hospital, but they got caught and were fired."

Georgia had a feeling she knew what was coming next.

"So I hooked up with some other people. But they kept hiking their prices, and it got to the point where I couldn't pay. And then Chad Coe shows up at the grocery store one night and tells me he's got a way out."

"He already knew about your habit? And your debts?"

Nyquist nodded. "He said he understood. And it wasn't really my fault. Lots of people get dependent on the stuff and run up huge bills. But the people he was working with would forgive the bills if I helped him out. In fact, he said, they'd even pay me money once the debt was settled."

"Sounds cushy."

Nyquist threw her a glance. "It wasn't that simple. They..." She bit her lip. "There was one condition."

"Coe told you this?"

"No. It was a couple of days later. Someone else. Don't know his name."

"What was the condition?"

"They said if I ever thought about throwing in the towel or telling someone about it, they'd take her."

"Christy."

She nodded. "At first I thought it was just an empty threat. You know, to scare me. But after a few months—it was last summer—I told them I didn't want to do it anymore. It was too dangerous. I mean, if I was caught..." She let her voice trail off and sniffed. She was close to tears. "Anyway, a few days later, Christy wasn't there when I got home from work."

"They kidnapped her?"

She nodded again. "Someone came to the apartment and convinced Mrs. McCune—she's an idiot, by the way—that he was my ex's brother and that they had a date to go to the Kohl Children's Museum."

"Was it Coe?"

"I never found out."

"Didn't Christy put up a fuss?"

"Not at all. She thought she was going to see her daddy. They told her they'd get her ice cream. She was only too happy to go with them."

Georgia nodded. "What happened?"

"They dropped her off before dinner. They really did take her to the museum, it turned out. I have no idea how. But she was fine. Happy, even. After she was asleep, I got a call. Someone with an accent."

"Accent?"

"Russian. Or something. Anyway, they told me not to try quitting again, or she wouldn't be coming back."

"Jesus." Georgia let out a breath. "Are you still—on the drugs?"

Nyquist didn't answer. Which was answer enough. "So you're into them for drugs, and now they've got you for your daughter, too."

Her eyes rimmed with tears. "Can you help protect Christy? I'm desperate. I just don't know how it got this far," she sobbed.

Georgia knew, but now was not the time to remind her. "I might be able to help, but I need to know more."

Nyquist ran a sleeve across her nose as if she was trying to pull herself together. "What?"

"Let me get it straight. You're involved in an illegal organ transplant business?"

Nyquist nodded, slathered a roll with butter, and bit into it.

"How does it work?"

"It's actually pretty simple. There's this organization called UNOS. It's kind of a consortium. Online."

"UNOS? What does it stand for?"

"The United Network for Organ Sharing."

Georgia pulled out her tablet and looked it up. UNOS had a contract with the federal government to run the country's organ transplant system. Any hospital could join the website, which, according to UNOS, was updated 24/7.

"Is that true? It's updated all the time?"

Nyquist finished her first roll and buttered a second. "Absolutely," she said around a mouthful of bread. "Member hospitals log on anytime they need to know what organs are available, who's got them, and most important, how fresh they are."

"Fresh?"

"See, the most important thing in this business is time. Most organs don't last long outside the body. Like hearts and lungs. They only last about four to six hours. Kidneys and livers can make it for about twenty-four hours with these new organ boxes they have. But after that you're asking for trouble."

"So you'd log on and see who needed what?"

"Right." Nyquist polished off the second roll. "There's a huge demand for transplants. Especially in the US. It's probably ten to one."

"Ten to one?"

"Ten organs needed for every one that's available."

Georgia reeled back. "That many?"

Nyquist nodded. "Some organs are supplied by family members. But when that's not possible and a hospital needs an organ, they post it on UNOS. I check it a few times a day, and if I find something, I let Chad know. He takes it from there."

Chapter 64

Georgia swallowed. She'd thought Chad Coe was simply involved in a baby-breeding operation. Now he was running an organ transplant business too? How did they get the organs? She gulped air as it came to her. The mothers. A wave of nausea climbed up her throat, and it was all she could do not to bolt. Nyquist seemed to understand Georgia's distress and stopped eating.

Georgia swallowed. She tasted bile. "So...," she said slowly. "It's your job to scout patients who need organs all over the country?"

"Oh no. UNOS divides the country up into regions. I only search from New Orleans to Minnesota. You know, the Midwest. A few months ago I found a woman who needed a lung in Texas, but that didn't go so well. The lung failed on the way."

Georgia didn't want any details. "How often do you find someone who needs an—an organ?"

"Like I said, demand is much higher than supply. Traffic accidents, cancer, old age, things like that."

"So what's your best guess? How many do you come across? How often?"

"In the Midwest? Probably three or four a week. But Chad doesn't supply them all."

Georgia blinked. "What happens after you give the names to Chad?"

"There aren't any names. Just hospitals. I don't know how he finds out who the patients are."

Georgia thought she knew. If he subscribed to the same private databases she did—and as a lawyer he could—he could identify individuals by studying their financial and medical records. People who required transplants in a specific area would run up sky-high bills from hospitals, clinics, and doctors. Coe could zero in and contact a potential patient. Pay them a visit, tell them about the service he offered. Like he did with the Glencoe couple.

Nyquist went on, seeming relieved to be talking about something other than her drug problem and daughter. "The thing is, when it comes to life and death, doctors—at least the ones I know—aren't that picky about where the organ comes from. Most of what they call the 'alternative solution' happens in the OR every day."

"Come on. You're not saying that doctors knowingly transplant black market organs?"

"Of course not. They probably don't know they're black market. I mean, if someone—an administrator or a lawyer or someone like that—assures the surgeon everything is kosher, what are they going to do? They want to save lives. And they don't have time to mull it over."

"You're talking about someone like Chad Coe?"

Nyquist nodded. "Then if the organ rolls up in an ambulance, and a guy in a uniform delivers it, has them sign a bunch of paperwork, and a lawyer already said it's okay..." Her voice trailed off.

All of which the Russian mob could provide. Georgia shifted. UNOS was being used as a chop shop for human parts. Which meant her sister, Savannah, could be part of the mix. Were they planning to auction off her baby to the highest bidder and then kill *her* for parts?

"When did you go on Chad Coe's payroll?"

Nyquist broke eye contact. "About nine months ago." She

stared at her soup. "At first, I just thought he was finding people who died in car accidents and things."

"When did you figure out what was really going on?"

"When he was able to come up with the..." Nyquist faltered. "...the exact organ for whatever was needed on UNOS. It wasn't rocket science."

Georgia nodded. Coe and his cronies had offered Nyquist a way out of her troubles, as long as she didn't have scruples. Which, apparently, she didn't. At least at the start. Best of all, the business had the cachet—at least the appearance—of legality. To be fair, though, if Georgia had a critically ill family member and someone like Chad Coe showed up with a solution to her problem, as he had for the Glencoe couple, would she question how he'd come up with it?

"And now you want to get out, but you can't."

Nyquist nodded. A long silence stretched between them. Then the woman cleared her throat. "What's going to happen? Am I going to jail?"

"Oh yeah," Georgia said. "Especially after I call the cops." She hesitated. "But before I make that call, you need to make your daughter disappear. As soon as possible. Send her someplace safe. And inaccessible."

She looked up. "I have a sister in Minnesota."

"Not good enough. If your sister has a phone, she can be found. Give her to someone who has no connection to you. Someone from your church, maybe. Your pastor might be able to help."

"Do I have to?"

"If you ever want to see her again. You know who you're dealing with. They don't like loose strings. And you are a big one. Who knows? They might have been planning to move you 'out of the way' at some point anyway."

Nyquist pushed her plate away, most of her salad uneaten. Anxiety spread across her face. "For how long? Christy, I mean?"

Georgia shrugged.

"Are you talking weeks? Months? A year?"

"I don't know."

"God, what if Christy doesn't remember me? She's only four."

"Maybe you should have thought about that before you hooked up with Coe."

Nyquist massaged her temples, her expression veering toward panic.

Georgia didn't like the woman and couldn't condone what she was doing. But by calling the cops, she was condemning an innocent little girl to a long time without her mother. She was on the right side of the law. So why was she often faced with shitty consequences? It wasn't fair. She blinked rapidly.

"Okay," she said. "Here's the deal. I'm going to give you the name of a good lawyer. I think she'll help you. But you need to go to her office right away. Like, now. I'll call and tell her you're on your way."

She scribbled Pam Huddleston's number on a piece of paper and slid it across the table.

Chapter 65

In her apartment Georgia pulled up a few articles about the black market in human organs. Organs Watch, a monitoring organization, estimated that more than fifteen thousand people a year were trafficked worldwide for their organs. Like the baby-breeding farms, most of the action was run by organized crime. But it was all overseas; aside from two articles, there was next to nothing about it in the US. One of the articles reported on clinics that sold organs to research facilities back in 1999. One company actually posted fees for various organs: a thousand dollars for a brain, five hundred for a heart, three twenty-five for spinal cords. At the time it was perfectly legal. The other story was about a Brooklyn rabbi who'd been part of an international transplant ring run out of Israel. That article called it an "unpunished public secret."

She understood why there was scant coverage of the issue. Still, she bristled at the hypocrisy. The media would have a field day if they looked into it. In fact, the journalist who broke it might even win a Pulitzer. So far, though, they hadn't. It was okay to write about human organ trafficking in Europe, Asia, or Africa, but, of course, no American would ever be that callous. Organ trafficking didn't exist here.

Except, apparently, it did. A sanitized, well-regulated system of organ trafficking with enough cracks in it for people to be killed for their body parts. She started to pace around her apartment. Who made the decisions? On what criteria? And how much money was at stake? If a brain cost a thousand dollars fifteen years ago, how much would it be today? Add in cuts to middlemen like Nyquist, Coe, and Lotwin, the facilities in which the body parts were harvested, the people who transported the organs, and, of course, profit, and selling organs could be as lucrative as adoption. Possibly more.

She kept pacing. She'd made the right decision to send Nyquist to Huddleston. Huddleston would call the cops, and with what Nyquist knew, they could pick up Coe and Lotwin once Nyquist made arrangements to safeguard her daughter. She stopped. She should call O'Malley. Tell him that the murders of Bruce Kreisman, the pregnant girl on Route 173, and the drive-by in Evanston were probably connected.

But not today. She didn't want the law showing up at the farm tonight. If they did, the guards might destroy any evidence of the operation, and that might include the girls. She needed to get there first. Examine the evidence. Find out if Savannah was there. Make a plan to get her out. And, hopefully, put her eyes on the boss of the operation.

Chapter 66

Georgia drove out to Capron later that afternoon. Driving through Harvard, she passed Harmilda, the fiberglass cow in the middle of downtown that celebrated Harvard's past glory as the "Milk Center of the World." Then she drove through Chemung, a small town between Harvard and Capron on Route 173. The town was all clapboard houses and a church, except for the Harleys parked at the gas station. She passed a Ron Paul billboard, then a couple of cell towers.

As she drove into Capron, a dirty layer of snow covered the roads, fields, and trees. She passed small ranch houses, a trailer park, and more churches. How did all these churches survive? She drove past the Village Café, where she'd stopped for coffee before, then turned off the main road. She drove past the field with rusted farm equipment. Unlike the first time she'd come here, when she followed Zoya, it was still light, and no snow was falling.

Another turn took her to what she now saw was Nichols Road. On one side of the road was an open field with spindly twigs poking out of the snow cover. She couldn't tell what the twigs had been but figured they were either corn or soybeans. The other side of the road was cut by a series of patchy driveways.

She spotted an ADT sign on the driveway Zoya had turned into and smiled. What good was an alarm this far from civilization? It would take hours for anyone to respond. She slowed about a hundred yards past and turned the Toyota around so she was facing the direction she'd come from. The driveway was now on her right. She parked at a sharp angle so that the hood of her Toyota was camouflaged in the brush but she still had a view down the road.

She spent the next two hours watching dusk turn everything purple, then black. She was bored, cold, and irritable. Staking out a farm on a cold February night wasn't the worst assignment she could imagine, but it came close. Another three hours passed before a scrim of light swam toward her. Headlights. A car.

Although it had to be more than a mile away, she went on alert. Most people had the sense to stay home on a night like this. Unless they had important business. She put on her gloves, grabbed her baby Glock, and slid out of the Toyota. The beam of the headlights, sharper now that they were closer, would expose her at any moment. She plunged through the brush at the side of the road. It led to a dense but narrow stand of trees that edged the property and provided a natural boundary from the road. Just as the twin beams of light reached the spot on which she'd been standing, she thrust herself through the trees.

And heard the trill of a cell phone.

Chapter 67

Georgia froze. A man was so close to her she could reach out and touch his sleeve. Did he hear her tramping through the underbrush? If he turned around, he'd see her. She'd be finished. She held her breath. After what seemed like an interminable time, he moved in the opposite direction and headed toward the farmhouse. His cell kept ringing. He fished in a coat pocket for the phone and brought it to his ear.

"Yah?" It was a deep voice, rough and guttural.

Georgia allowed herself to exhale.

"*Da*. Okay." The man slid the phone back into his pocket and changed direction, walking up the driveway away from the farmhouse. She heard the sound of a car door opening. Jesus! She hadn't known she was this close to another vehicle.

The man who'd answered the cell called out in what sounded like Russian. A second voice, sounding sleepy, replied. Then the passenger door opened, and she heard two men exit the vehicle.

Guards. Good to know.

Behind them loomed a dark structure. A barn? Toolshed? She'd have to check it out later. Carefully, silently, she turned back to the approaching car. It was rolling into the driveway, headlights illuminating the two guards, one of whom raised an arm in greeting. She hunched her shoulders and tried to disappear behind a tree. Thank God it was dark.

The car was a dark sedan. Maybe a Beemer. Two figures were inside: driver and passenger. The car stopped on the driveway, the passenger door no more than ten feet from her. The engine cut out, and the man in the passenger seat climbed out. Georgia squinted to get a better look at him. When she saw who it was, she gasped.

Chapter 68

Savannah—Three Months Earlier

Over the next six months, time had no meaning for Savannah. Lost in a yawning black maw of dope and sex, she measured its passage by how often she got her fix. She spent most of her time in a fog, but occasionally—usually when she needed another fix—a burst of clarity would puncture the numb curtain. By then, though, her awareness of how low she'd sunk was too intense, too horrifying, and she'd have to back away and allow the fog to envelop her again.

After Turdball caught her in the backyard of the fleabag hotel, he threw her in the back of a van and took her someplace new. She had no idea where it was, but it wasn't a long drive. Turdball parked, hauled her out, and practically dragged her up a four-story walk-up. When he pushed her through the door of a dingy apartment, she was thrilled to see other girls. She counted eight. But none of them spoke English, and as she started to explore, her joy turned to despair. It was a two-bedroom apartment, and they all appeared to sleep in one room. The other room was filled with clothes on metal racks, all come-hither outfits, low-cut tank tops, short skirts, and stiletto heels. She guessed she was supposed to share them with the others.

By the next day she realized all the girls were addicted to heroin, that they were all whores, and that the ring was operated by the couple who had brought her first taste of heroin. They'd seemed so friendly. Friendly enough to fuck her blind.

Now, though, both the man and woman—she never learned their names—were all business. They no longer smiled, and they rarely spoke English. She found out later they were Ukrainian, not that it mattered. The only thing that did matter was that she was now their employee, and everything was different. She was expected to work nearly twelve hours a day on her back. Instead of getting smack from them every day, Savannah now had to pay for it. She had to pay for her food, too, although she was never hungry. And she had to fork over seventy-five percent of her earnings to the couple after the last john headed back to the suburbs or the north side or his job.

Which meant she was up shit creek. Sex was a cash business, and she made about five hundred a night. By the time she handed over nearly four hundred, she had barely a hundred left for dope, and the good stuff cost at least fifty a hit. The Ukrainians would extend credit, but even Savannah knew it was a ploy to keep her dependent on them. She'd never make or keep enough to get away from them. That was their plan. A Ponzi scheme in reverse.

Chicago was oppressively hot and dry that summer. Even air-conditioning did little to relieve it. And yet she was supposed to look good. Five, maybe six times a night, in clothes that had been worn by seven other women. The heroin helped dull her awareness, but a few impressions seeped through anyway. The smell of the men and their cum, briny and thick. Stray pubic hairs on her body, which made her skin crawl. The way most johns kept their eyes screwed shut, as though looking at her would turn them into stone. Their body odor, rancid and dirty or drenched in cologne. Either way, it was all repulsive. Yeah, sure, she'd fucked for money back in Colorado. But it was her choice. She decided who, when, and where. No more.

The other thing she found curious during her rare moments

of lucidity was the medications they were given. Antibiotics but no birth control pills. When she asked the woman who had "recruited" her about it, the woman lied and said they were birth control pills. But Savannah had seen the bottles from which the pills were doled out, and the labels said amoxicillin or Cipro. She tried to ask the only other girl who spoke a smattering of English about it. But the girl, who wore a world-weary air, didn't understand or wasn't in any shape to give advice and shrugged.

The biggest event of the summer occurred in August, when a second American was brought in. Another blonde, the girl wore the same dazed look as the others, and Savannah wondered if she'd met up with Lazlo. She gave her a few hours to get acclimated, then approached her with a simple "Hi."

The girl's eyes widened; she told Vanna later she hadn't thought anyone else spoke English. Her name was Jenny and she was from Kansas City. They could talk only in snatches—the couple had armed handlers like Turdball monitoring them—but she told Vanna a familiar story: an abusive family, druggy parents. Jenny wanted something better. She'd come to Chicago on the bus. Met a guy named Lazlo at the bus terminal.

That confirmed it. Savannah had been set up from the beginning. Lazlo was a recruiter. His assignment was to find fresh "stock," and he was paid off with sex and money. She winced. She didn't have the heart to tell Jenny.

Chapter 69

Savannah

A few nights later they were getting dressed when the couple left the apartment. That in itself wasn't unusual; one or both of them often left for hours at a time, probably to lure another girl into heroin and sex. Two men were assigned to guard the girls. One of them would take whomever he wanted into the clothing room to fuck, while the second stayed in the living room with the others. The women, listless and dull eyed, didn't seem to care. After what they went through on a daily basis, no further humiliation was possible. When the first guard emerged, it would be the other's turn.

This time was different. The couple usually handed out assignments before they left, including what street corner the girls were to supposed to hang out on, or what fleabag hotel they were supposed to find. But this time they didn't. Once the couple had gone, Vanna caught a furtive look between the guards, as if they knew they had to behave. Had the Ukrainians been fingered by someone and were they now trying to flee? The other girls didn't seem to notice—or care—that the couple was gone, but Vanna knew something was off.

At the same time she was powerless to do anything about

it. She hugged her knees and rocked on the floor. She stopped when she heard footsteps thumping up the steps. Male voices murmured on the other side of the door, but she couldn't make out the words. For a fleeting moment she thought the men were cops and she was just moments from freedom. But when she heard their harsh, Slavic words, which she now knew was Russian, she sagged and resumed rocking.

The door opened, and three men came in. They were all well dressed in jackets that looked expensive, designer jeans, and soft leather boots. One man seemed to be in charge, and he gestured to the other two. They cruised around the living room, hauling each girl to her feet. Most were too high to stand on their own, and the men had to support them.

The leader looked each girl over in turn, squinted, and cupped her chin in his gloved hand. Then he shook his head, and the men released their grip. The girls slid to the floor. The leader moved on and motioned to the next.

The men proceeded around the room, closing in on Vanna and Jenny. Vanna made herself pay attention. Why were the men checking them out? Did they want a party? An orgy? She studied the man in charge. He had pale blue eyes, almost hooded, but they contrasted sharply with his black hair. Most of the Russians she'd come across had light complexions; his dark coloring gave him a slightly Asian look. He was sinewy and slim, and his clothes fit him like a second skin. He wasn't what you'd call handsome, but there was something about him. It was hard to look away.

As he approached, she scrambled up from the floor. But she was unsteady on her feet, and the two men grasped her under her armpits. She tried to shake them off. The leader raised one eyebrow, as if surprised anyone had the energy or motivation to fight. He moved a step closer and grasped her chin in his hand. Vanna tossed her head, trying to loosen his grip, but the more she wriggled the tighter he squeezed, until she couldn't move. Her jaw locked and pain shot through her.

When he had her where he wanted, he smiled. It was a strange, crooked smile, a smile that didn't reach his eyes. Mustering her courage, she stared back at him, trying to suppress the fear skittering around in her. She wasn't prepared when his crooked smile deepened, as though her efforts amused him. He dropped his hold and stepped back, pulling his gaze away from her face. He examined her from head to toe. Then he grabbed one of her arms turned it over. When he saw the tracks on her veins, his smile faded, but he looked at the other two men and nodded.

They seized Vanna and shoved her against the wall nearest the door, then motioned for her to sit. The leader moved on to Jenny. She was weak and flaccid and couldn't stand. Still, he examined her, looked back at Vanna, then his men, and nodded again. The men pushed Jenny onto the floor next to Vanna.

When he had finished checking out all the girls, he waved his hand and left the apartment. Vanna heard his boots clumping down the stairs. One of the men grabbed Jenny, the other Vanna, and forced them out and down the steps. Vanna's final thought before she was hustled into an SUV was that the leader had done everything without saying a word.

Chapter 70

Savannah

When Savannah was herded into the back of the SUV, the nip in the air told her summer was over. Of course, she wasn't wearing much of anything, but one of the men threw a blanket over her and Jenny. They needed it. The sky was inky dark, and she had no idea where they were, except that they were barreling down a highway. After what seemed like a long time, the driver turned off, and a fresh, piney scent replaced the gritty smells of the city. The smell made her feel oddly optimistic, although there was no reason to be.

They turned off a two-lane road onto a narrow lane thick with woods on both sides. Rolling down the uneven road, they eventually reached a patchy driveway, which led to a farmhouse well recessed from the road. An unattached barn lay farther away. The men parked the SUV and motioned for Vanna and Jenny to get out. Floodlights mounted to the walls of both house and barn illuminated the surroundings, but all Vanna could see were bare branches waving in the wind.

Inside, the farmhouse was unusually clean and neat. No dirty dishes lying around, no trash piled up, worn but comfortable furniture. The kitchen looked good enough to cook in.

An older woman, round, with dark hair piled on top of her head and the faint trace of a mustache, motioned them to a set of stairs.

"Where are we?" Vanna asked.

The woman didn't answer. Had she not heard or did she not speak English?

"Who are you?" Vanna said.

The woman shook her head, still not talking, and started up the steps. About halfway up, she stopped, turned around, and gestured for Vanna and Jenny to follow. The second floor contained four bedrooms. Vanna peeked in one as they passed. The room contained not much more than a bed and dresser, but like the rest of the place, it looked clean. At the end of the hall was a bathroom with older fixtures, but again, it was cleaner than most of the bathrooms she'd seen since she left Colorado.

The woman turned on the shower above a claw-footed tub. She opened a chest of drawers, handed both girls a washcloth and towel, and gestured to the water. Vanna didn't need any more encouragement. She peeled off her clothes and stepped into the tub; it was the first real shower she'd had in months. As she lingered in the hot, steamy water, she wondered if she could scrub away the past few months as easily as the grit from her body.

After they showered, the old woman led Jenny to one room, Vanna to another. A faded green bathrobe lay on the bed. It wasn't new, but the terry cloth was soft and comfortable. The woman beckoned her back down to the kitchen. A few minutes later, Jenny came down too, also wearing a bathrobe, but hers was white. She flipped up her hands as if to say, "What the fuck?"

Vanna shook her head. She didn't understand either. The cleanliness and concern were a universe away from the way she'd been treated. All she knew was that she didn't want it to stop.

The older woman busied herself at the stove and minutes later set down two steaming cups of tea in front of the girls. Vanna sipped hers, wondering whether she was dreaming or whether this was real. She felt herself smile wide enough that her lips curled.

It would be her last for a long time.

Chapter 71

Savannah

V anna slept more soundly that night than she had since she'd stepped off the bus in Chicago. Still, she woke early. She knew why. She was ready for a fix. Somehow she had to communicate that to the woman who'd taken them in. She and Jenny would have to drive into town—wherever that was—to score. They'd need money, too, she realized worriedly. When they'd been taken from the apartment, they had no time to gather anything, including the few twenties Vanna had stashed inside her pillow case.

She went down to the kitchen in her bathrobe. Through the window the morning sun glittered through the trees, splashing a riot of yellow, orange, red, and brown over the surroundings. When had it become fall? she wondered. How had she missed it? Fall was her favorite season. It meant a new grade in school, new clothes—and her father.

Her little corner of the universe had been perfect. Her mother met Denny when they moved to Flagstaff; they'd married a few months later. Vanna was born a year after that. Her dad taught at the community college, and he spent more time with her than any of the other kids' dads did with their kids; he even enjoyed her dress-ups and tea parties. When her mother called her a "daddy's girl," he would laugh and wink at Savannah like they shared a secret. When she started school, it was Denny who dropped her off in the morning and picked her up in the afternoon. He was going to his classes; she'd was going to hers. They were a team.

Until the freak ice storm that happened in January eleven years later. He dropped her at school in the morning but wasn't there to pick her up in the afternoon. She'd stayed at school so long they finally called her mother, who couldn't come to the phone. Instead the principal spoke to a neighbor who said her daddy had been in an accident on the highway. An eighteen-wheeler skidded on the ice and smashed into his car. He was killed instantly. Savannah never forgot the moment she heard he was dead. She was twelve and was wearing a new pair of shiny black boots he'd helped her choose. The next day it was sunny and sixty-five degrees.

Now she tore her eyes away from the window. The woman sat at the kitchen table, tiny white headphones dangling from her ears. The sight of an old woman listening to an iPod or iPhone was funny, and Vanna almost giggled. When the woman noticed her, she pulled out her earbuds, rose, and went to the fridge. She took out milk and a loaf of bread. Then she went to a cabinet and fished out a box of Cheerios. Vanna wasn't hungry and she didn't want cereal; the only thing she did want was a hit. She approached the woman, who was taking a bowl out of another cabinet, and stayed her hand.

"No. No cereal."

The woman threw her a disapproving scowl. "*Da*. You eat."

Vanna scrunched up her nose. "I'm not hungry."

"*Da*," the woman repeated. "You eat. You must."

Vanna squinted. "So you do speak English?"

The woman tipped her head from side to side. "A leetle."

"Great." Vanna pasted on a smile. "Listen. I need a ride into town. Can you drive me?"

The woman's gaze was cool and direct. She turned away and put the bowl back in the cabinet.

Vanna was confused. "You understand, right? I need a ride into town. Or Chicago. Now."

The woman turned to face her. She held up her index finger. "You stay. Here."

Vanna blew out a breath. "Look, I don't know your name, and you've been great to take us in, but we really need to go into town."

"Vanna," a voice called. Vanna spun around. Jenny. In her white bathrobe. "Hey," Jenny asked, "did you find any clothes in the drawers or closet?"

"I didn't look."

"Well, I did, and there's nothing there. Not a thread."

Vanna turned back to the woman. "Look, lady, we need our clothes. Where's the stuff we were wearing last night?"

But the woman refused to answer. She got out the same bowl she'd offered Vanna, the Cheerios and the milk, and gestured to Jenny.

Jenny sat at the table. The woman nodded and poured cereal into the bowl.

"She doesn't understand a fucking word we're saying." Vanna blew out a breath.

The woman put the cereal and a spoon in front of Jenny.

"You see a car anywhere?" Vanna asked.

Jenny shook her head. "The van took off."

"Dammit." Vanna started to pace. "She's got to have a car." She stopped and brightened. "I bet it's in the barn."

Jenny dug into her cereal.

Vanna scowled. "How the fuck can you eat?"

Jenny shrugged. "I'm hungry."

"Yeah, well, if we can't find her car, we're up shit creek." She headed toward the kitchen door. "I'm gonna check out the barn."

But the old woman, suddenly as fleet-footed as a ballerina, intercepted Vanna before she reached the door. "No." The woman grasped her arm and shook her head. "You stay in. No go out."

"Let me the fuck go!" Vanna tried to shrug her off, but the woman's grip was surprisingly strong.

"You go up now. Bed." The woman said.

"You can't do this. I'm not a prisoner!" Vanna cried out.

"You stay. You see." The woman nodded and guided her toward the stairs.

Vanna opened and closed her mouth several times as if she wasn't sure whether she wanted to throw a tantrum or cry. The woman's expression remained stoic. Vanna narrowed her eyes, took another look, and stomped out of the room.

A few hours later Vanna's stomach began to tighten. The cramps started twenty minutes after that. She'd had food poisoning from a lobster roll years earlier, but the pains from these cramps were much sharper. Beads of sweat ringed her neck and forehead. She made it to the bathroom just in time.

While she was dealing with the cramps, diarrhea, and sweat, her skin started to itch. That worsened as well, until she felt as if bugs were crawling over her body. She scratched everywhere, but it didn't help.

She staggered into Jenny's room. Jenny was fast asleep. How the hell could she sleep? Shouldn't she be as sick as Vanna? Then she knew. Jenny had been on junk for only a week or so, not the five months Vanna had been hooked. Her withdrawal would be easier. Vanna frowned. She wanted to wake Jenny up. Why should she suffer alone? Meanwhile, the urge for a fix, somewhere, anywhere, tore through her. If she didn't get it soon, she was going to die.

She hurried down the steps. The old woman was at the table again, earbuds trailing a white cord to her phone. Vanna wanted to rip the fucking cord away from her head and strangle her.

"Please...," she wailed. "I need it. I need it bad."

The woman glanced up, but her expression was stony. She didn't even bother to remove her earbuds.

Despair thickened Vanna's throat. The morning sun disappeared from the window. It must be almost noon. She tried another tactic. "Hey, what's your name?" She wondered if her voice sounded as frantic as she felt.

The woman hesitated, then squinted as if she knew the ruse. She took off her earbuds. "I Zoya."

"Zoya." Vanna pasted on a smile. "Do you have a daughter, Zoya?"

There was no response. In fact, the woman stiffened as if Savannah had struck her.

"Well, if you did, you wouldn't want her to suffer, would you?"

Zoya pressed her lips together. "You stop talk. Go up."

"Up? You mean high?" Vanna, close to the end of her rope, purposely misinterpreted the woman's words. "Thank God. Where is it? I can do it myself, you know."

Zoya rose and shooed Vanna toward the stairs like a misbehaving dog. "Up, up. You go bed. I come soon."

"No!" Vanna shouted. Panic rolled over her. Fresh sweat soaked the back of her neck. "You just said I could score. You promised!" She knew she wasn't making sense, but she glanced around wildly, trying to home in on something, anything, that would stem the overpowering urge for a fix.

Then she remembered the barn. The woman's car had to be in there, didn't it? She inched around the table toward the door, preparing to bolt. This time, though, Zoya didn't try to stop her. With a shriek of victory Vanna reached the door and twisted the knob. Nothing happened. The door was locked. She looked for the release. She couldn't find it. She whirled around.

"Open this door!" she commanded.

Zoya just looked at her.

"Open it, you goddammed witch!"

Still no reaction.

Vanna screamed. And then screamed again. She screamed over and over until she was hoarse and the screams turned into tears. With her back to the door, she sank to the floor. She couldn't stop crying.

Zoya went to Vanna, grabbed her by the arm, and pulled her to her feet. Vanna tried to resist, but whatever strength had propelled her this far vanished. Or else Zoya was a hell of a lot stronger than she looked.

"You go to bed. You sick."

Vanna kept crying.

Zoya half pushed, half dragged her up the steps. She shoved her into the bedroom and locked the door.

Chapter 72

Savannah

The next four days were torture. Excruciating pain pummeled Vanna in waves. Her legs buckled, and she couldn't walk—even to the bathroom. At the peak, she thought her joints and muscles were going to explode. When the pain did recede, her fingers, arms, and legs felt lethargic and weak. Opening a drawer was impossible. So was twisting a doorknob, assuming it wasn't locked, which, of course, it was. Then there were the cramps, which gnawed at her gut and radiated down to her crotch but were a thousand times worse than menstrual cramps. The bouts of diarrhea were so fierce she couldn't control them, and full-body sweats left her wringing wet, except when they alternated with chills that couldn't be controlled even with three blankets.

Zoya laid plastic sheets on the bed. She brought Vanna Imodium and vitamins, but Vanna's lips were so swollen and cracked she could barely open her mouth wide enough to swallow. A sour taste in her throat slithered up to her tongue, making her mouth taste like clay.

Eating was out of the question, despite the toast and endless cups of tea that Zoya brought. She almost threw them in the woman's face. After the first day, she didn't see Jenny at all, but when she heard moans and screams coming from the other bedroom, she knew Jenny was going through withdrawal too.

There was no respite. Insomnia claimed her and she couldn't sleep. Occasionally she dozed, but most of the time she lay in a semiconscious state of misery. Her legs had acquired what those late-night TV commercials called restless-leg syndrome, twitching and moving on their own. By the third day, she begged Zoya to kill her.

"I can't do this anymore. I'm going to die. Just kill me now. Please."

Zoya shot her a pitiless expression.

That night she was woken by the sound of a car crackling on the snow and gravel. It seemed to be heading past the house to the barn. She thought she heard a woman cry, but it was muffled, and she could have been dreaming. The next morning, the car had vanished, and everything was the way it had been.

By the fourth day, the symptoms were still there, but they didn't seem as fierce. Vanna still felt like she had a bad case of flu, but she managed to get down half a piece of toast and a few sips of tea. On the fifth day, although she wasn't sure how much time had passed, the diarrhea subsided, and she even took a full-fledged nap.

The next morning she actually got out of bed, unsteady, and was taken to the bathroom. She gazed at herself in the mirror. An ugly girl with ratty blond hair, a gaunt face, alabaster skin, and huge eyes stared back. Vanna turned away. She didn't want to see the human wreck she'd become.

Chapter 73

Savannah

The next few weeks passed in hues of gray. The physical symptoms of withdrawal subsided, but Vanna's emotional state was shaky. Bouts of listlessness during which she didn't have the energy to get out of bed alternated with irritable, manic periods. She didn't want to live; she didn't want to die. She spent most of her time in her room, wondering how her life had come to this.

One morning she was lying on her bed when she heard a voice. "Vanna."

She sat bolt upright. The voice was her father's. She knew it better than she knew her own. She gazed around the room in a panic. Where had it come from? How was it possible? She slid off her bed. It took only about two seconds to search the tiny room—there was only the bed, a chest of drawers, and an empty closet. She looked under the bed. Nothing. She threw open the closet door. Empty. She sucked in a breath. She'd been so sure.

She lay down again, trying to make sense of what she'd heard. It must have been a dream. She must have been dozing. But it was so real. His inflection, his tone, the underlying warmth in his voice. Was it just a heroin dream? Or was it something else? If felt as if he'd reached down from heaven—or wherever he was—to let her know she was on his mind. That everything was okay. That he was there and he loved her.

She blinked back tears.

Chapter 74

Savannah

Savannah wasn't sure whether it was the dream, as she came to call it, or the fact that she hadn't been hooked on dope for more than six months, but by the following week Vanna was better. The personality changes and mood shifts heroin was known to trigger seemed to ebb, and she felt stronger. More competent and lucid.

In retrospect, Vanna realized Zoya must have noticed it too, because one afternoon she came back to the house with a Walgreen's bag and shook it out on the kitchen table. Two pregnancy tests fell out. Zoya made both Vanna and Jenny pee on the sticks. Zoya's eyebrows rose as she read the results. She eyed Jenny and Vanna from top to bottom. Then she walked out, as she usually did, leaving Savannah and Jenny with the guards. The girls snatched the sticks off the table and studied the results. Jenny's test was positive; Vanna's wasn't. Vanna heaved a sigh of relief. Jenny burst into tears.

"Crap, Vanna. What am I going to do?"

Vanna shook her head. "I don't know. How did it happen?"

Jenny wiped the back of her hand across her eyes. "That's a stupid question."

"What I mean, is, do you think you were pregnant when they were shooting us up?"

"I think I'm about three months. So I had to have been." Fresh tears streamed down Jenny's cheeks. "Which means the baby might be deformed or something, you know?"

"That's okay. You not going to keep it, anyway."

Jenny stopped crying and looked at Vanna. "What do you mean?"

"Just tell Zoya you want an abortion. There's still time. I'm sure they'll say yes. They don't want you having a baby any more than you do."

Jenny sniffed. "I—I don't know."

"Jenny, you have to. This"—Vanna waved her arm to encompass the kitchen, the farm, their entire situation—"this is not the time or the place to have a baby. Promise me you'll ask, okay? Tell them you'll do anything to get it out of you. And then we'll figure out a way to get out of here."

Jenny bit her lip. Then the guards cut them off and took them up to their rooms.

Vanna was dozing when Zoya returned that afternoon. She came awake when she heard the woman's heavy tread on the stairs. Vanna frowned. There was more than one person on the steps. Zoya came into her room followed by a pudgy man in a suit. Thin, dark strands of hair in a comb-over failed to hide his baldness. He was carrying a black bag.

"Who are you?"

"A doctor."

She eyed him suspiciously. "Sure you are."

Zoya cut in. "You no talk. He doctor. Take blood."

"Why?"

"We want to make sure you're healthy," the man said.

"Healthy? You want to make sure I'm healthy? Where were you when I needed you?"

"I'm just going to take a little blood. Make sure you don't have any STDs or AIDS."

Vanna ran her hand through her hair. "Oh fuck. Just get it over with."

Mercifully, the doctor was quick. Once he had a couple of vials of blood, he nodded to Zoya and left the room.

Zoya closed the door. Vanna hadn't noticed, but Zoya was carrying a familiar white bag with a red bull's-eye. She placed the bag on the bed and slid out the contents. Inside was a silver-sequined tank top, the skimpiest black shorts Vanna had ever seen, four-inch heels, and tubes of mascara, eye shadow, and blush. She told Vanna to put on the clothes.

Vanna's spirits sank. Was she being sent back to the hookers? Her throat closed up in fear. "But I don't want to."

Zoya squinted and shoved the clothes closer.

"I don't want to go back there," she pleaded. "Please."

"You pass test, you no go."

"The blood test?"

"No." The woman shook her head. "You see."

"What about Jenny? Is she having the test too?"

Zoya shrugged.

"Why me?"

But Zoya didn't answer. She waited while Vanna tried on the clothes. Then she nodded. "You take off now. Rest." She locked the door and left Vanna's room.

Chapter 75

Savannah

Sometime after dark Zoya came back up to help Vanna dress.
When Vanna had pulled on the skimpy clothes, Zoya
motioned her into the bathroom. Vanna had been avoiding
the mirror since she'd caught that glimpse of herself, but putting
on her makeup required her to look. The sunken-eyed, hollow-
cheeked face that had stared back at her a month earlier was gone.
Instead her reflection showed an attractive, fresh young woman.
Her hair was longer now, and when Zoya pinned it up in a twist,
Vanna almost smiled. Even her cheeks had a rosy glow.

Zoya herded Vanna down the steps to the living room, a large
space with no furniture except two easy chairs, an end table, and
thick green drapes covering the windows. Track lighting illuminated one end of the room; the rest of the room was in shadow.
Almost like a stage. She was aware that a man was reclining in one
of the easy chairs near the pool of light, but she couldn't see who it
was. Zoya stopped at the entrance to the room, and a brief conversation took place in Russian. It ended with the man's voice calling
out of the dark.

"*Da.*"

Zoya rotated a dial on the light switch, and the track lights brightened. Then she nodded at Vanna. "You go."

Vanna flipped up her hands. "Where?"

Zoya pointed to the center of the room. "Stand. Turn around."

"Why? What the fuck is going on?"

"Just do," Zoya hissed.

Vanna shot her an irritated glance but moved to the middle of the room under the lights. She paused, unsure what to do next. She was aware that the man in the chair was watching her, and she realized with a start that this was the test. She *was* on a stage, of sorts. She raised her hand to shade her eyes.

A voice came out of the darkness. "Put hand down."

She hesitated. The man had a thick Russian accent, but at least he was speaking English.

The voice deepened. "Now."

Vanna dropped her hand. Who was this man?

"Turn around," the voice said.

Vanna turned.

"Other way."

She turned back.

"Put hands behind head. Look up."

She tilted her head up, but the glare from the lights was too bright. She squeezed her eyes shut.

"Open eyes and walk across room."

She felt like a bug under a microscope. She flashed back to biology lab in high school. She and a geeky kid named Stewart were supposed to dissect a frog so they could examine the creature's delicate muscles and joints under the microscope. She couldn't do it. She told him she'd give him a BJ if he did it himself. He happily complied.

"Now back."

Pulled back to the present, Vanna backtracked to the center of the room.

Another silence. Then, "You look better than last time I see you."

"Who are you?"

"A friend."

After what had happened to her over the past six months, she knew that was bullshit.

"You okay now?"

She didn't answer.

"We clean you up."

"Why?"

"I buy you."

"You bought me?" Her voice spiked. She hadn't imagined anything worse than being forced to be a whore. On the other hand, if he'd bought her maybe there was. But something told her she couldn't show him she was afraid. She pretended to be pissed off. "What the fuck for?"

The man laughed; a rough, harsh laugh that wasn't a laugh at all. Terror bubbled in her throat, but she forced herself to keep up a front. This was America. "Lincoln freed the slaves, remember?"

The man's laughter faded. "You no like? I take you back to apartment, drugs, fucking."

Chapter 76

Savannah

Vanna gulped air. She didn't want to go back to the filth,
the whores, the heroin. She didn't know what was going
on, but this man was now clearly in charge of her, and at
least for now, she had to play along. She let out her breath and
pretended to think. Then she planted one hand on her hip, angled
it out, and smiled seductively. "I guess I'll stay." She paused. "So?
Did I pass?"

He didn't answer.

"What's your name?" she called out.

More silence. "C'mon. Make one up if you want to. I need to
call you something."

Then, "I am Vlad."

Vlad? What kind of a name was that? She shaded her eyes
again and tried to make out his features. She couldn't. "Well,
Vlad. What happens now?"

A throaty chuckle came from the shadows.

Vanna was suddenly tired of the bullshit. "Okay. Tell it to me
straight. What do I have to do to get out of here? How much do
you want?"

He sidestepped the answer. "Where is home?"

"Colorado."

"Why you leave?"

A sharp memory of her mother bit into her. Why hadn't they been able to make it work after her father died? Maybe Vanna should have been more caring. Her mother was as broken as she was. Maybe they could have patched each other up instead of ripping each other to shreds. Vanna needed someone who cared whether she lived or died. Maybe, over time, she could have broken through her mother's problems and found that love. Her father would have wanted that.

"Tell me," Vlad said.

She shook her head.

"Okay. What is *your* name?"

"Vanna."

"Vanna? What name Vanna? For TV show?"

"It's short for Savannah. Hey, do you think we could turn down the lights? I'd really like—"

Ignoring her request, he cut her off. "Why you come Chicago?"

She pressed her lips together. He didn't have to know.

"I waiting, Vanna." He emphasized the word "Vanna."

She kept her mouth shut.

"Is big secret?"

She shook her head.

"You tell me. Now." He sounded irritated.

Vanna considered it. Maybe it wasn't such a big deal. He'd probably heard the story before. "My mother and I weren't getting along. So I came to see my sister."

There was a sudden pause. Then, "You have sister here?"

"Well, a half sister," she replied. "Look, if it's money you want, I can borrow some to pay you off," she lied. "Really. Just give me a chance."

"Where is sister?" His voice grew cool. The throaty laugh was gone.

"I—I don't know. Things happened so fast..." Her voice trailed off. Maybe she shouldn't have brought up Georgia.

"You want I call?"

Vanna looked at the floor. "She doesn't know I'm here," she said softly.

She heard him shift. Had she made a mistake? Maybe she should never have mentioned Georgia.

"What is sister name?"

She didn't answer.

Even though she couldn't see Vlad, she had a sense he was leaning forward. Waiting. "Tell me her name."

Again, she shook her head.

"Vanna, you want make you talk?"

Vanna ran her tongue around her lips. She had fucked up. But there was no way to unring this bell. She had to tell him. "Her name is Georgia."

"Georgia? Georgia what?"

"Georgia Davis."

Once again, a silence so long and deep that it seemed to suck all the air out of the room. What had she done? She wrapped her arms around herself protectively. Finally, Vlad cleared his throat. What came out of his mouth next shocked her. In fact, it scared the shit out of her.

"Your sister...she is police?"

She went rigid. How could he know that? Who was this man? Why would he think Georgia was a cop? A mental alarm blasted her brain. She had to fix things. Fast.

"There's no fucking way my sister is a cop," she blustered. But even as she said it, she recalled her mother telling her how *she'd* married a cop in Chicago all those years ago. That man had been Georgia's father. It *was* possible. But how did this man know?

Her thoughts were interrupted by the rustle of movement. Vlad stood up and came toward her. She lifted her chin, like an animal sniffing the air.

When he came into view, she took a step back. She recognized him. He was the man in the leather jacket who'd come to the hooker apartment a month earlier. Who'd chosen her and Jenny and brought them here. Whose orders had been obeyed without his saying a word.

She looked him over. Muscled and well built, he was the type she wouldn't mind fucking. Skin so pale it was milky, eyes so icy blue they could probably cut glass. High cheekbones, a nose that looked like it had been broken once or twice—but who cared about that?—and a mass of thick hair, black and silver, particularly at the temples. Still, there was something wild and dangerous in his face, something that made her feel there were no boundaries he wouldn't cross. His expression was cold and detached. He stared at her as if she were nothing more than a lump of clay.

"A sister. Police. Georgia Davis." His gaze turned calculating, as if he was putting things together. Finally he smiled, as if he had just figured it out. But it was an odd, crooked smile, a smile that highlighted his sharp features but did nothing to warm his face. "Well, well. How you say? It is small world."

She recoiled.

He called out something in Russian. Out of the corner of her eye, she saw, or maybe felt, Zoya, who was lurking at the entrance to the room, stiffen. He talked to Zoya, whose eyebrows rose sky-high. Then he switched back to English. "How you say? This is my lucky day."

Vanna took a step back, but he closed in, invading her space, moving so close she could smell his aftershave. She didn't recognize it. An icicle of fear slid up her spine.

He cupped her chin in his hand, still with that strange, crooked smile. "I think we have fun now. How you say? Kill birds with stone?"

"Kill two birds with one stone," Vanna murmured.

"Yes." Vlad paused. "We see how good a cop sister is." He grinned as if he was very pleased with himself. "Zoya. Go into kitchen. Get paper. Pencil. We plan."

Vanna shivered. Her bravado vanished. Something was off. Really off.

Vlad turned back to her with a cold smile, one that, curiously, reminded her of her mother in one of her moods. Then the smile vanished, and he gazed at her with barely disguised contempt. "You now gonna be my favorite girl."

Zoya came back into the room with paper and pen.

Vlad motioned to Vanna. "Bring her to me in an hour."

Chapter 77

When Georgia was still a cop, her boyfriend, Matt, a detective on the force, had come home with one of the strangest stories she'd ever heard. He and his partner, Mike Green, now happily retired and fishing in Wisconsin, were running down a burglary ring at Northbrook Court, an upscale mall on the North Shore. The targets included jewelry and high-end apparel stores as well as a wildly successful electronics store. They were sure it was an inside job—apparently the thieves had keys to the stores—but they didn't have enough evidence. They'd been brainstorming how to proceed when Green had an idea.

A few hours later Matt found himself with Green in front of a modest ranch house tucked away on a nondescript residential Northbrook street.

"Why are we here?" Matt had asked.

"You'll see," Green replied.

Green rang the doorbell. The woman who opened the door was middle-aged and plump and wore enough jewelry on her wrists, fingers, and ears that she jangled when she moved. Her eyes narrowed when she saw them. Matt had the feeling she knew they were police.

"You have appointment?" she said in a thick Slavic accent.

Mike Green nodded. "Tell him it's Mikhail."

The woman turned toward a door on one side of the hall and opened it. Matt could see a flight of stairs. He heard her jangle as she took the steps down.

"What's going on?" Matt said quietly.

Green put his finger to his lips.

The woman returned, beckoned them inside, and closed the front door. Then she threw an imperious wave toward the open door. "You go down."

They did. She closed that door too. Matt, halfway down the steps, promptly let his hand stray toward his holster, but Mike shook his head. "You're not gonna need it."

Georgia interrupted Matt at that point. "What the hell was going on? Where were you?"

"We had entered the throne room of one of the most powerful Mafiya leaders in Chicago."

"The what?"

"The throne room," Matt said. "You remember in the *Godfather*, how on the day of his daughter's wedding, Marlon Brando received people who wanted favors in his office?"

Georgia nodded. "Right. He wasn't supposed to say no because it was his daughter's wedding. I always thought that was just Hollywood bullshit."

"Not really," Matt said. "This guy saw people in his basement. They called it the throne room. And it kind of looked like one. He sat at one end in a La-Z-Boy recliner, and there were chairs and things set up theater-style in front of him, like he was the pope granting an audience. That's where he did business."

"And you were there because..."

"We needed a favor."

"Huh?"

"We told him we knew he wasn't behind the burglaries, and—"

"Wait a minute. How did you know that?"

Matt grinned. "We didn't. But Mike played to his ego."

Georgia raised her eyebrows.

"He said he was sure the guy wouldn't have been involved in such an amateur job. That the people who ripped off the stores didn't even have the brains to fence the stuff in Milwaukee or Minneapolis. That we'd already found a lot of the goods in Chicago. And that it was just a matter of time before we got to the source."

"Was any of that true?"

"Of course not."

"But he believed you?"

"Not a word," Matt went on.

Georgia scowled. "I don't get it."

"He knew what we were saying and why we were there. It was a kind of code."

"In what way?"

"He knew we were getting heat from the village and the mall developers and the chain stores inside the mall. We needed an arrest," Matt said.

"You told him that?"

"We didn't have to. He reads the papers. Or someone read them to him. He knew."

"So what happened?"

"He gave up the guys who did the job."

"So it *was* him who did the job?"

"Probably."

"And you let him skate?"

"He was clearly in charge. The boss. Maybe the boss of bosses. The burglaries were penny ante stuff. He knew we needed him to scratch our back, and we all knew we'd have to scratch his somewhere down the road."

Georgia felt a chill. She knew there was a thin line between lawmakers and lawbreakers, but she'd never thought that applied to the people she worked with every day.

"But...," she'd stammered, searching for something to say, "I thought the Russians weren't that well organized, you know, not like the Outfit."

"They've had twenty years to learn," Matt said. "Anyway, the guy told us he'd done his good deed for the decade...and not to come back."

"Did you?"

"Nope. And of course, his lead was good. We cracked the case."

Now Georgia ran her hand up and down her arm. She got up from her desk and went to the window. Another frigid night, the moonless sky threatening to close in and swallow everything on the ground.

After telling her the story, Matt had sworn her to secrecy, and she'd respected that. She hadn't thought about it at all.

Until this morning.

Chapter 78

She knew the man in the Beemer last night. Knew him well, in fact—he'd been her last case as a cop. She was investigating the murder of a woman captured on a video surveillance tape. The tape had been brought to her by Ellie Foreman. It wasn't a snuff film, but it might as well have been. They learned that the victim had been in the clutches of a former lieutenant in the Soviet military. After the USSR collapsed, he sold weapons off a base in Soviet Georgia. When that dried up, he emigrated to the States and ran hookers, drugs, and small arms deals. Eventually he partnered with a prominent Chicago developer, Max Gordon.

His name was Vlad. No last name. Just Vlad. Now, ten years later, he apparently had resurfaced. Running a hooker ring, a baby farm, and an organ transplant business.

Georgia threw off the blankets, got out of bed, and brewed a pot of coffee. She couldn't take Vlad by herself. He and his men would be well armed and itching for combat. She might be able to get inside, deal with one or two of them, but she would need reinforcements on the way out.

She didn't want to go to the police—it still wasn't a solid case for them—too many maybes and what-ifs and too little evidence. If they did decide to get involved, they'd screw it up. Cops were not known for their delicacy. They'd storm the farm with massive firepower; if she was there, Savannah would be caught in the crossfire. She didn't want to get Jimmy involved, either. Whatever happened would complicate their relationship, assuming they still had a chance for one. She needed outside help. Powerful help.

The coffeepot beeped. She poured a mug, drank half, then showered and dressed. While she was blow-drying her hair, the notion took shape. It was crazy. Even subversive. But it was a way to fight fire with fire.

She stared at the phone. Matt was trying to put his life back together, and she'd promised herself she wouldn't exploit their relationship. Then she thought of the times he'd exploited her for one thing or another. Of course, she'd let him. She'd hoped that would make him love her more.

She took in a breath. She wasn't sure if it was a good idea, but her options were limited, and she couldn't waste time. She punched in Matt's number.

Chapter 79

It was noon when she pulled up to the house in Northbrook. A modest redbrick ranch house with a couple of pin oaks in front, their branches now skeletal and scrawny, the place wasn't showy, and it seemed to fit in with the other homes on the block. Matt was already there, his engine idling. She slid out of the Toyota and walked over.

A dirty leaden overcast hung low, and the February day was bitter. Matt rolled down the window.

"Thanks, Matt. I appreciate this."

He nodded. They hadn't seen each other in months, but neither offered the normal pleasantries. "Unless you tell him the whole truth, you know, it's gonna blow up in your face," he said.

Matt wasn't a big man, but he was powerfully built. And wiry. With curly dark hair and almond-shaped eyes that were almost feminine, he still made her catch her breath. He wasn't wearing his glasses today. Georgia felt a pang. Glasses gentled him, even gave him a sensitive air, unusual for a former cop.

He seemed to know she was appraising him and smiled. That broke the spell. She'd been outed. The case of nerves that had been roiling her gut since she called him returned. "You're coming in with me, aren't you?"

"I have to. He won't see you otherwise. Actually, to be fair, he might not see us at all. We'll have to get past his bodyguards."

She nodded.

"One more thing," he added. "If we do get in, don't laugh."

She frowned.

"As I recall, some of—I guess—what you'd call his furnishings are pretty strange. But for God's sake, when you see them, don't crack a smile. You're in the throne room."

Puzzled, Georgia frowned. Together, they walked up three concrete steps to a small porch. Matt pressed the bell.

A woman who was probably in her sixties but trying for forty opened the door. Wearing an expensive-looking warm-up suit, with perfectly coiffed hair and manicured nails, she had a face on which work had definitely been done. The woman stared at Matt, and a moment later recognition lit her face. This woman was sharp.

"You remember me." Matt sounded surprised.

The woman dipped her head from side to side: maybe yes, maybe no. Georgia fidgeted. She hated the way some people made that casual gesture in response to a question or comment, as if the answer was ultimately unknowable or not that important to begin with.

Without saying a word the woman stepped back from the door. Behind her were two brawny men, not even bothering to hide their pistols. She nodded to the men and pointed her index finger. She turned away, opened a door, and thumped downstairs.

One of the men growled. "Hands up."

Matt raised his arms. Georgia followed suit. Each of the men frisked them thoroughly. Then the second man grunted. Georgia lowered her arms.

"It's the same woman," Matt said quietly. "It's got to have been ten years since I saw her."

"I got it."

"I guess it doesn't hurt to be married to a woman with a photographic memory."

Georgia wondered if that was somehow directed at her. She didn't have a photographic memory. Then she stopped. She was falling into the same pattern she used to when she was with Matt. Wanting to measure up. Wondering if everything he said was an indirect allusion to her. She shifted again.

The woman came back up and nodded to the guards. One of them opened the door wider. Georgia walked into a stifling house, the heat way too high for February. A few feet away was the open door. The woman gestured toward it.

"You go down."

Georgia tried to flash the small group a polite smile, but the woman had already turned away.

As soon she descended the steps, Georgia realized she was in a foreign place. The staircase itself was ordinary, its walls paneled in a dark woody color. But the floor of the main room, which stretched the length of the house, was covered with thick shag carpeting. No one had shag carpeting now. It was a cocoa brown, not that different from the paneling covering the walls. The dark, bearish color screamed "man cave."

As if to complete the surroundings, she spotted a huge Rottweiler at the far end of the room. His brown markings matched the rug and walls. He raised his head, scrutinized Matt and Georgia, sniffed, then lowered it again. Had it not been for a series of track lights on the ceiling that cast a glare over everything, the room would have been gloomy and claustrophobic, and with the dog, even dangerous. And to make it even more threatening, two additional bodyguards hovered at the other end of the room.

But the most bizarre aspects of the man cave hung on the walls, and she soon figured out what Matt had meant earlier. The walls were an homage to singer-songwriter Barry Manilow. A framed autographed poster of Manilow hung on one section of paneling, a framed collection of concert tickets on another. A leather jacket encased in a plastic or glass case hung on another wall, accompanied by an eight-by-ten black-and-white photograph of the singer in, presumably, the same jacket. More photos festooned the other walls, some with Manilow's arm around an elderly man with thick white hair. Georgia bit her lip to avoid a grin. The only section of wall that wasn't a tribute to the singer was filled with an ornate gold crucifix.

Under the crucifix sat a La-Z-Boy recliner, upholstered in brown leather, with two chairs in front. Reclining in the chair was a big man with a shock of white hair that rivaled Boris Yeltsin's. Like his wife, he wore an expensive-looking warm-up suit, but his bulged in all the wrong places. The man in the Manilow photos.

He appeared to be a benevolent grandfather until you looked at his hands. Rough and calloused, with stubby fingers, those hands told Georgia he could, and probably did, do all manner of things. At the moment they were folded in his lap, and he was watching Matt and Georgia with sharp eyes that belied his casual pose. Indeed, his presence was so powerful it seemed to blot out the rest of the room. Even the Barry Manilow displays faded into the background. Georgia understood why they called it the throne room.

He pointed an index finger at Matt.

"My wife says you back," he said in a gravelly and thickly accented voice.

"She has a good memory."

"I tell you not to."

"You did. But I'm not here for me. And I'm not a cop anymore."

He shifted his gaze to Georgia. "You cop?"

She shook her head.

"So why you here?"

Matt gestured toward Georgia. She took a breath. The basement smelled of dog, boiled cabbage, and sweat.

She got to the point. "I think a gang from your part of the world is running a baby ring, trafficking women to get them pregnant and then adopting the babies out."

Chapter 80

The Russian mobster's eyes narrowed. She could hear the bodyguards shift behind her. "Why you care? Not your *beezniss*." Business.

Georgia gestured to the chair. "May I?"

He shrugged. Georgia figured she had about a minute before he threw them out. Or worse.

She and Matt sat in the chairs in front of the recliner. They weren't much more than folding chairs, rigid and uncomfortable. Purposely, of course. Make the supplicant uneasy.

"So who run this ring?" the man asked.

Georgia glanced at Matt, then back at him. Was she being played? He had to know. Carefully, she said, "That's why we're here. I think it's someone you know."

The man raised his hands, palms up. "You think I tell if I do?"

Georgia nodded. "I do."

He canted his head. "Why I tell you?"

"Because I think he's cutting into your turf. Again. And you want him out of the way."

Her comment elicited an intense look. He narrowed his eyes. "Go on."

Georgia told him about the man who'd been gunned down in Evanston a few weeks earlier. "I kept wondering why it was so public. You know, when you guys don't get along, bodies turn up in ditches. Or the lake. But this was right out in the open. On an Evanston street.

"After a while I wondered if the guy who was killed was informing for you. That you were running a double?"

"Who you think running this gang?"

She hesitated. Then, "Vlad."

He blinked and folded his arms. She could sense the bodyguards behind her go on alert. Even the dog picked up his head.

She was on the right track.

"How you know?"

"I saw him." She told him about the Capron farm. "Look—uh—sir—" She didn't know what to call him. Neither Matt nor he had told her his name. But his features softened almost imperceptibly at her words. She took it as a good omen. "If I've been able to piece together this much, the cops will too, at some point, and they'll be coming after you, even if you're not involved."

The softness vanished, and a suspicious glare came over him. "And you will make *sure* they know."

She raised her palms, mimicking the same gesture he'd made just a moment ago. Two could play this game. She heard Matt's sharp intake of breath. She wasn't sure where her courage was coming from, but she barreled on.

"At the very least there will be a mountain of shit thrown your way. And"—she hesitated—"my sister is mixed up with them."

He leaned forward. "You sister?"

She nodded and explained the note that had been stuffed in her mailbox, the DNA test she'd done. "She's pregnant, and she needs my help. I want to get her out. And I'm pretty sure the man who delivered the note was the guy gunned down in Evanston."

Boris—she decided to call him that, at least to herself—lifted his eyebrows.

"So you go in with *heem*"—he yanked a thumb at Matt—"and get her out."

"He's not involved. It's just me. That's why I'm here. I need backup. But I don't want to involve the cops."

His eyebrows arched higher.

"They'd screw it up. Everyone will end up dead. Including my sister."

He deigned to give her a slight nod.

"But I can deliver Vlad to you. And if *you* or your *krysha* get involved, you'll be able to take him out. Consolidate your turf. Maybe even add to your lines of business."

Boris leaned back, grabbed the handle at the base of the recliner, and pushed it forward until he was sitting upright. Suddenly, he was three feet closer, almost on top of Georgia. She swallowed. If he was trying to intimidate her, he was succeeding. She heard the bodyguards moved closer.

"No baby ring," he said firmly. "No is steady *beezniss*. Babies is problems. Need to put up women. They cannot work. No drugs. Is too much—how you say—out of pocket. Plus the women, they go crazy. They want escape. Even keep babies. No. Not good *beezniss*."

It was Georgia's turn to raise her eyebrows. He knew a lot more than he had let on. Was he already getting a cut? She couldn't ask; he'd never admit it. She had to use her final card.

"I haven't told you everything," she said slowly. "Whoever is running it has an extra business on the side." She told him about the human transplant organs.

He was quiet. Then he inclined his head, his expression flat. "How you know?"

She shrugged, but his knowing expression indicated she might have given him too much. If Boris was involved in the ring, or knew who was, he might realize what a threat she posed to the operation. She would leave this room a marked woman. She wouldn't know when or how, but they would come for her.

No. She wouldn't—she couldn't—live that way, no matter what the consequences. She figured she had one final shot. She

decided to go for broke. "So, sir, or whatever you call yourself.
What proof do I have that you're not part of it?"

He leaned forward in the recliner and stared at her. Shit. She'd
blown it. He was going to destroy her. Maybe shoot her right here
and now. She held her breath. She sensed Matt doing the same.
He must have been shitting his pants.

But then Boris did something totally unexpected. He cracked
a smile. "Because you still alive."

She let his words roll over her, then let out a breath. He was
right. She chose her next words carefully. "Does that mean you
are not in league with Vlad?"

Boris templed his fingers. "What you think?" Always a strate-
gic move to answer a question with a question.

She glanced at Matt. He nodded. "I think he's a monster. At
least he was ten years ago when I dealt with him."

Surprise spread across Boris's face. "What happen ten years
ago?"

"You remember when his network fell apart? When Max Gordon was taken down?"

Boris nodded.

"That was me. And another person."

"You?" He frowned as if he couldn't—or wouldn't—believe
her. Then he shook his head. "I help finance. I lose much money."
He waved a dismissive hand. "Banks. Skyscraper. Is all fake. I
never trust him."

"I watched Vlad kill his wife. Then jump into the Chicago
River. He went back to the Ukraine."

Boris nodded. "I hear he back."

"He is." Georgia was telling him something he already knew.
"I saw him."

The man's shoulders hunched as if he was about to sigh. "You
know, of course, he is worse kind of bad. He play with people. Like
cat with mouse before it pounce."

Georgia nodded. "He may be setting me up." She explained
how she'd been able to find the warehouse, Chad Coe, Zoya, and

Claudia Nyquist. "He's letting me get close to my sister. I'm good, but not that good. He's setting a trap. He wants revenge."

Boris kept his mouth shut.

"Just tell me one thing. The man he gunned down in Evanston—he *was* your man, wasn't he? Vlad was sending you a message. Toying with you, too. Or trying to, right?"

Boris kept his mouth shut, but a calculating, measuring look came over him.

"Look, I want my sister alive. And we both want this bastard gone," she said. "I can bring you to him. But I need help."

He didn't answer.

"Hey, I risked everything to come here. I've told you what I know. Please. Give me *something*."

He gestured to the Manilow jacket on the wall. "Is bad timing. I go show in Vegas. He like my son, you know. I know him for years."

Georgia glanced over her shoulder at the jacket, then at the crucifix. "Then you know what a crime against nature it is to kill a young woman."

Boris shifted uncomfortably.

"Here's what I propose," she went on. "I will set a time for your men to meet me out at the farm. It will probably be within the next twenty-four hours. I'll call you—or one of your *krysha*, if you're at—out of town." She just couldn't say the words "at a Barry Manilow concert."

"I'll wait for an hour; then I'll go in. If they don't hear from me within a few minutes, it means I got in trouble. The likelihood is I'll be dead, but I don't matter. I want your men to get my sister out alive." She paused. "Then do what you want to Vlad."

"An eye for an eye," Boris said.

"A sister for a sister."

Boris didn't say anything for what seemed like forever. Georgia wondered what he was thinking. Finally, he said, "Here is number you call. When you ready."

She nodded and handed him a card with her number. "Just

in case you need it." She leaned back in her chair. "So does that mean we have a deal?"

Boris smiled enigmatically. "Maybe yes. Maybe no."

She gritted her teeth. She'd have to be satisfied with that.

Chapter 81

"Holy shit. You were amazing! We could have been killed!" Matt said. They had stopped at Max's, a popular deli on the North Shore, famous for its kosher-style-but-not-really-kosher food. "I couldn't believe your—um—balls."

"That's me. Balls of steel," Georgia said.

He grinned.

She smiled back. "Honestly, I was shaking in my shoes. At one point I thought he was gonna off me right then and there." She scanned the menu, which was a tall multipage laminated book. "I hate these things. There are way too many choices. How can you possibly decide?" Georgia went on. "I couldn't believe the Barry Manilow shit. Was that for real?"

"A hundred percent. In fact, it's worse since I was there. He's obsessed."

"How did it start?"

"No idea." He paused. "Wishful thinking?"

That brought a giggle from Georgia. It felt good to laugh with Matt. It had been years. In fact the entire day so far had been almost surreal: her reunion with Matt, the visit to the Russian Mafiya boss, now lunch at Max's. She was about to tell him when the waitress, a middle-aged woman in black pants and white shirt, brought over a bread basket and a bowl of sliced pickles.

"So what'll it be, kids?" the waitress said in a tired voice.

Georgia ordered matzoh-ball soup. Matt ordered a corned beef sandwich. She wanted to tell him Benny's were better but resisted.

After they ordered, Georgia picked up a slice of pickle. "I couldn't figure out how well he knows Vlad." She bit into the pickle. "A guy like him has to know pretty much everyone in the—uh—community, don't you think?"

Matt's tone was sober. "They all know each other. And you're right not to trust him. They're bad people. Even him."

"I get it."

"Were you bullshitting back there?"

"What are you talking about?"

"That stuff about the Russian mob guy killing his wife."

She leaned back. A flicker of annoyance shot through her. "Not at all. Happened down near the old Sun-Times building."

"How did you get involved?"

"You remember Ellie Foreman?"

Matt frowned. "Video producer, right?"

Georgia nodded. "Someone sent her a videotape of a woman being murdered. She turned it over to us. Former Superintendent Olson let me work the case. I found out the vic had been in his clutches." She took another slice of pickle. "The asshole was into all sorts of shit. Running hookers, drugs, small arms deals. Then he got involved with a Realtor."

Matt's features hardened.

"Don't worry. It wasn't Stuart Feldman." She heard the edge in her voice. She and Matt had broken up after he fell in love with Feldman's daughter, Ricki.

"Damn! Where was I?"

Georgia hesitated just a beat. It was always about him, she thought. Aloud she said, "Who knows? Israel probably."

"Ahh." He picked up a bialy, slathered it with butter, and bit into it. "So what happened to him? Where'd he go?"

"They dragged the river but never found a body. I heard he went back to the Ukraine to nurse his wounds."

Matt chewed his bread. Georgia picked up another slice of pickle. The waitress brought Georgia's soup and made a big deal of putting it down. Georgia was aware of Matt watching and smiling as she wolfed down the pickle. They were her favorites. Did he remember?

"A lot can happen in a few years, Georgia," he said.

She got the sense he wasn't just talking about the Russian Mafiya. She looked over. Gray hairs were threaded through the black curly waves she knew so well. Still. She steered the conversation back to Boris.

"So do you think he'll back me?"

Matt considered it. "Depends on how he analyzes the situation. But I do know one thing."

"What's that?"

"You made an impression. I don't think a woman has ever talked to him like that." He cleared his throat. "You made an impression on me, too."

Chapter 82

"You've changed."

She stiffened. "People do." She needed to change the subject. She didn't want to deal with what she suspected was coming. "By the way, you ever hear of a doctor named Richard Lotwin? Used to be a surgeon. Maybe he still is."

Matt shook his head.

"He was accused of malpractice. Twice. Both times at Newfield. Maybe ten years ago."

He frowned. "Wait...I think I did hear something about that. Wasn't he dumped from the hospital?"

"Right."

"Why? I mean, why do you want to know?"

"It's something I've been working on."

"Something to do with this?"

She stopped talking then, and spooned soup into her mouth. The waitress brought Matt's sandwich and gave them a peculiar look, as if she wasn't sure what their relationship was. Georgia returned the look. The woman retreated.

Matt picked up half of his sandwich. He looked Georgia up and down, then put the sandwich back on his plate. "I was wrong, you know."

Georgia let a beat of silence go by. "About what?"

"You never told me the way you felt. I never knew where I stood."

That was a crock of shit, she thought. They had been lovers. They'd lived together almost a year. He was supposed to know how she felt.

"You always kept things bottled up," he added.

What was he doing? Trying to rewrite history? He had dumped her for Ricki Feldman. It had nothing to do with communication.

Or did it? Even if it did, what did it matter? It was yesterday's news. If it made him feel better to think she was at fault, so be it. She knew the truth. She started to open her mouth to say something to that effect when an image of Jimmy floated into her mind. Communication skills. Jimmy. She hadn't called him back.

Damn Matt. He had a point.

She put the spoon down. "I—I was dealing with all sorts of things."

"Like whether you wanted to be a cop."

She nodded. "And a Jew."

"I should have known when you started taking conversion lessons," Matt said.

"It never occurred to me I'd have to spell it out."

"I was an asshole."

"Yes, you were." She waved her spoon. "But that's in the past."

He looked at her, his face wide open. "What are you saying?"

Georgia couldn't believe what came out of her mouth next. "I think you're right. We should have communicated better. I should have told you how much I loved you. We were both at fault." Another powerful vision of Jimmy strafed her brain. The two of them in her bed. At the pancake house. At the movie. Then Jimmy embracing Saucy Hat.

"Are you saying there might be another chance for us?" Matt reached for her hand.

She pulled it back and let the silence grow. It was okay with Matt. Comfortable. Familiar. But none of the old sirens wailed.

Her skin didn't tingle. It was over. Really over. All she could think about now was Jimmy. She knew what she had to do. "Hey, thanks." She smiled.

"For what?" He looked lost.

"For coming today. And for lunch. I need to go."

"Right now?" He motioned to her soup. "You hardly touched it."

"Take it home for dinner." She grabbed her coat, flung it on, and hurried out to the parking lot. A frigid wind had kicked up, and her fingers ached with the cold. Still, once inside the Toyota, she made herself dig for her cell and punched in Jimmy's number.

He picked up right away. "Georgia?" He sounded relieved, happy, and pissed off, all at the same time. "Are you all right? God! I've been so worried. I must have left a dozen messages."

"I know. I'm fine. I—I'm sorry for not calling you back. It was—well—I was...hey, do you have a minute?"

"Of course."

"Who was that woman you put your arms around two nights ago outside the restaurant, around six? The one with the"—she couldn't say the word "saucy"—"hat?"

"What are you talking about?"

"Wednesday." It was Friday now. "I drove out to a farmhouse in Capron. Then I drove to Lake Geneva, hoping to catch you. It was snowing, remember? And I saw you go inside the restaurant with another woman. You were—pretty cozy."

He hesitated. It was the longest minute Georgia could remember. Then,

"Oh. Her. Marianna is my cousin. I've known her all my life. She just lost her husband. A sudden heart attack. No warning. He was barely fifty. I was trying to comfort her." He paused again. "Why the hell didn't you come in?" Then he answered his question. "Oh."

Georgia swallowed. "I should have, Jimmy. I was wrong. We—no—I need to communicate better. I'm not real good at it. I don't trust easily. But I want to try."

"We both will."

He was letting her off the hook. Her heart melted.

"Um, where are you now?" he asked.

"In my car."

"Have any plans for the rest of the day? And night?" She felt his smile through the phone.

"I do now," she said.

Chapter 83

A narrow band of sunlight crawled across Georgia's bed the next morning on its way toward Jimmy's cheek. When it reached his eyes, he'd wake up. Meanwhile Georgia watched and listened. His slow, even breaths mingled with the sounds of a Saturday morning: the slam of a door, the catch of a car engine, the whoop from one of the kids across the street. A profound contentment spread through her. She was where she was supposed to be. She pulled the sheet up to cover her body; the morning chill was taking its toll. The rustling couldn't have been much more than a whisper, but when she looked back at Jimmy, his eyes were open.

"Good morning." He smiled and reached for her. She let herself be folded into his arms. He tightened his hold. She let out a breath. His hands moved up and down her back, lightly stroking her skin. She closed her eyes and concentrated on every sensation.

Over coffee and croissants at the coffee shop in Evanston, Georgia debated whether to tell him about Boris, the farm, and her plans. If she did, he'd go all cop on her again. He'd hook up with the Boone County Sheriff, the Harvard police, maybe bring in his own men. They'd take over. She couldn't chance it. Then again, Jimmy would find out soon enough when the cops announced they had Nyquist, Coe, and Lotwin. He would be pissed she hadn't trusted him enough to confide in—no—"communicate" with him.

She was between a rock and a hard place. If she told him, her part in the operation would be over; if she didn't and he found out, their relationship would be over. She winced. Either way, she was aware that this one was on her. She was still keeping secrets, precisely what she'd just promised not to do.

Jimmy bit into his croissant. "What's wrong? You look like you've lost your best friend."

She brushed her fingers across his cheek. "I want you to know something."

"What's that?"

"I never thought I could feel this way about a man. Thank you."

He finished chewing. "Shouldn't that be cause for celebration?"

She tried to smile brightly. "I hope so."

"Assuming I feel the same way."

She felt a rush of heat on her face. "I didn't say it to trap you. Or make you say something you don't want to."

His eyes crinkled up at the corners, and he flashed her a grin. "Don't you think I know that? You're the least devious, Machiavellian person I know."

She kept her mouth shut.

He glanced at his watch. "I need to get going. I'm working today."

She nodded.

He stood up, leaned over, kissed her.

"We'll continue this conversation tonight. You want to drive up?"

Chapter 84

Later that afternoon Georgia stocked up with as much gear as she could think of: a thermos filled with coffee, another jug in which to pee, a Maglite, a ski mask that covered her nose and cheeks, sandwiches, boots with rubber soles, and of course, her baby Glock. She loaded an extra magazine and stowed it in the glove compartment, made sure her cell was charged, and brought the charger. She strapped a .22 to her ankle and wedged it into her left boot. It wasn't the most original place for a throw-down, but like a good scout, she wanted to be prepared.

At the farm she parked in the same place as before and prepared to wait. To pass the time she reviewed what she knew. Chad Coe had visited a surgeon. Then he showed up at the home of a Glencoe man who needed a kidney transplant. Then he'd driven to the Evanston apartment where Claudia Nyquist lived. Nyquist later confessed she was helping him traffic organs. Then Chad Coe had gone up to the salon where Zoya worked. Zoya had led her here.

Yes, it was mostly circumstantial. There was always the chance she had it wrong. And there was one missing piece. Vlad needed a place to harvest the organs. He couldn't use a real hospital—way too risky. Same with the EmergenC clinics that had sprung up since health care deregulation. A private clinic or hospital would be best.

She remembered a cosmetic surgeon's office on the North Shore, right on Green Bay Road in Kenilworth. Privately owned, it boasted an operating room, recovery suite, even patient rooms. In fact, it was a small hospital, intended for nose jobs and breast augmentation. Still, as far as she could tell, it had the same equipment as a surgical OR. It made her wonder if the farm was the site for a similar place. There had been some kind of structure behind the guard's car when she'd staked out the other night.

She checked her cell. No texts or messages. She downed some coffee from the thermos. Its smell was better than the taste. She took a few bites of a ham sandwich. As dry as sawdust.

Finally it was twilight, then dark. Georgia took a few breaths to center herself and slipped her Glock in her shoulder holster. She grabbed her cell and climbed out of the Toyota.

Chapter 85

Georgia trudged through the stand of trees between the Toyota and the driveway. The snow beneath her boots crunched. Some had melted in the past two days and seeped into the dirt, leaving patches of bare ground that gave off a fresh, earthy scent. Although it was still February cold, the smell reminded her that spring would be coming.

She wanted to snap on her Maglite but couldn't risk it. She listened to the silence instead. She thought she might have heard a faint whisper. Was it a TV inside the farmhouse? One of the guards? Or just the night breeze?

She edged around the last of the trees but stayed half-hidden among the bare branches. A shabby barn stood about a hundred feet from the house, partially surrounded by trees and brush. This was the structure she'd seen the other night. A window was cut into the side closest to her. She needed to look into that window. A dim spotlight mounted on the side of the barn angled in her direction, but the throw of light was too weak to penetrate the tight weave of the branches where she stood.

Two cars were parked beside the barn. One was Zoya's red sedan. The other was a dark-colored SUV. The same vehicle from two nights earlier. And now that she had time study it, she realized the van could be the SUV used in the Evanston drive-by.

She squinted, trying to pick out the plate—she remembered it started with 633. But the SUV was parked at an odd angle, and she couldn't make it out. She was about to head over for a closer look when two men on foot emerged from the gloom. The guards. She shrank back into the trees.

They approached from the far side of the barn. One had a flashlight pointed at the ground, but it wasn't powerful, and she couldn't make out either man's features. They talked in low tones. They circled around the front of the barn and disappeared.

She waited. Ten minutes later, they came around again, but this time they closed in on the SUV and climbed inside. The dome light snapped on, and she saw them pass a bottle back and forth. Perversely, that gave her hope. If they spent the night loaded on vodka, maybe they'd fall asleep and she would have a chance.

Half an hour later the men were still in the car. Georgia's feet and fingers had gone numb, and despite the ski mask, her nose was runny. She had to retreat to the Toyota. She was halfway through the copse of trees when the doors to the SUV slid open again, and the men got out. Their conversation was louder now, and punctuated with broad laughs. They made another circuit of the barn, stumbling occasionally, their boots tramping the under-brush. This time, though, instead of going to the SUV, they headed toward the house. A door slammed.

She waited another ten minutes. The sky began to spit a cold, stinging rain, not cold enough for sleet but strong enough to hamper visibility. Only crazies would be out in this. Good. She needed every edge.

Slowly she crept past the cars to the barn. She was about a foot away from it—and the window—when a second set of lights suddenly flickered on, brighter and more powerful than the first. She froze. Her heart thumped in her chest. Had she been made? She stood absolutely still, a rabbit caught in the glare of light. But there was no alarm. No shouts. No movement. The lights must be connected to a motion sensor. Shit. She should get back to her car. They must have noticed the light.

But she was so close. All she needed was a quick peek through the window. A few seconds. Then she would leave. She closed in. The window was covered with something on the inside: brown paper maybe. Or a canvas drop cloth. She was catching no breaks tonight. Then she looked more closely. One corner of the covering had drooped or the paper had torn, leaving a tiny portion of bare window. The glare from the lights made it difficult to tell. She shaded her eyes and squinted.

And sucked in a breath. Followed by a triumphant exhalation. Although the window was grimy and streaked, she could clearly see the gleam of metal. And several pieces of equipment, including a gurney, different colored tanks for gas and oxygen, an assortment of instruments. In the center of the area was a table. A light fixture hung over it. Thick drapes cordoned off the sides. She was looking at an operating suite. A place where Dr. Lotwin delivered babies, killed their mothers, and then harvested their organs.

She hurriedly fished out her cell and took a few pictures. She'd found what she was looking for. She tapped her phone app. She'd programmed in the number of the Russian mob guy she and Matt had visited. Time to call in the cavalry. She'd told Boris they should give her an hour—it would take them at least that long to get here. If they came at all. Not ideal, but it was the only insurance policy she had.

She tapped on "Boris" and was waiting for a connection when she felt it. The spitting rain was cold, but the barrel of the gun against her neck was colder.

Chapter 86

Savannah—One Month Earlier

Vanna was pregnant. She'd never been pregnant before, but, like her mother used to say, "Sure as eggs is eggs," she knew. She hadn't seen her period for more than two months, and the cramps that always preceded it never materialized. Her boobs were bigger, too, and tender. She wasn't showing, at least yet, but she would be. Soon.

When Vanna told her, Jenny, already five months pregnant, said, "How could you be? You've been here. You haven't been doing tricks."

The girls were kept in separate but adjacent rooms at the farm. They'd discovered a vent in each of their rooms at roughly the same location. If they lay down beside them, they could communicate.

"Keep it down," Vanna said in a whisper.

"But how did it happen?" Jenny's voice grew quieter.

"Vlad. He checked me out a couple of months ago. Made me parade in front of him downstairs in hooker clothes. He's been coming out here a few times a week."

Jenny's voice went flat. "So it *is* you."

"What are you talking about?"

"The guards said Vlad had a new girl. But they weren't sure who it was. I should have known."

"I didn't ask for it," Vanna said.

"Yeah, I know." But there was a judgmental quality in Jenny's voice, as if Vanna could have done something about it if she wanted. "Enjoy it while it lasts."

"What are you saying?"

"He's had all of us."

"You're kidding." Vanna couldn't help feeling deflated.

"Yup." Was there just a hint of "I told you so" triumph in Jenny's voice? "And now I'm pregnant."

"But that was—while we were on the junk, wasn't it?"

"Yeah. And now he ignores me. Like I was the one who fucked up. Even though they were the ones who put us on the shit."

"How come you never told me?"

"I thought you knew. I thought he was fucking you too. And now"—Jenny's voice caught—"he is."

Vanna kept her mouth shut. Vlad had come out to see her just two days ago. In fact, she was getting used to him. He could be cruel; then again, there were times he was quite sweet. At least to her. One night after they fucked, she thanked him for getting her off the dope.

He nodded. "No one should be on that poison."

She curled up next to him, something he rarely allowed. "When you're on it, you don't think it's bad."

He actually put his arm around her.

She snuggled closer. "Anyway...," she said, "now I know you care."

When he bought her a pair of earrings for Christmas, dangly things that sparkled in the light, she was sure of it. She was different from the other girls. She and Vlad had something special.

Now Jenny interrupted her thoughts. "This isn't good, Vanna. When we were downtown, there were rumors. The girls—when they get pregnant—a lot of them disappear. And never come back."

"What do you mean?"

"Just that. After they go into labor, they're gone."

"What do you think happens to them?"

"What do *you* think?" Jenny whispered.

Vanna swallowed. "No. I don't believe it. He probably just sells them to other pimps."

"But what if he doesn't?"

Vanna hesitated. "It—it makes no sense."

It was Jenny's turn to be quiet.

"And," Vanna added, a chill running through her, "it would mean we're next."

Chapter 87

Savannah

That night Vanna couldn't sleep. At one point she heard the crunch of cars on snow and gravel. She'd heard them before, but her room was on the other side of the house and she'd never actually seen the cars or the people in them. She only knew they hadn't come into the house. Once she thought she heard a woman cry out, but when she asked, Zoya said she must have been dreaming.

Then there was the barn. All the time she'd been at the farm, no one had allowed her near it. She'd tried. One of the guards, Sergei, was almost human. He nodded when he saw her; even smiled once or twice. She begged him to let her go for a walk, and he consented, but, of course, he went with her. Anytime she ventured in the direction of the barn, he steered her away. Which, of course, made her more curious.

Now she wondered if the cars arriving at night and the barn were connected to what Jenny had told her. She didn't see how. She wasn't even sure Jenny was telling the truth. Girls who got pregnant, and there did seem to be a lot of them—four or five in the time she'd been at the farm—were probably given abortions, then sold.

If she'd learned one thing about sex trafficking, it was that there was always a supply of new girls. Fresh off the bus, duped into thinking they were going to be nannies, actresses, or models. Once snared by assholes like Lazlo, they were sold into trafficking, then hooked on heroin so they couldn't buy their way out. Except for the ones who got pregnant. Like her, they were forced into withdrawal. But Jenny had a point. She never saw any of the pregnant women once they delivered.

If that was true, though, why was Vlad coming out here three times a week to have sex with her? And why was he fucking other girls, many of whom, according to Jenny, got pregnant as well? It made no sense. And yet, if it *was* true, she and Jenny were sitting ducks.

She didn't want to leave. For the first time since she'd come to Chicago, for the first time since her father died, in fact, she'd found a sort of security. Sure it was crazy to think that being trafficked was stable. But Vlad had rescued her from the worst of it, and she didn't have much to do except wait for his next visit. She wasn't stupid enough to call it love, but it was *something*. He came to see her regularly, they had sex, they talked. She liked that part—the talking—best of all. They were getting to know each other.

But now Jenny was saying that it wasn't real. That they were in danger. A tiny voice nagged Vanna and said Jenny was right. Vlad wasn't her father, and the voice said he couldn't be trusted. She would be smart to put some distance between herself and the farm.

Reluctantly, she and Jenny hatched a hasty plan. The next night they waited until it was late. Zoya allowed them to keep emery boards in their rooms, and they managed to tear them into pieces and wedge them into the back plate so that the door locks didn't completely catch. They piled on as much clothing as they could, which wasn't much since they no longer had boots, coats, or hats, and crept down the stairs. They sneaked out of the house and even made it partway down the driveway before a pair of bright lights kicked on and the guards soon overpowered them. After they threw them back in their rooms, Vanna heard Zoya on the phone.

Chapter 88

Savannah

The next morning Vanna was driven to a warehouse somewhere in the bowels of Chicago. Eight girls were already there, and the place was filled with camp cots, sleeping bags, makeup, and trash. Like in the apartment she and Jenny had been kept in before she'd gone to the farm, a clothing rack held all sorts of hooker clothes that, presumably, were shared. The women ate only one meal a day, usually sandwiches from a nearby deli. Most of the girls didn't speak English, but they chattered incessantly, so much that Vanna had a persistent headache. The only peace she got was when they were out hooking. For some reason she was no longer sent on booty calls. She spent the entire day inside the cramped quarters of the warehouse.

The only consolation was that Sergei had come with her. She tried not to think how low she'd sunk to consider a Russian goon her ally; it was clear he was supposed to keep an eye on her. But she smiled when he brushed by, and when they were the only ones in the warehouse, he would perch on the edge of her cot. He didn't speak much English, nor she Russian, but they were able to communicate through pigeon English, pantomime, and gestures.

Sergei, Vanna learned, was not only a guard, but also Vlad's part-time chauffeur. She asked him where Vlad was; she hadn't seen him since they'd brought her here, and that was nearly a week ago. Was her "relationship" with him—she wasn't sure what else to call it—over? Or was Vlad punishing her because she tried to escape? Did he know she was pregnant?

Sergei shrugged. "I not know. No ask."

Vanna pursed her lips. "Am I going to be here forever?"

He shrugged again, implying, at least to Vanna, that she was better off not knowing.

Chapter 89

Savannah

A week later the cold was so bitter that the space heater's red coils seemed like a bad joke. It was about ten at night and all the girls were out. Vanna was huddled on her cot in sweats and a blanket that Sergei had managed to rustle up. It was ironic—if she'd still been turning tricks, she wouldn't be cold. She was hungry, too, and about to ransack everyone's belongings for a candy bar or cookies when a car pulled up outside.

The door slammed, and a man came in through the back. She recognized the burly bull of a man: one of Vlad's bodyguards. He took a look around but gave no sign he recognized Vanna. Then he went back out. Another car door opened and closed, and a moment later, Vlad strolled in. Vanna's pulse sped up—she couldn't help it—and a kernel of hope took root. Was he here to take her back? Forgive her? She scrambled off the bed and started toward him.

The look on his face made her halt midstride. No crooked smile tonight. No enthusiasm, not even a glint of desire. His expression was blank. Vanna took a step back and ran one hand, then the other, up and down her arms. She couldn't remember ever feeling this cold.

"They say you try to run." His voice was as neutral and flat as his face. But that, she'd learned, was Vlad at his most dangerous. He was sizing up his prey. Making adjustments. Soon he would strike. "After how I treat you, Vanna?"

She hung her head, hoping a sign of submission would win him over.

He reached his hand out toward her. She cringed, expecting him to slap her—or worse. But all he did was finger one of her earrings.

She couldn't meet his eyes. When he'd given the earrings to her, he'd ordered her to wear them all the time. She did. Now she waited for him to tear them off her ears, waited for the excruciating pain and blood and bits of skin that would follow. Instead he dropped his hand.

"Look at me."

Slowly she raised her head. His eyes were chunks of ice. There was no anger in them, but no forgiveness, either. She could have been a chair or table as far as he was concerned. She swallowed. Rage she could deal with. Lust, too. But this—this glacial emptiness—terrified her, and her composure evaporated. His presence sucked out her teenage arrogance, cynicism, and know-it-all attitude, as if he'd run a huge vacuum cleaner over her psyche. The only thing left was fear, and an overwhelming desire to make it go away. Maybe if she tried to please him, tried hard, she could regain her position as Vlad's chosen.

She tried to muster some of her flirty ways, but they wouldn't come. Instead the words slipped out. "I'm sorry."

"I could kill you," he murmured after a long pause. "No one would know. No one would care."

Maybe he should. That would solve her problems. What did she have to live for if he didn't want her anymore?

"You like that, wouldn't you?"

She jerked her head up. Was he reading her mind?

He closed in. This time she was sure he would strike her. She squeezed her eyes shut. Her mother had predicted it. Her teachers, too. She would come to no good. She was just a two-bit junkie whore who gave boys blow jobs in their cars. She deserved whatever was coming.

But Vlad's punch didn't come. She felt him cup her chin in his hand. She opened her eyes. He was staring at her, his eyes narrowed, as if he was trying to figure something out. Finally, a tiny crooked smile curled his lip.

"But I no kill you."

She swallowed, unsure whether the wave of emotion rolling through her was relief or regret.

"You pregnant."

Again, she was taken aback. How did he know? "Does—does that make you happy?"

Another crooked smile. Then he turned and called out to Sergei, who appeared from the depths of the warehouse. Vlad spoke in Russian. Sergei stole a glance at Vanna, disappeared, then returned with a cardboard box, which he handed to Vlad.

Vlad tossed it to Vanna. She didn't catch it fast enough, and it fell to the floor. "You know what to do."

She bent down and picked up the box. A pregnancy test kit. Of course he could tell she was pregnant. If he'd impregnated as many girls as Jenny claimed, he would know the signs. And if he didn't, Zoya would.

He waved a hand toward the bathroom. "You bring back stick."

Five minutes later she emerged from the bathroom, clutching the white plastic strip with a pink cross on one end, indicating a positive result. She passed it to him. He examined it, then nodded. "This is gut."

She tried out a smile. "Yes. It is. I'm having your baby." She hugged herself, pretending to be happy. "Can you forgive me, Vlad? I'll never leave you again, I promise. I just want to have our baby. Together." She wondered how many other girls had said the same thing. Would it make any difference?

Vlad looked around. She followed his gaze. No one had

cleaned up the warehouse. The blankets on the cots were messy and crumpled; clothes and toiletries were scattered; trash littered the floor. But Vlad's expression was absorbed. He wasn't registering the scene. He was planning something, working things through.

Finally he turned back. "You want back to farm?"

She nodded. "More than anything in the world."

He walked over to a small mound of trash on the floor and picked up a crumpled sandwich wrapper from the deli. He held the edge of it between his fingertips, as if it was contaminated by dangerous microbes, and backtracked to Vanna.

"You do this, I take you back."

"Anything." She smiled in a way she hoped was both seductive and submissive.

"Take." He dangled the wrapper in front of her.

Chapter 90

Savannah

"Sergei," Vlad called. "Bring pen."

Again Sergei materialized out of the gloom with a ballpoint pen, which he gave to Vanna.

Vlad motioned toward her cot. "Sit."

She sat with the wrapper and pen.

"Make this good English." Then he told her what he wanted her to say.

Her smile lost some of its wattage. "I can't do that."

"You do." The icy look was back.

Vanna bit her lip. "But—but she's my sister."

"And I am father of baby."

"I don't want to see her." *Not now. Not like this*, Vanna thought.

"You no do? If not, easy to fix."

She would be dead before morning. Along with the baby. She squeezed her eyes shut. She didn't want to die after all. "Okay. Okay. I'm sorry. I'll do it."

Despite the cold, she was sweating. She wrote on the wrapper.

"Make English good."

"I will. I am."

Georgia, I am your half sister, Savannah. I'm in Chicago and I'm pregnant. I need your help. Please find me.

When she was done, she handed it back. "Why do you want her to find me?"

"Not your business."

Her stomach knotted. "Why? Do you know her?"

"I say not your business."

She blinked rapidly. She'd taken it as far as she could. She'd have to try another tack.

"We not finished," Vlad said.

"What do you mean?" She felt the knot tighten.

"Sergei. Envelope."

Sergei passed her a white envelope, which Vlad made her address. Georgia lived in someplace called Evanston. On Wilder Street. She didn't know where Evanston was but figured it had to be close. She wondered if there was any way she could warn her sister. Vlad cut off her thoughts.

"Now give me hand."

Vanna cocked her head. "Why?"

Vlad reached into his pants pocket and pulled out a knife. It looked like a Swiss Army knife, but thinner and sharper. Savannah gasped. She'd done what he needed. Now he was going to kill her. The blood left her head in a rush.

"Give me hand," he said in a businesslike tone.

She tried to slip it into the pocket of her sweatpants. He was going to cut it off.

"Now." He motioned.

There was nothing she could do. She extended her palm and looked away. Whatever was going to happen would be now. She felt a prick on the tip of her index finger. She turned back to gaze at her hand. A drop of blood oozed out. She stared at the blood, wondering what the hell he was doing. Then Vlad took the sandwich wrapper and rolled her finger across a corner of the wrapper until it was smeared with her blood. He handed it to her.

"Fold and put in envelope," he ordered.

Vanna slipped the wrapper inside.

"Now lick closed."

She did.

Vlad took the envelope, gave it to Sergei, and issued orders in Russian. Sergei nodded.

Without another word Vlad turned around and left the warehouse as suddenly as he'd come.

Chapter 91

Savannah

Once Vlad left the warehouse, Savannah's anxiety bubbled to the surface. Something was very wrong. Vlad knew Georgia. She didn't know how, but she knew her sister was in danger. And it was her fault. She had to do something. She pulled her gaze from the door Vlad had gone through and rubbed a hand down one arm. As she did, an idea came to her.

She continued to briskly rub her hands up and down her arms. "I'm fucking freezing," she said to Sergei. "Can I borrow your coat?"

Sergei flashed her a puzzled look.

"Your coat." She pointed to his coat and pantomimed draping it around her shoulders. Sergei hesitated, uncertainty flooding his face.

"Please. I'm so cold."

Finally he nodded. He took off his jacket and passed it to Savannah. She put it on and flashed him a brilliant smile. "Thank you so much."

She went back to the camp bed. She couldn't do it right away. She had to wait. She stretched her arms, yawned theatrically, and lay down, curling up on her side. Sergei looked as if he approved.

Why not? With her asleep, he could relax his guard. She pretended to be sleepy and closed her eyes, all the while mentally counting seconds. When she got to three hundred, she rolled to the other side, As she did, she furtively slipped a hand into the front pocket of his jacket. Where he kept his cell.

Her fingers brushed something metallic. It was there! She closed her fingers around it, trying hard not to let her triumph show. She counted to three hundred again. Then she slowly got up, swung her legs over the bed, and stood.

"Bathroom," she said when Sergei also rose from his chair.

He nodded.

She headed to the bathroom. Sergei didn't go with her, but he followed her with his eyes. She went in and closed the door. Her heart banged in her chest. She fished out the cell, sat down on the toilet, and dialed 4-1-1, timing her pee so that it trickled out at the same time the recorded voice came on the line. When it was time for her to speak, she flushed the toilet and whispered.

"Georgia Davis. Evanston. Wilder Street."

"One moment."

Savannah impatiently pressed the phone against her ear. *Hurry up.* Finally, when the recorded voice told her she could be connected at no additional charge, she pressed the button. She couldn't believe it. She was actually going to talk to her sister. For a fleeting moment, a burst of pure joy skipped up her spine.

Georgia's line rang. At the same time, Sergei banged on the door.

"Give back, bitch."

She kept her mouth shut.

"Hello?" a woman's voice said on the other end.

"Savannah, now."

She heard her sister's voice. "Hello? Is anyone there?" And then, "Sam, is that you?"

"No, I won't!" Savannah said.

The door to the bathroom swung open, and Sergei stormed in. He bent over her and snatched the phone away.

"No!" she yelled.

Sergei raised the phone to his ear. Savannah could hear her sister.

"Sam, are you there?"

Savannah had no way to reply.

Sergei broke the connection.

Chapter 92

Savannah

Savannah was relieved when Jenny called through the vent the next morning. At least *she* was still there.

"Where were you?" Jenny whispered. "I was so worried."

Vanna told her about the week in the warehouse and how Vlad had made her write a note to her sister.

"Why would he do that? Does he know her?"

"Apparently. I tried to call her." She explained how she'd "borrowed" Sergei's phone but it hadn't worked. "I still need to warn her."

"About what? You have no idea what he's up to."

"I know that, but somehow I need to tell her not to come looking for me."

"But you just wrote a note asking her to do just that."

Vanna let out an impatient breath. "Jenny, it's a trap. Vlad *wants* her to come looking for me."

"Why?"

Vanna wondered how another human being could be so dense. "I just told you I have no idea." She paused. "Maybe Sergei knows."

"Sergei...the guard?"

"He was my watcher at the warehouse. He may know what Vlad's planning. Maybe he could warn her for me."

"Oh sure." Jenny voice was laced with sarcasm. "He'll definitely go out of his way for you. Especially after you tried to rip off his cell."

"Other than that, he's been nice to me."

"I'm sure he has. But Vlad pays him a lot of money to guard us. How are *you* going to pay?"

"I'll let him do whatever he wants," Vanna said after a beat.

"I don't know about that." Jenny went quiet. Then she changed the subject as if she didn't want to know any more. "Speaking of plans, something happened while you were gone."

"What?"

"There's a new girl."

"Here?"

"Yes."

"Pregnant?"

"About to deliver."

"Is she a blond?"

"Of course."

"Shit. What's with him and all the blond girls?"

"I don't know," Jenny said.

"Maybe he thinks he can charge a higher price for babies that have blond mothers. Or something like that. Have you talked to her?"

"Not yet. Her English isn't so good. But she speaks Russian. She and Zoya were talking."

"Well now, that's interesting."

"Why?"

Vanna felt another flash of irritation. Jenny should have been able to figure it out. It meant that Vlad's business was growing so fast he was now recruiting girls from overseas as well as the US. But more important, it meant this girl could listen in on what Zoya and the guards said to each other. She could eavesdrop on Zoya's end of a phone conversation, too. And if she could translate what she heard, a bunch of new possibilities had just turned up.

* * *

Later that day Vanna managed to get Sergei to take her for a walk. It was a mild day for February, and the ground was so soggy from melting snow that clumps of mud stuck to her gym shoes. She didn't care; she'd found the shoes in her closet and they were two sizes too big. As they made their way past the barn, she let out a breath and asked if he'd warn Georgia for her.

"I don't have money to pay you. But you and I can have our own private party afterward." She flashed him what she hoped was a seductive smile.

His eyes narrowed. He gazed at her with a frown on his face. Then he shook his head. "Too danger. If Vlad find out, I am dead."

"Not if no one tells him. I won't. Neither will you."

"He find out."

"How?"

Sergei shrugged. "He has ways. He check cell sometime."

A wave of guilt rolled over her. With her luck, he'd check Sergei's phone today. Sergei didn't deserve Vlad's wrath. No one did. "I'm sorry for using your phone." She paused. "But, if he finds out, I'll take the blame. I'm probably going to die anyway."

Sergei eyed her without speaking.

"Look, I don't care. It's too late for me. But my sister—she has a life. I don't want her to come into contact with Vlad. It's too dangerous. You know that."

Still no answer. They walked to the edge of a stand of trees and turned around.

"Have you delivered the letter yet?"

"Today."

She clapped her hands. "That's perfect. Go ahead and deliver it, but then hang around and tell her to ignore the whole thing."

He looked doubtful, which, perversely, filled Vanna with hope. It meant he was considering it.

"And don't forget what we're gonna do afterward," she purred.

Sergei didn't say anything, but he stopped walking. "I have daughter. In Ukraine."

Vanna stopped too. "Then you know how important it is to protect her. All I'm asking is that you help me save my sister."

"And if Vlad's men follow?"

"Vlad trusts you. You're his driver."

He rolled his eyes, as if that was meaningless in the great scheme of things. Then he started back toward the house. "I make no promise."

The thought occurred to her that he might be setting her up. That he might double-cross her, run to Vlad, and tell him what she wanted. But she had played her last card. She just had to pray he wouldn't. She touched his arm and pulled it toward her. "Will you at least try?"

He shrugged.

"You know where Wilder Street is?"

Chapter 93

Savannah

Two days passed before Vanna and Jenny found themselves in the kitchen at the same time as the new girl, whose name was Ivona. Sergei hadn't come back to the farm, and a new guard with greasy hair and a full beard was on duty when Zoya was away. He smelled like he hadn't showered in months, and Vanna didn't want to think about what could be trapped in his beard or under his fingernails. He stationed himself with his back to the door and scowled at them.

Vanna tried to ignore him. She was worried about Sergei. Sometimes he did disappear for a few days doing errands for Vlad. She convinced herself that's what was he was doing and concentrated on Ivona.

The girl had brown eyes and limp, straw-like hair that hung to her shoulders. Except for her belly, she was waiflike and pale. Her teeth were yellow and crooked—she could have used an orthodontist. But that would be a luxury for a Russian immigrant.

She tried to draw the girl out, using the same combination of pigeon English and gestures she'd used with Sergei, but Ivona wouldn't make eye contact and sat hunched over, as if she was folding into herself, trying to disappear.

"When are you due?" Vanna asked. She shot a glance toward the guard. He stared back, his expression hard and flat. She'd assumed he didn't understand English; now she wasn't sure.

"Nothing." Ivona said only the one word, but her Slavic accent was heavy.

Vanna shook her head. "When does baby come?" Vanna patted her own belly.

Ivona looked up. "Soon."

"Vlad?" Vanna asked.

Ivona nodded.

Vanna felt a stab of anguish. Another girl impregnated by Vlad. Jenny was right. She, Vanna, was just another girl who had been knocked up. Nobody special. But then, why had he treated her like she was? Had she imagined it? She fingered her earrings.

"Where are you from?" Vanna asked.

"Latvia," Ivona answered without looking up.

"How long are you here?"

"My cousin come Northbrook. He meet Vlad. Vlad say to tell me I get big job here. Make much money."

"So when did you come?"

"One year."

Vanna gave her a cheerless nod. Another soul who thought the streets of America were paved with gold.

Now Ivona looked up. "How long you?"

"About six months."

"But you American. Her too." She motioned to Jenny.

"So what?" Jenny said. "We're all in the same boat."

Ivona frowned. "Boat? What boat?"

"She means situation," Vanna explained.

"Maybe, maybe no."

"What does that mean?" Jenny asked.

"Maybe you okay."

"What do you mean 'okay'? How could we be?'"

Ivona gazed long and hard at Jenny. "You know."

"Know what? What are you talking about?"

The guard started toward them. Zoya didn't like the girls talking among themselves, and she must have told him to break up any conversation that lasted more than a few seconds. Ivona spoke sharply to him in Russian. The guard stopped. She held up her palm and wiggled her fingers.

"Stupid peasant," Ivona said. "I say we talk nail polish."

"Ivona," Vanna said impatiently. "Tell us what you mean by 'okay.'"

Ivona lay her hand down on the table. She gazed at Vanna with an expression that said she had nothing left to live for. Then she heaved a sigh. "I tell." She paused and stole a glance at the guard. "Before here I in apartment. Girl start to have baby. They take away. She not back."

Vanna remembered they were supposed to be talking about nail polish. She spread her hands like Ivona. "Maybe they adopted out the baby and put the girl back on the street. That's what they do. It's their *beezniss*," she said mimicking a Russian accent.

The guard jerked up his head. Vanna bit her lip. That was a mistake.

Ivona shook her head so forcefully her pale hair flew around her face. She tapped her lips. "No. I speak Russian. Guards talk."

"About the girl?"

"About all."

"What about them?"

Ivona leaned toward them. Her voice dropped to a whisper.

The smelly guard scowled and took a step forward. Vanna guessed they had only a few seconds before he forced them back to their rooms.

"The babies adopt. But the mothers...they kill. Then sell parts. To hospitals."

Jenny blanched. "What? That's crazy. How do you know?"

Ivona pointed to her ear. "They say can get lots money for heart or liver, so they sell. And kill mother."

Jenny clapped a hand over her mouth.

"That can't be true," Vanna spit out. "You're lying."

Ivona threw Vanna a patronizing look just as the guard hurried over. He forced them to stand, marched Ivona upstairs, and slammed the door. Then he did the same to Vanna and Jenny.

Chapter 94

Savannah

Three nights later, sometime after midnight, Ivona started screaming so loudly that Vanna awoke from a deep sleep. She hurried to her door and twisted the knob. But the door remained locked, and she no longer had a nail file to pick the lock. Ivona's screams intensified and were interspersed with curse words in both English and Russian. She was in labor.

Finally, she heard the thud of feet on the stairs, and Zoya's voice, speaking urgently to someone. The smelly guard, probably. Metallic clinks followed as someone fumbled with the key. The door squeaked open, and Zoya shouted in Russian. Ivona yelled back and the two of them went at it, back and forth. Then Zoya thumped back out into the hall. She started muttering. Vanna leaned her ear against the door. Zoya was making a call on her cell, she thought. But with Ivona's screams and the guard, who was now yelling as well, it was hard to be sure.

A few minutes later Zoya's voice could be heard, now calm and quiet, talking to the guard. Vanna heard a grunt—the guard? Footsteps shuffled. Ivona's screams reached a fevered pitch, but they seemed rent with something new. Despair, Vanna thought, and deep sorrow. Vanna heard the guard hustle Ivona down the stairs and out the door, but her cries reverberated through the house. Where were they taking her? For a moment there was a lull. Then Vanna heard another blood-curdling shriek, followed by heavy silence.

Chapter 95

Savannah

The next morning Vanna called to Jenny through the vent. There was no reply.

"Jenny?" Vanna raised her voice. "You awake?"

Still no answer.

Goose bumps spread up and down her arms, and her skin crawled with fear. "Jenny?"

Was she still asleep? Or down in the kitchen? Usually they were taken downstairs together. She lay in her bed, worrying a hand through her hair until she heard a tread on the stairs.

Someone knocked on the door. "Get up," the voice said harshly. Vanna's stomach flipped. Whoever it was spoke English without an accent.

She threw on sweats. A new guard unlocked the door and entered. Shaved head, not too tall, but barrel-chested and built like an eighteen-wheeler. He wore jeans, a sweatshirt, and a holster with a gun belted around his waist.

"Who are you?" Vanna asked.

"Your worst nightmare."

"But where is—"

"Shut up. Or you'll end up like your friend."

What was he talking about?

"Downstairs." He pulled out his gun and aimed it at her. "And remember this is loaded."

Vanna made her way down the stairs. Something was very wrong. No one had ever pointed a gun at her. Where was Jenny? Where was Sergei, for that matter?

In the kitchen Zoya was on her cell. The smelly guard was by the door, but the new guard stayed only inches away, invading her personal space.

"Sit," he ordered.

She did.

Zoya disconnected and stared hard at Vanna. "What you know?"

Vanna was confused. "About what?"

"Jinny," Zoya said, pronouncing the e like an i. "I know you talk through vent. What she say?"

"Nothing." Vanna looked around, her fear rising. "Where is she?"

Zoya's lips pressed into a grim, tight line. "What she say you last night?"

"Nothing." Panic skipped up Vanna's spine. "What happened?"

The new guard and Zoya exchanged glances. Zoya threw him a nod, and he spoke. "Your friend managed to escape last night during the—when the other girl was screaming."

Vanna's eyes went wide. "Jenny?" She didn't think Jenny had it in her to run. Especially by herself.

"Yeah, well, she didn't make it far."

Vanna froze.

"We eventually found her on 173 near Harvard. Let's just say..." He hesitated. "...she won't be coming back."

Chapter 96

Savannah

Before they locked her in her room again, Vanna heard on the radio that the body of a young blond pregnant girl had been found on Route 173. She'd been stabbed multiple times. Vanna's stomach pitched, and she ran to the bathroom to vomit. When she returned, the announcer reported that police were still investigating another murder a few days earlier in Evanston. That time it was an Eastern European man, gunned down from an SUV in a drive-by. One look at the new guard, defiant yet proud, was all it took. Sergei was dead.

No one cared whether she lived or died. Not Vlad. Not Zoya. Not her mother. Not the half sister she didn't know but hoped would somehow rescue her. All she had was the memory of a loving father, and he was dead. She was alone. Nobody's child. Her life wasn't worth a sheet of used toilet paper. The first time she'd heard the expression, she thought it was just the cynicism of an acne-scarred kid she went to high school with. She knew better now.

Chapter 97

The two guards hustled Georgia into the farmhouse. They
stripped off her coat, her fisherman's sweater, and her
boots. They found her cell phone and her baby Glock right
away, as well as the throw-down in her ankle holster. Georgia
tried to concentrate on her surroundings, looking for a way to
escape, but she was now wearing just a tank top, jeans, and socks,
which were soaked through. Although the kitchen was warm, its
heat seemed to mock how cold she was, and she couldn't stop
shivering.

The men cuffed her hands behind her back, tied her to a
kitchen chair, and stuffed a gag in her mouth. Then they con-
gratulated themselves with shots of vodka. They talked in Russian, but one rubbed the back of his hand across his mouth and
laughed, all the while throwing lewd grins at Georgia. The other, a
dopey smile on his face, thumped his glass on the table whenever
he wanted another shot. Georgia didn't need a translator.

Someone with a heavy tread thumped down the stairs.

"*Chto proishodit?*" a sandpapery voice called out. Georgia knew
that voice. The guards quieted, and a moment later Zoya came
into the kitchen. When she spotted Georgia, she halted midstep.
At least Georgia had the satisfaction of seeing the woman's jaw
drop.

"You!" Zoya's eyes narrowed to slits.

Georgia didn't answer. The guards exchanged worried glances. Evidently they were afraid of the woman.

Zoya folded her arms, and her expression went flat. She stared at Georgia for a long moment. Then she said in clear English, "Put in dead girl's room."

Georgia flinched. Had that been Savannah's room?

* * *

Great PI she was, Georgia thought after they dragged her upstairs, threw her into a bedroom, and locked the door. Unspeakable things were happening in this place, and she was powerless to do anything about them. She hadn't seen her sister and had no reason to think she was at the farmhouse. Savannah could be anywhere: downtown, uptown, in the suburbs, in a ditch. She had no way of knowing if her call to the Russians went through, either. It was possible the cavalry wouldn't come. She had screwed up. She wouldn't make it out alive.

It was late, but a silver moon threw luminous stripes across the room. Bars hugged the windows, and the double lock on the door was out of reach, since her hands were cuffed. The guards had, however, taken the gag out of her mouth, believing, apparently, that she wasn't the type to scream. They were right. At first she thought she might be able to work the cuffs off, but she couldn't, and even if she could, she had nothing to help her pick the lock.

She lay on the bed on her side and let out a dejected sigh. She must have dozed off, because the moonlight was weaker and the stripes had disappeared when she opened her eyes. A quiet hiss was coming from across the room. Was it the heat flowing through a vent? She squeezed her eyes shut to focus. The hissing stopped. Then it started again, and she realized that was what woke her. She rolled toward the sound. The bedsprings squeaked.

The hissing stopped abruptly, and a tiny voice whispered. "Hey, is anyone there?"

Instantly alert, Georgia bolted from the bed. The words were coming from the corner, nearly at floor level. She tiptoed over, found a vent, and squatted next to it.

"Who's there?" she whispered back.

"Who are you?" the voice whispered.

No cat-and-mouse game here. "I'm Georgia Davis."

"Oh my God. I'm Savannah."

Chapter 98

"You're alive!" Georgia breathed. "Are you hurt? How long have you been here?"

Savannah giggled through the vent. At least Georgia thought it was a giggle. "I can't believe it! Is it really you?"

"It is." Georgia felt her throat get thick. She blinked rapidly. "Tell me everything."

Savannah breathed in through her nose, and Georgia realized what she'd thought was a giggle was actually a sob. "It won't do any good."

"Don't say that." Georgia felt her eyes fill. She wished she could wipe her eyes with her sleeve but her hands were tied. "Tell me what you look like."

"I don't know. I guess I'm pretty. Blond. Blue eyes. But I'm too thin."

"I wish I could see you. How old are you?"

"Almost sixteen."

"How long have you been in Chicago?"

"Since last March."

"Where did you come from?"

"Denver."

"I never knew about you, you know."

"I just found out about you, too. Mom told me."

Long-buried memories surfaced for Georgia. Her mother holding her hand in the supermarket. Taking her to school on her first day of kindergarten. Watching her rip open Christmas presents. And then the long days and nights after she'd gone and Georgia waited for her to come back. She wanted to ask Savannah what her mother was like, but now wasn't the time. "Why'd you leave?"

Savannah hesitated. "Long story."

"We've got time."

Savannah explained how she'd run away, how she'd ended up in Chicago, how she'd met Lazlo, which led to trafficking and heroin, which led to Vlad. Then she stopped. "Wait. Why are you here? Didn't Sergei warn you?"

Surprised, Georgia sat back on her haunches. "About what? I got your note a while ago. I've been looking for you ever since."

"But I told you not to."

Georgia frowned. "No, you told me to find you. That you were pregnant and you needed me."

"Oh fuck. I told Sergei to tell you to ignore it. He forced me to write it. I— "

"Sergei?"

"No. Vlad."

"You know Vlad?"

"Of course I know Vlad. I'm pregnant with his baby. He and I—hey, wait. How do you know Vlad?"

"Hold on. Are you saying that Vlad forced you to write me that note?"

"Yes. Exactly. It was a trap. I even tried to call you. But the guard snatched the phone away."

The call she'd gotten while she was investigating the flash rob. It hadn't been a butt dial. She frowned, remembering something else. "But your DNA was on the napkin. I had it tested."

"He pricked my finger and made me smear it on the wrapper. He knew you'd do that. He's been trying to reel you in."

Georgia remembered Boris talking about Vlad playing cat and mouse. Leaving bread crumbs to trap his prey.

"The next day I begged Sergei to set you straight. Instead he was killed. Vlad must have found out I'd sent him and had him killed." Vanna let out a strangled sob. "Oh fuck. Now he's going to kill me, too."

"Stop. Sergei's murder wasn't your fault, Savannah. Sergei was a double. A stoolie. He was working for someone else in the Russian mob. One of Vlad's enemies. Vlad killed him to send that guy a message."

"How do you know that?"

"I've been trying to find you for a few weeks. In the process, I've discovered a lot of things."

"How did you know it was Vlad?'

"I saw him in a car two nights ago." She ran her tongue around her lips. There was one piece of the puzzle she still didn't understand. "But how did *he* figure out you were my sister?"

Savannah hesitated. "It was my fault," she said. "When I first met him, I bragged. I told him you'd get me out of here."

"You told him my name?"

Her voice cracked. "I—I told him I had a sister here and he asked your name. Then..." This time her voice broke. "...he asked if you were a cop."

"What did you say?"

"I said I didn't know. But then I remembered Mom saying *she'd* been married to a cop in Chicago, and I figured...well, it was possible."

A cold weight settled in Georgia's chest. "I was. A cop."

"I thought so. As soon as he heard your name, he began to plan. And then later, when he was fucking me, he started talking all this crazy shit. About dangling bait on a hook. Figuring out how to get you to come to him." She was sobbing now. "I'm sorry, Georgia."

With a rush of comprehension, the scale of it all became clear to Georgia. She'd told Boris she suspected she'd been played. She had. Set up from the beginning. Everything she'd done or discov-ered about Zoya, Chad Coe, Lotwin, and the baby-breeding and organ businesses had been orchestrated by him. The DNA, the note, Claudia Nyquist, too. It was an elaborate trap set by a vin-dictive thug. The irony was that against all odds, it had worked. Her jaw clenched.

She was about to ask Savannah more when someone with leather soles on their boots clattered up the stairs. Seconds later a key twisted the doorknob of her room.

Chapter 99

Georgia threw herself back on the bed just as the door flew open. A man she hadn't seen before was silhouetted in the doorway. He gazed around with suspicion, as if he thought she'd been up to something but wasn't sure what. Then in perfect English, he said, "Vlad is on the way. He wants to see you."

"Will you please uncuff me? I'm harmless."

The man hesitated, then shook his head. "Only if he says so."

She wanted to ask the guy if he always did exactly what Vlad said but thought better of it. He seemed like the type who'd tell Vlad she was trying to drive a wedge between them. Which, of course, she was.

He closed the door and relocked it, then banged on Savannah's door with the same message. His boots clomped as he went back down the stairs.

An assortment of emotions roiled Georgia: relief, joy, a sense of achievement that she'd found her sister. But they were tempered by mounting apprehension. How was she going to get them out of here? She had nothing to work with. The man she was up against had every advantage.

She went back to the vent.

"Savannah?"

"Yeah?" Her sister sounded desolate.

"Tell me something," Georgia asked. "You're sure Vlad is the father of your baby?"

It took her a moment to answer. "Yes," Savannah breathed. "He fucks all the girls. I thought I was special. And I was. For a while." She paused. "Georgia, are you a blonde?"

"Yeah. Why?"

Her sister sucked in a breath. "Never mind."

Georgia sat back. Vlad was impregnating girls, sowing his seed, creating tiny beings who might be adopted and whose mothers were later murdered for their parts. What kind of monster runs such an evil three-ring circus? What kind of person harbors such deep hatred? Was Savannah going to be killed after she delivered? She had to come up with something to save them both.

Savannah cut into her thoughts. "What are we going to do?"

Her voice was small and desperate. She was waiting for Georgia to take the lead. To be the big sister. To save her. But how?

"Tell me about the layout downstairs."

"Well, you already saw the kitchen and the stairs. If you cross the hall instead of going up, there's a living room. Vlad put track lights in there for inspections."

"Inspections?"

"When he gets a new girl, he makes them parade around the room while he decides which ones he's going to fuck and which he pimps out." She hesitated. "I was his girl longer than anyone else."

Georgia frowned. "You sound like you're proud of it."

"He wasn't all bad. He got me off dope. And had a doctor examine me."

Georgia jerked her head up. "A doctor?"

"He took my blood. To make sure I didn't have an STD. Or AIDS."

And figure out what your blood type is, Georgia thought.

"Vlad gave me a pair of earrings for Christmas," Savannah went on. "And you know, sometimes I used to catch him staring at me. I was never sure whether he wanted to hurt me or love me. But then he would break into that strange smile of his and make a joke. Or throw himself on top of me and make love."

"Make love? Are you kidding?"

"It wasn't always just sex."

Sure, Georgia thought. Her sister had a case of Stockholm syndrome. "Except that he impregnates whoever he wants and kills them afterward."

"You know about that?"

"Yes."

"I just found out," Savannah said. "A girl, my friend Jenny, used to have your room. But she couldn't handle it and tried to run away. She"—her voice cracked—"she's dead now."

Georgia put it together. "Was she the girl they found on Route 173 a couple of weeks ago?"

"Yes."

"She was your friend?"

"Yes."

"I'm so sorry, sweet—" Georgia cleared her throat. "So what do you know about Zoya?"

"She works for him. She's around a lot, especially when girls go into labor."

"Is she a midwife?"

"A what?"

"Never mind." Georgia was quiet. Then, "Didn't you used to be at a warehouse in downtown Chicago?"

"Vlad moves us around a lot. Apartments, warehouses, the farm. We're always coming or going."

Of course they were. Vlad had to stay one step ahead of the law as well as the johns, whores, and guys like Bruce Kreisman.

Savannah cut into her thoughts. "Georgia, are you still there?"

"I'm thinking."

"He'll be here in a few minutes. What are we going to do?"

"Can you handle a gun?"

"I—I...no," Savannah said, her voice crestfallen.

"Well, you're in for some on-the-job training. I assume he'll keep us under tight guard. And he'll probably keep my hands cuffed. I'll do my best to think of a diversion, and if it works, you're going to have to find a gun. They took my Glock and my revolver. Do you have any idea where they'd be?"

"They usually keep them in the kitchen."

"Good. If you can find them, go for the revolver. You know, the one that looks like a cap gun. It's smaller and easier to use. All you have to do is aim and squeeze the trigger. Try to shoot your way out, then run like hell. Hitch a ride to the police station and have them call Jimmy Saclarides in Lake Geneva."

"Who's he?"

"A friend. Say the name so I know you know it."

"Jimmy Saclarides."

"Good." But it wasn't good. Not at all. Savannah didn't know it, but you couldn't really call what she'd said a plan. All they had was a wish and a prayer.

* * *

The crunch of tires on snow and gravel signaled Vlad's arrival. A car door slammed.

"Oh fuck. He's here!" Savannah cried. "Shit, shit, shit."

Her sister was losing it. Georgia had to keep it together. Tension tightened her neck and shoulders, but she forced herself to think. They needed to create a diversion so Savannah could look for the gun. But what? Finally, an idea came to her. It wasn't much, but it was better than nothing.

"Savannah, listen to me. I have an idea."

Chapter 100

Minutes later footsteps clattered up the stairs again. By the sound of it, more than one set. Keys jangled, and Georgia's door swung open. A guard she hadn't seen before crooked his finger, and when she rolled off the bed, he grabbed her shoulders and shoved her out the door. In the hall a second guard, the man who spoke perfect English, fumbled a key into Savannah's room. His entry was cut short.

"Fuck you," she yelled. "Don't you dare come in. I'm not ready."

"Well, get ready. Vlad wants you downstairs pronto."

The guard holding Georgia uttered something sharp in Russian. The guard who spoke English rolled his eyes. Georgia's guard pushed Georgia toward the stairs. Her wrists were still cuffed, and she was off balance. She had to focus to keep from falling. When they got to the bottom, the guard turned her away from the kitchen into the living room.

It was a good-sized room with bright track lighting at one end. The rest of the room lay in deep shadow, but she made out a couple of easy chairs with a small table between them. A man filled one of the chairs. The guard pushed her into the lit area. The illumination from the track lights was blinding, and she squinted.

She needed to shade her eyes. The guard released her but stayed a few feet away, his hand on his holster.

Out of the darkness came a male voice in heavily accented English. "Welcome, Georgia Davis."

She kept her mouth shut.

"It is long time." There was a rustle and the man disentangled himself from the chair.

Unlike the other night, he was now in the light. Georgia took a good look. She recognized the high cheekbones, the sharp Slavic features, and the pale blue eyes that glittered like diamonds. His hair was more silver now, but on him it looked good. He was casually dressed in a sweater and leather jacket. He just missed being handsome, but she could see why women were attracted to him. Still, something was off. She tried to figure out what. Was it his flat expression? The smile that didn't reach his eyes? No. Something else.

She turned, mentally calculating how many steps it would take her to get to the kitchen.

"I wait for you long time." Vlad blocked her view by moving in front of her. He crossed his arms.

"I'll bet," Georgia said.

"You and other woman took my life."

He was referring to Ellie Foreman, who was the first to discover that the money Max Gordon had been laundering was Vlad's. And with that Georgia realized what was off. They had ruined his life; he'd barely escaped and had returned to the Ukraine, humiliated and broke. Yet now he was behaving in a restrained, almost pleasant manner, as if they were chatting about the weather, not his undoing. The degree of self-control that required had to be enormous.

"You seem to have survived," Georgia said. "Like a cockroach."

He gestured to the guard in the room with him. "Bring me water."

The guard scurried out and returned with a filled glass from the kitchen.

"Not that," Vlad knocked the glass out of the man's hands. It fell and smashed into pieces, spilling water on the hardwood floor.

The guard jerked back. Georgia winced at the sudden violence.

"Bottle. Bottle water," Vlad seethed. He gazed at the broken shards of glass, ground the heel of his boot, crushing them into smaller bits and pieces. "Pick up. Now."

The guard nodded, bent down, and tried to sweep up the pieces with his hand. Blood oozed from his palm.

"Stop. Stupid. Get bottle."

The guard bolted from the room with the remnants of the glass.

Vlad reverted to the icy calm he'd shown earlier. Georgia pressed her lips together. His unpredictable mood shifts were going to be dangerous.

"Yes. I survive," he said pleasantly. He hadn't reacted to her cockroach remark. It must have sailed over his head. "And now...how do you say in English? Turn around we play?"

"Turnabout is fair play," Georgia said, her voice low.

"Yes. Turn-around is fair play. You see, I not forget."

Georgia remembered Vlad had been a soldier. He could be ruthless, but the men in his unit were devoted to him. His wife, Mika, had said he would rule the world one day. She was only half joking. Georgia decided her only option was to make him lose his cool. If he did, maybe he would make a mistake. She just needed one. A tiny misstep would give her an opening.

"Did you have a nice swim in the river?" she asked.

He smiled lazily, as if he knew what she was trying to do but wouldn't let her bait him. "They say cockroach survive World War Three."

Chapter 101

A pair of heels clacked down the stairs, and Savannah's voice called out. "Vlad, baby? Is that you?"

A second later, Savannah sashayed into the room, followed by her guard. Vlad turned around and gaped. Georgia did too. It was the first time she'd laid eyes on her sister, and her appearance left little to the imagination. She was wearing next to nothing: tiny glittery pasties on her nipples, a pair of slinky black panties, fishnet stockings, and four-inch stiletto heels. Her long blond hair shone in the light, and her makeup had been carefully applied. Her skin, and there was a lot of it on display, was rosy, taut, and smooth.

She was drawn to her sister's face. It was a young face, a face that needed to mature. Still, she was a knockout. Big brown eyes, a tiny nose, a perfect complexion, and full lips that were bowed in just the right way. Despite what she'd gone through, she still wore an eager, hopeful expression, and when she broke into a smile, as she did now, she couldn't have looked more alluring. Georgia understood why Vlad kept coming back to her.

Savannah hurried over and threw her arms around Vlad. "I'm so happy to see you. Where have you been? I've missed you!" She flashed him a brilliant smile. *Too much*, Georgia thought. *Tone it down*. But Savannah pressed her cheek against his, nuzzled his neck, and dropped kisses on him. The second guard, who had come back in the room with a bottle of water, stood by helplessly, apparently unsure what to do.

Vlad shoved her away. "Stop! You pregnant!"

Undeterred, Savannah continued to flash him a dazzling smile. "Yes, and it's your baby! We made it together."

Georgia frowned. It didn't sound like she was faking.

"I do not fuck woman with child. Go. I talk with sister." He took the bottle of water and waved it dismissively in her direction.

"But, Vlad, I want you to come upstairs and make love to me. Just us." Her voice was pleading now. Almost begging. "You love me. I know you do."

"Love? Who can love a whore?"

"That's not true." Savannah stiffened, and her voice grew shrill. "I know you love me. The earrings."

Vlad's expression was steely. "I take them off dead girl."

Savannah's lips tightened into a thin, grim line.

Vlad motioned to the guard, but before he could grab Savannah, she spun around to Georgia. Bitter hostility spread across her face. "It's *your* fault he doesn't want me," she cried. "Why did you come here? I don't want you. No one does." She raised her hand and slapped Georgia across the face.

She'd expected it, but the force of the blow brought tears to Georgia's eyes. She reeled back, her cheek stinging.

Savannah slapped her again. "Get rid of her, Vlad. Now!"

Georgia swayed unsteadily. She would have collapsed, but the guard hurried over to break her fall.

"Take her away." Vlad pointed toward Savannah.

Savannah's guard grabbed her and tried to drag her out of the room, but in a surprising show of force, Savannah struggled.

"No! I hate her. She's the reason you don't want to be with me!"

Vlad set the unopened water bottle on the table and rubbed the back of his neck, as if he wasn't sure what to do. Savannah kept ranting, sounding hysterical now. There was a thin line between acting and real life. Had Savannah crossed it? Finally, Vlad spat out something in Russian, and the guard dragged her sister across the room. Vlad motioned to the stairs.

Georgia's spirits sank. Their chances had been slim to begin with, but she'd hoped the ploy of having Savannah attack Georgia would force him to remove her from the room. Then Savannah would have the chance to find a gun. But the strategy had failed. Georgia's stomach churned. But she had to try.

"You've had a good run, haven't you, Vlad? Women falling all over you, a lucrative operation, lots of money, whores, and drugs. And, of course, babies."

Although Savannah was no longer in the room, they could hear her crying. It sounded like she was in the kitchen. Definitely not upstairs. How had she managed that? Georgia felt a flicker of hope.

Vlad ran one hand up his other arm, stroking himself in a self-conscious way. Only athletes did that, she thought. And narcissists. But the action helped him regain his equilibrium, because when he turned back to Georgia, he smiled. "It is good business."

He was back in control.

She kept going. "Business? Is that what you call a baby-breeding ring where the babies and their mother's organs go to the highest bidder?"

His tongue snaked over his lips. His smile broadened. "You know nothing about my business. People are happy. They get baby. Other people live because of me. I run—how you say—unselfish business. For others."

Georgia wanted to spit. "Sure it is. And I guess that absolves you for killing their mothers and selling their body parts?"

His smile vanished.

Good. She was getting to him. "Well, Vlad? What do you say to that?"

He was quiet. Then, "I lose ten years because of you."

Keep him talking. Something would happen. "You're about to lose a lot more. I know about Chad Coe. And Dr. Lotwin. And the woman at the hospital who scouts transplant organs. They're all being picked up as we speak. How long do you think you have before the cops get here?"

"I let you find out." He shrugged. "And if cops come, my people know what to do. So do I." He shot her a smug look.

Savannah was weeping in earnest now, loud, wracking sobs that knifed through Georgia's heart. Vlad gazed at Georgia with a curious look. It wasn't desire or lust or even hate; it was more like satisfaction—satisfaction that he held the ultimate power. That he could get people to do whatever he wanted whenever he wanted. He was so absorbed in his self-importance that he failed to notice a distant whine whispering through Savannah's cries.

Chapter 102

It was faint, but it sounded like cars approaching. The sounds grew louder and more distinct. Definitely car engines—more than one—closing in on the farmhouse. Now Vlad cocked an ear. Brakes squealed. Car doors slammed. Men's voices shouted. Vlad gestured to the guard holding Georgia.

"Who is here?"

The guard flipped up a hand.

"*Zhopa!*" he hissed. "Go see."

The guard pulled out his gun and hurried into the kitchen. Savannah's cries stopped. Georgia heard the guard shout something in Russian. The screen door squeaked as it was flung open.

Vlad glared at Georgia. "It is cops?"

Georgia shook her head, but she knew who had arrived. The Russians. Her call had gone through. Vlad started toward her, his hand raised as if he was going to hit her. At the same time they heard a commotion in the kitchen. A series of shots rang out. They came from outside, but close enough to cause alarm. A woman shouted in Russian. Zoya.

His arm still raised, Vlad listened. His eyes widened. He pulled out his pistol. "Come!" He shoved Georgia across the living room away from the kitchen, one hand jabbing the pistol into her back. When he reached the other side, he swept aside a pair of drapes with his free hand. Behind them was a patio door. He slid the door open. Georgia shrank back at the rush of frigid air.

"Go," he ordered. "Outside. Now!"

Georgia took a tentative step. A floodlight flicked on. Georgia wheeled around and yelled toward the kitchen. "Do it, Savannah! Now!"

Vlad pushed her through the door, which caused her to stumble and fall into the snow. But before she could use her fall to knock him off balance, he grabbed her arm and yanked her back upright. Then he shoved the barrel of the gun against her temple.

"Vanna!" Vlad called out, his voice tight. "Come back and watch me kill sister."

A grunt came from the kitchen. A rustle and thud followed. What was happening?

Georgia tried to take stock. They were in the backyard of the farmhouse. But the throw of the floodlight was dim, and she couldn't make out how big the yard was. Or whether there was a way out. She began to shiver. She had only seconds before Vlad pulled the trigger.

"Vanna...," Vlad insisted. "This is last chance."

Goddammit, Georgia thought. Where was Savannah? Had she found a gun? Or was she taken down? Why didn't Boris's men come around to the back?

More shouts from the front. A burst of machine-gun fire. The lights inside the house flickered. Then silence. A shout here and there broke through, but then a vast stillness reclaimed the night.

Though the light wasn't the best, Georgia saw patches of red flare on Vlad's face. A bright anger suffused his eyes. Georgia sensed he was waging a fierce internal struggle. Why didn't he pull the trigger? Was he trying to assess the damage? Perversely, that gave her a burst of courage. She hadn't followed his bread crumbs all the way out here just to lose everything. Could she throw him off balance with a jab of her elbow or foot?

Vlad called out in Russian. It was clearly a question, but all she could make out was the word "Zoya." He was asking Zoya what was going on.

There was no answer.

Chapter 103

Georgia fisted her hands, digging her nails into her palms. She was preparing to land a karate kick in his groin when Savannah entered the living room from the kitchen. She'd taken off her heels, but she was still practically naked. Her face was ashen, and her eyes had a glazed sheen. She was clutching a large butcher knife, but she was trembling. She walked toward the patio door.

"Zoya is dead."

Vlad moved Georgia in front of him as a shield. His voice was unsteady. "Good job, Vanna, my love. She was bitch. Give me knife. You right. We together now."

Savannah didn't move.

He thrust his pistol hard into Georgia's temple. "Okay. Then watch. I shoot sister."

Before Savannah could reply, Georgia bent forward, drew her foot up, and smashed it into Vlad's groin. He staggered back. His pistol fired and fell just beyond the pool of light. Georgia checked herself. No wound. The shot had gone wild. She shouted to her sister. "Grab the gun, Savannah!"

But Vanna was still brandishing the knife. She closed the distance between herself and Vlad and tried to thrust the knife in his chest. He twisted away at the last minute, and it only nicked his arm. He lurched forward and snatched the knife from her.

Panic streaked through Georgia. "The gun!" Georgia tried to motion with her chin. "Over there. Shoot him. There are bullets in the chamber." But as she said it, she realized Savannah didn't know what that meant.

Savannah spun around and headed toward the gun. She was fast, but so was Vlad. Brandishing the knife, he reached the spot where the gun had fallen at the same time as Savannah. Savannah fell on top of the gun, but Vlad threw himself on top of her and tried to plunge the knife in her back.

Georgia screamed. "Stop! Kill me instead!"

Suddenly a series of shots rocked the air, sending a stream of sharp, deafening retorts across the yard. Vlad let out a groan. The knife fell from his hand. A pool of blood seeped out beneath Savannah, staining the snow pink. His? Or Savannah's?

Georgia spun around. One of Boris's men stood at the edge of the yard in deep shadow. She couldn't see him clearly, but she could see his assault rifle still aimed at Savannah and Vlad.

She let out a breath.

The man lowered his weapon, dipped his head as if to acknowledge a debt paid, then melted into the darkness.

Georgia hurried over. Neither Vlad nor Savannah moved. She approached with caution. The wounds on Vlad's body—she could see three or four—bled freely. The Russian mob guy was some shot. But what about her sister?

"Savannah. Are you okay? Say something. I need to know that you're alive."

There was no answer.

"Savannah?" Georgia was desperate. "Please. Answer me, baby. Are you okay?"

This time she heard a whimper. "Get him off me," Savannah said. "I can't breathe."

Chapter 104

Five minutes later, thanks to Boris's men, Vlad's body was moved and Georgia's cuffs were off. Savannah couldn't stop shivering, and her teeth chattered; she'd spent the last ten minutes lying practically naked on the snow. Georgia took her upstairs and helped her into dry clothes.

Her sister was unusually passive and gazed at Georgia as if she was a stranger. Shock, Georgia thought. "Savannah, you were a hero out there. You saved my life. Do you get that?"

Savannah didn't answer.

"It's over now, baby. And it's all good." She smiled at her sister and ran a hand down her cheek. Savannah's expression didn't change.

The sound of distant sirens split the air. Her sister tensed.

"Shit!" Georgia said. "Come on, baby. Talk to me."

Savannah took her time. "They're all dead," she whispered.

"Who?"

"Zoya. Jenny. Sergei. Vlad."

"But we're okay. You and I. We made it."

Her sister didn't answer, and Georgia wasn't sure she understood. The sirens grew louder.

"Listen. You stay up here. I'll deal with the cops."

Georgia hurried down into the kitchen. Zoya's body lay on the floor, oozing blood from a gaping wound in her back. Georgia felt a spit of pity. Zoya didn't know it, but when Lotwin had killed her son, he'd doomed her, too.

Savannah hadn't had time to find the guns, Georgia realized, so she grabbed a knife instead. How had she managed to kill Zoya? She figured they'd have time to talk about it. Months. Even years.

She looked around and found a broom closet. Opening it, she saw it was filled with assault rifles and pistols, among them her baby Glock. She snatched it, then opened the door and went outside.

Chapter 105

The night was cloaked in darkness. The only illumination came from the floodlights on the barn and the muted light from the kitchen. Still, Georgia counted eight Russian mobsters in the shadows, their weapons drawn. She made out a few assault rifles and a long gun; the rest were pistols. A different shade of black that didn't quite belong hugged the ground near the barn, and when she squinted, she spotted two bodies. The guards. The faint odor of cordite lingered. Georgia placed her Glock on the ground and raised her arms in the air. "I'm Davis."

One of the men, apparently the leader—he could have been the one who shot Vlad, but she wasn't sure—barked something in Russian. The others holstered their weapons.

"Thank you. You took down a really bad guy." The wail of sirens was loud. "Now, get the hell out of here before the cops show up."

The men didn't need to be told twice. They hurried to their cars, both Beemers, Georgia noted, threw open the doors, and keyed their engines. Once they got to the road, both cars raced toward the highway, passing two squad cars hurtling toward them from the opposite direction.

The squad cars careened up the driveway and screeched up to

the farmhouse. Six officers spilled out, their weapons drawn. The first one out was Jimmy.

He spotted Georgia, then the two bodies near the barn. He raised a megaphone to his mouth. "Police. Drop your weapons and get your hands in the air."

Georgia threw her hands in the air. "It's over, Jimmy."

"What the fuck are you talking about?" His voice was ice-cold. "There are two bodies over there."

She glanced over. A dull pain throbbed against her temples. How was she going to explain them without giving up the Russians? She owed them. She looked back at Jimmy. His face was sliced into shadow and light, but she could tell he was angrier than an F5 tornado. His furious breaths clouded the air.

The screen door behind her banged, and Savannah emerged, already shivering. Jimmy stared at her, then back at Georgia, as if to say, "This better be good."

"I'll explain everything at the station."

He took almost a full minute to reply, and when he did, his voice was still tight. "Okay, men. We're good. Back off."

"You sure, Chief?" one of the officers called.

He nodded. "Take these two to the station. The rest of you start working the scene."

Georgia let out her breath. She trudged over to Jimmy and handed him her Glock. "You'll find more bodies inside. One is Vlad. I shot him. My sister stabbed the woman in the kitchen. Her name is Zoya. We were held prisoner and threatened at gunpoint. We managed to turn the tables on them. It was self-defense."

"And them?" He swept his hand toward the bodies on the snow.

Georgia glanced over, hunched her shoulders, then gazed evenly at Jimmy.

"I guess they had an accident."

Chapter 106

B ack at the Lake Geneva police station, Jimmy recused himself from the case, and Georgia was interrogated by his
second-in-command. A detective from Harvard ques-
tioned Savannah in a separate room. Georgia laid out the story:
the sex trafficking, the baby breeding, the harvesting of organs.
The officer, stunned at first, grimaced as she continued, gradually
moving his chair away from her, as if Georgia and the story she
was telling him were both contaminated.

She told him about Chad Coe, Claudia Nyquist, Richard
Lotwin, Bruce Kreisman, and the Glencoe couple. He told her
Riverwoods police had picked up Chad Coe, who'd decided not
to talk; Northbrook cops arrested the doctor, who did. Detectives
paid a visit to the Glencoe couple but concluded they were innocent dupes.

It was afternoon the next day before she and Savannah were
allowed to see each other.

"Are we going to jail?" Savannah asked nervously.

Georgia saw the dark rings under her sister's eyes. Neither of
them had slept. "I doubt it." She shot Savannah what she hoped
was a reassuring smile.

"Because Jimmy is your friend?"

"He is. But he has a job to do." Georgia changed the subject.

"Let's talk about you. Did you tell them about the trafficking ring and what Vlad did to you?"

"I told them everything."

"Good."

"At least that creep Lazlo will be off the streets," Savannah added.

"He's just the beginning," Georgia said. "I hope they wipe all of them off the map." She hesitated. "Savannah, at the farmhouse, how did you manage to stay downstairs after Vlad told the guard to take you up?"

Her sister beamed. "I pretended to fall and twist my ankle. You know...in those heels. I said I couldn't get up the steps. That I needed to sit for a while. Then when all the shooting started, the guard ran outside, and I grabbed the knife."

Georgia grinned.

Chapter 107

That afternoon just before dusk the Lake Geneva police
released them. Jimmy wasn't around, but Georgia understood. She had broken so many rules even she wasn't sure
on which side of the law she belonged. She'd asked a Russian
Mafioso who loved Barry Manilow for a favor; she'd helped his
men go free after they complied; she'd tampered with evidence;
she'd lied about who killed whom.

But somehow it had worked. Vlad and Zoya were gone, and
her sister was safe. The only unknown was Jimmy. She'd failed to
keep her promise to communicate; she'd gone right back to her
guarded ways. It wasn't going to be easy—this relationship stuff. It
would take time. She only hoped once he realized why she'd done
what she did, he'd forgive her.

She unlocked the door to her apartment and settled Savannah
on the couch. The girl fell asleep almost immediately. Georgia
went to a closet, pulled out a blanket, and draped it over her. Her
sister was a train wreck. She would need a lot of healing. But
under that tough-girl exterior was a vulnerable young girl who
just needed to be loved unconditionally.

Hell, you could say the same thing about *me*, Georgia thought.
Maybe they could help each other heal. She had much to learn
about her sister. How they were alike, but how they were different,

too. She suspected Savannah was stronger than she was. She'd survived sex trafficking, a heroin addiction, and Vlad's control, and she was still mostly sane. That indicated a powerful resilience Georgia wasn't sure *she* possessed.

In the kitchen she ran cold water, cupped a hand, and drank directly from the faucet. After the baby came, Savannah ought to go back to school, but Georgia wouldn't force it. The past nine months had been quite enough of an education. Maybe Georgia would call Reggie Field. Have him hire Savannah to work part-time at his store.

She dug out her cell, ordered a pizza, then at the last minute added a salad—Savannah needed healthy food. As she rummaged in a cabinet for plates, she looked around. She was going to need a bigger place. She took out plates and utensils, marveling at what life could throw at you. In a month she'd gone from a loner to a woman with a sister, a niece or nephew on the way, and a boyfriend she wanted to keep. What was next—a frigging dog?

She went to the window. It had begun to snow. Soft, plump flakes that glittered in the light and eddied to the ground where they knit a blanket of white. Georgia pulled the shade down and went back to her sister.

Acknowledgements

Special thanks to Jerry Silbert for his legal expertise; Jim Bentley and Tim Thoellecke Jr. for their help with DNA reports; Mike Green, former deputy chief of police, Northbrook, Illinois, for police procedure; Pam Hutul and Rosemary Mulryan for information about adoption procedures in Illinois. To Cara Black, too, for her advice, suggestions, and generally being the best traveling partner around. Finally, to my friend Tania Tirraoro. You are one of the most talented women I know.

Any mistakes are mine alone.

Made in the USA
Middletown, DE
10 December 2023

45265912R00215